CHARLIE BONE

AND THE

BEAST

ALSO BY JENNY NIMMO

CHARLIE BONE
AND THE
BEAST

CHILDREN OF THE RED KING

BOOK 6

JENNY NIMMO

ORCHARD BOOKS
AN IMPRINT OF SCHOLASTIC INC.
NEW YORK

Library of Congress Cataloging-in-Publication Data available

ISBN 10: 0-439-84665-X
ISBN 13: 978-0-439-84665-3

10 9 8 7 6 5 4 3 2   07 08 09 10 11

Printed in the U.S.A. 23
First Scholastic edition, June 2007

Cover illustration © 2007 by Chris Sheban
The text type was set in 11-pt. Diotima Roman.
The display type was set in Latino–Rumba.
Book design by Alison Klapthor

For Max and Molly Philo — one day.

CONTENTS

Beatrice Bloor
b.1835
Witch.

Maybelle Bloor
b.1833
Endowed.

Bertram Babington Bloor
b.1840
Having read Mary Shelley's *Frankenstein*, Bertram, a scientist-magician, tried to make a human being. He was not successful.

m.

Donatella da Vinci
b.1845
Daughter of an Italian magician. She assisted Bertram but was electrocuted during one of his experiments.

Gideon
b.1875
Mathematician. Knighted for tutoring a royal prince. Sir Gideon was not endowed or interested in magic.

m.

Gudrun Solensson
b.1876
Amateur singer.

Ezekiel
b.1902
Spoiled, cunning, flawed magician. Continued his grandfather's experiments.

m.

Hilda Hansoff
b.1902
Botanist. Fatally poisoned by a rare plant.

Bartholomew
b.1930
Unendowed. Mountaineer. Lost in the Himalayas.

m.

Mary Chance
b.1930
Dancer. Danced herself to death when Bart disappeared.

Masie Jo
b.1935
Widow.

Note:

Charlie Bone can hear the voices of people in photographs and paintings. In certain circumstances he can meet them.

Harold
b.1955
Unendowed, but interested in his grandfather's experiments.

m.

Dorothy de Vere
b.1957
Violinist.

Manfred
b.1985
Hypnotist.

Yorath Yewbeam b.1850 Shape-shifter. **m.** **Vera Kuragina** b.1862 Hypnotist.

Grace Bloor b.1885 Painter. Unendowed. Lived with her son and grandson, Paton, until she died, aged eighty. **m.** **Manley** b.1884 Soldier. Killed in 1918 in the Great War.

Yolanda b.1900 Shape-shifter. Inherited her father's castle. Never married.

Henry b.1905 Disappeared when he was eleven. Unendowed.

Daphne b.1908 Clairvoyant. Died of diphtheria in 1916.

James b.1910 Unendowed. Historian. **m.** **Solange Sourzac** b.1912 French actress. Fell and broke her neck in mysterious circumstances while visiting Yolanda's castle in 1964.

Monty Bone b.1937 Pilot. Died 1963. **m.** **Grizelda** b.1937 Unendowed.

Lucretia b.1942 Matron. Unendowed.

Eustacia b.1947 Clairvoyant.

Venetia b.1952 Designer of magic clothes.

Paton b.1957 Power-booster.

Amy Jones b.1967 Store assistant. **m.** **Lyell** b.1962 Pianist. Disappeared in 1994.

Charlie b.1992 Picture traveller

Note:

When James Yewbeam's wife, Solange, died, his four daughters went to live with their evil great aunt, Yolanda, who turned them against their father. Yolanda also tried to steal Paton, but James resisted her.

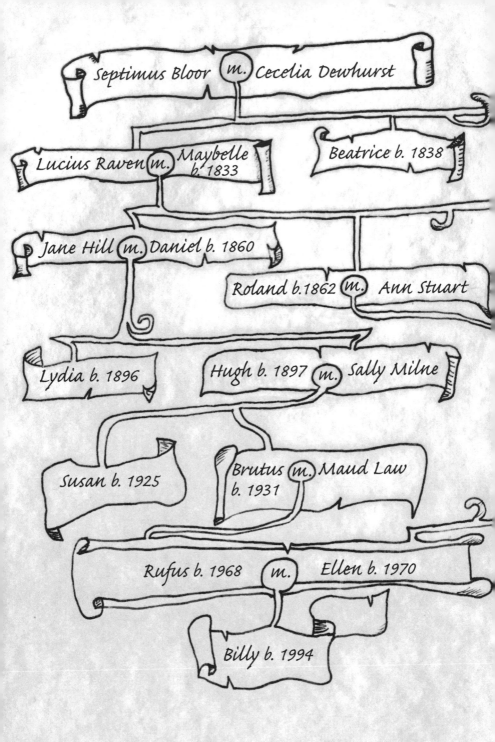

Bertram m. Donatella da Vinci
b. 1840

Evangeline b. 1865

Everard m. Harriet Hayward
b. 1900

Thomas b. 1932 m. Leah Lee   Timothy b. 1934

Note:

Maybelle gave the mother-of-pearl inlaid box
to Evangeline. Evangeline gave it to Hugh and
Sally on their wedding day. Hugh and Sally
gave it to Rufus and Ellen on their wedding
day. Rufus gave it to Lyell Bone for safe-keeping.

THE CHILDREN OF THE RED KING, CALLED THE ENDOWED

THE ENDOWED ARE ALL DESCENDED FROM THE TEN CHILDREN OF THE RED KING.

MANFRED BLOOR — Teaching assistant at Bloor's Academy. A hypnotist. He is descended from Borlath, elder son of the Red King. Borlath was a brutal and sadistic tyrant.

NAREN BLOOR — Adopted daughter of Bartholomew Bloor. Naren can send shadow words over great distances. She is descended from the Red King's grandson who was abducted by pirates and taken to China.

CHARLIE BONE — Charlie can travel into photographs and pictures. Through his father, he is descended from the Red King and through his mother, from Mathonwy, a Welsh magician and friend of the Red King.

IDITH AND INEZ BRANKO — Telekinetic twins, distantly related to Zelda Dobinski, who has left Bloor's Academy.

DAGBERT ENDLESS	Dagbert is the son of Lord Grimwald, who can control the oceans. His mother took the gold from drowned men's teeth and made them into charms to protect her son. Dagbert is a drowner.
DORCAS LOOM	An endowed girl whose gift is the ability to bewitch clothes.
UNA ONIMOUS	Mr. Onimous's niece. Una is five years old and her endowment is being kept secret until it has fully developed.
ASA PIKE	A were-beast. He is descended from a tribe who lived in the northern forests and kept strange beasts. Asa can change shape at dusk.
BILLY RAVEN	Billy can communicate with animals. One of his ancestors conversed with ravens that sat on a gallows where dead men hung. For this talent he was banished from his village.
LYSANDER SAGE	Descended from an African wise man, Lysander can call up his spirit ancestors.
GABRIEL SILK	Gabriel can feel scenes and emotions

through the clothes of others. He comes from a line of psychics.

JOSHUA TILPIN   Joshua has magnetism. He is descended from Lilith, the Red King's oldest daughter, and Harken, the evil enchanter who married her.

EMMA TOLLY   Emma can fly. Her surname derives from the Spanish swordsman from Toledo whose daughter married the Red King. The swordsman is therefore an ancestor of all the endowed children.

TANCRED TORSSON   A storm-bringer. His Scandinavian ancestor was named after the thunder god, Thor. Tancred can bring wind, thunder, and lightning.

OLIVIA VERTIGO   Descended from Guanhamara, who fled the Red King's castle and married an Italian prince. Olivia is an illusionist. The Bloors are unaware of her endowment.

PROLOGUE

Charlie Bone lives in a city that holds many secrets. They are hidden in the walls and buried under centuries of dust.

The city began nine hundred years ago with a castle. It was built by Charlie's ancestor, the Red King, so-called because of his red cloak and the burning sun emblazoned on his shield. The Red King was African; he was also a magician.

When the king's beloved queen, Berenice, died, he went to grieve in the forest. He believed that his ten children were safe in the hands of wise councillors and kind nurses. Besides, each child had been endowed with an extraordinary power.

At that time, the country was a violent and lawless place; murder and robbery were rife. On his way home, the king found that his considerable powers were needed to help the poor and oppressed.

He donned a suit of chain mail and a helmet with a plume of red feathers. Then, conjuring up an invincible sword, he rode out to defend the troubled and helpless people.

For five years the Red King fought tyrants, murderers, and plundering nobles. When he finally returned to his castle, he found that five of his children were gone and the other five were using their endowments to wreak havoc on the surrounding countryside. It was these children and their heirs who began the city's history of dreadful magic and wickedness. Unable to fight his own children, the brokenhearted king left his castle forever.

Charlie's grandmother and her three sisters all have a part in the evil. While Lyell Bone was spellbound they sent Charlie to Bloor's Academy, a school run by a family with an especially violent past. Charlie is often afraid of the Bloors and their allies, but, so far, he has resisted all their attempts to crush him, for he has friends among the descendants of the Red King, friends who use their unusual endowments to help him.

With his own talent for traveling into the past through pictures, Charlie is beginning to learn the city's secrets. It is a dangerous pursuit, but Charlie has his friends to support him and a firm trust in the enduring power of the Red King.

NOT-QUITE-HUMANS

You might think it was rather careless of Charlie Bone to lose his father a second time, especially when he had only just found him. They had been apart for ten long years, spellbound years for Lyell Bone, a time spent in deep forgetfulness, when he could remember nothing of his past or even recall his name.

This time, at least Charlie knew where his father had gone. He was taking Charlie's mother on a second honeymoon. What could be better than to get away from cold, dark February days, to watch whales and dolphins roll through a sunlit sea? They had asked Charlie to join them, of course, but he had politely declined. His parents needed to be alone and, besides, there were things that he had to attend to at home. A few mysteries to clear up.

At that moment Charlie was standing by the gate of the house where he was born. It was an old, red-brick building, with a steep slate roof and four steps up to a blue front door. Charlie and his mother had left the house when he was two, and he couldn't remember it at all. Even the name was unfamiliar to him: Diamond Corner — it stood on the corner of Diamond Street and Lyme Avenue.

Charlie was twelve now, a boy of medium height with dark, unruly hair and walnut brown eyes. A boy who was ordinary in every way except one: He was a picture-traveler, a talent he had inherited from the legendary Red King.

Beside Charlie stood a very tall man with strong, finely chiseled features and straight black hair that almost touched his shoulders. He wore a long, dark coat and the brim of his black hat had been pulled down, as if to shade his eyes, though there was not the slightest glimmer of sunlight on this murky Sunday afternoon.

"Needs a lot of repair," the man remarked, looking at the dark holes where slates had fallen from the roof.

"I wish I could move in right now, Uncle Paton," said Charlie.

"You won't have to wait long," said his uncle. "They're starting work next week, builders, painters, plumbers, and roofers."

"Let's have a look." Charlie opened the gate and walked up the overgrown path. His uncle followed, jangling a bunch of keys. As they drew closer they noticed a light in one of the lower windows.

"Someone's in there." Charlie ran up to the door. His uncle, only a pace behind, leaped up the steps and fitted one of his keys into the lock. The blue door swung open and Charlie stepped inside.

A stale, mildewy smell filled the hallway. The floorboards were damp and dusty, and strips of ragged wallpaper hung from the dark-stained walls. Charlie trod as lightly as he could, but the bare boards creaked with every step he took. He quickly opened a door to his left and looked into the room where he had seen the light. It was empty. Uncle Paton nodded at a half-open door on the other side of the room. "The kitchen," he whispered.

A shuffling sound could be heard. It was difficult to make out where it came from. Charlie sprang across the room, his uncle's heavy footsteps pounding after him. But the kitchen too was empty. A sharp bang sent Charlie bounding through the kitchen and into the hallway. The back door swung open, hitting the wall behind it with another loud bang. A blast of cold air hit Charlie as he squinted outside. He was just in time to see two figures slip through a broken fence at the end of the yard.

"Hey!" cried Charlie, running through a sea of long, dried grass and weeds. When he reached the fence he peered into the narrow gap. But the intruders had vanished.

"Could have been tramps." Uncle Paton kicked at a pile of newspapers in a corner. "Let's go, Charlie."

"Can't I go upstairs?" begged Charlie. "I want to see if I can remember the room where I slept."

"Go on, then." Uncle Paton followed Charlie up

the stairs. When he reached the top, Charlie stood and stared at the two doors in front of him. There were two more leading off a hall to his left, and another on his right. He chose this last one.

"You did remember, Charlie!"

"I just guessed," said Charlie. He pushed open the door. "OH!"

It was impossible to move any farther into the room. Every floorboard had been lifted. Some stood against the walls, others lay scattered on the narrow planks that supported the floor.

"How very odd!" Uncle Paton peered over Charlie's shoulder. "I didn't know the builders had started already."

They looked in the other rooms. Every one was in the same state; floorboards were wrenched up and thrown carelessly into corners or strewn across the thin planks.

"Looks like someone's been searching for something," Charlie remarked.

"A pretty desperate search," his uncle agreed. "I

imagine they did the same downstairs, but relaid the boards in case anyone looked through the windows."

"I don't like to think of strangers coming in and trashing my old home," said Charlie.

As they went downstairs they kept an eye open for any sign that the boards might have been pulled up. And this time they noticed the splintered wood, the nails that had been unscrewed, and the slight wobble in the banisters.

"It might be a good idea to change the locks," said Uncle Paton, when they were standing in the street again. "I'll tell the agents."

They began the walk home to number nine Filbert Street. Uncle Paton was thinking about the intruders and failed to notice that the streetlights had come on. Before Charlie had time to warn him, his uncle carelessly glanced upward and the light over his head gave a loud pop and exploded.

Uncle Paton ducked as a shower of glass rained down on his head. "Bother! Bother! Bother!" he cried.

Paton Yewbeam, another of the Red King's

descendants, had inherited an unfortunate endowment. If he so much as glanced at a light that was on,
whether it was in a window, a building, on the street,
or at home, the element would reach such intense
heat that the bulb inevitably exploded. So Paton rarely
left home in the daytime. Traffic lights, brake lights,
and shop windows were all at risk from his unhappy
talent. And he found it very embarrassing.

This time Uncle Paton's accident had revealed
something. In the bright flash that momentarily filled
the street, two figures could be seen cowering beside
a hedge. The moment lasted less than a second but
their faces were printed sharply in Charlie's mind.
They looked . . . not quite human.

Charlie had blinked against the shower of glass
that fell onto his uncle. When he opened his eyes
again, the figures had vanished.

"Come on, Charlie, let's get out of here before
someone sees us." Uncle Paton took Charlie's arm
and pulled him away from the scene of his crime.

"Someone did see us, Uncle P.," said Charlie. "I

think it might have been THEM. You know, the intruders. But they weren't exactly people. If you know what I mean."

"I do not." Uncle Paton gripped Charlie even tighter. "Quick, quick! Over here."

Charlie found himself being dragged across the street. A fast approaching car gave a warning hoot, and Uncle Paton hauled him onto the sidewalk.

"What did you say about not-exactly people?" Uncle Paton tugged the brim of his hat. Now even his nose was hidden.

"They were weird, Uncle P.," Charlie panted. "I can't explain."

"Try," commanded his uncle. "I want to know what kind of creatures we're up against."

Uncle Paton set off again at his usual breakneck speed. Charlie had to make little skipping movements in order to keep up with him. "It's not fair," Charlie complained. "Your legs are twice as long as mine."

"I want to put distance between myself and the streetlight," Uncle Paton snapped. He turned a corner and slowed his pace. "Now, try again. What made these things inhuman, Charlie?"

"They were a bit hairy for one thing," said Charlie. "And their eyes — their eyes, well, I think they were too far apart for a human, they were more like dogs — or, or —"

"Wolves?" his uncle suggested.

"Maybe," Charlie said cautiously. "If wolves have yellow eyes."

"Hmmm. Why do I think that the Bloors have something to do with this? Tell me, did your father mention anything that he might have left at the old house?"

"Nothing," said Charlie. "But then there were so many things that he'd forgotten." He smiled to himself. It was enough that his father had remembered his mother and himself. "His memory is coming back, though. Every day something new pops into his head. Maybe when he comes home again he'll be completely recovered."

"And that's what they're afraid of." Uncle Paton came to a standstill.

"Who? What?" asked Charlie.

"Listen, Charlie. We believe that Manfred Bloor hypnotized your father because he caused old Ezekiel's accident. But I have come to believe that there was more to it. I believe your father was hiding something that the Bloors wanted. Perhaps they hoped that under hypnosis he would reveal its hiding place. But this never happened. And now they're afraid that he will remember and find whatever it is before they do."

Charlie couldn't imagine what had led his uncle to his conclusion. But Paton Yewbeam had an inquiring mind. He was writing a history of the Red King, and his room was crammed with huge books that covered every subject Charlie had heard of, and a lot more that he hadn't.

Diamond Street lay on the outskirts of the city, and it took Charlie and his uncle nearly an hour to get home. By that time dusk had fallen and a thick mist was creeping through the streets. Curiously it smelled of salt, though the sea was at least thirty miles away.

Charlie's grandmother Maisie met them at the door. She had the look of someone who's had a nasty shock. "Grandma Bone's back," she whispered, turning out the hall light in case of a Paton accident.

"Back?" said Paton loudly. "Why on earth . . ."

"Shhh!" Maisie put a finger to her lips. "Come in here."

Charlie and his uncle followed Maisie into the kitchen. The table had been set, and while Maisie ladled mushroom soup into three bowls, she told them about Grandma Bone's dramatic arrival.

Grandma Bone was Paton's sister. She was twenty years older than he, and they'd never gotten along. She didn't even get along with her only son, Charlie's father. As soon as he'd come home after ten long years imprisoned in Bloor's Academy, Grandma Bone had moved out. She'd gone to live with her three sisters at the end of a grim and gloomy alley called Darkly

Wynd. Charlie had hoped he would never see her again.

"She's still got a key," Maisie told them. "She marched in, dumped her bag in the hall, and said, 'I'm back!' 'Why?' I asked. Well, that was wrong for a start. 'Anyone would think you were sorry,' she said. 'I am,' I said. 'I thought you'd gone for good.'"

Charlie began to giggle. Paton asked, "But what is her reason, Maisie? Why has she returned?"

"A wedding!" said Maisie.

"Whose?" begged Paton.

"Your youngest sister, Venetia. She's getting married next week."

Charlie choked on his soup. "Great-aunt Venetia? Who on earth would want to marry her?"

"Who indeed, Charlie love," said Maisie. "But some poor man is soon going to rue the day."

"How extraordinary." Paton stared at Maisie in disbelief.

"Grandma Bone is very put out," Maisie went on, "but her sisters are all for it apparently."

"Phew." Paton blew on his soup, which couldn't have been that hot because he'd already swallowed several spoonfuls without a murmur. He was trying not to show it, but anyone could see that he was utterly baffled and extremely shocked.

Uncle Paton's four sisters were each as bad as the other. They loathed their only brother and spent their lives tormenting him just because he didn't agree with their morals and made very sure they knew it. All four of them were mean, spiteful, arrogant, dishonest, and greedy. In fact, Charlie couldn't find enough words to describe how horrible they were. None of them had ever given Charlie a kind word, let alone a birthday present, not even Grandma Bone.

Maisie had saved the best part of her announcement till last. "The worst of it is, he's got children," she said dramatically. "What do you think of that?"

"Children!" Charlie shuddered. "Poor things. Imagine Great-aunt Venetia being your mother?"

"Impossible." Paton suddenly looked up.

Charlie had his back to the door and failed to see Grandma Bone walking up behind him.

"I'm glad I'm not your mother," said Grandma Bone testily. She marched over to the fridge and opened it. "There's nothing in here," she complained. "Nothing but cheese and old bones. No paté, no mayonnaise, and not even a sniff of salmon."

Maisie gave a huge sigh. "How was I to know you'd come hunting in here, with your fussy stomach and your dainty mouth? Sit down, Grizelda, and I'll give you some mushroom soup."

"No, thank you." Grandma Bone plonked herself in the rocker by the stove.

Paton frowned. He had been meaning to get rid of the rocker. No one else ever used it. It had been a constant reminder of Grandma Bone's gloomy presence. If only he'd thought ahead and chopped it up for firewood a day earlier.

Creak! Creak! Creak! There she went, with her eyes closed and her head nestled into her chin. *Rock! Rock! Rock!* The sound was enough to curdle the soup.

"So." Paton found a voice at last. "I hear you've fallen out with your sisters, Grizelda."

"They're your sisters, too." She snorted. "Marriage indeed. I never heard of such rubbish. Venetia's fifty-two. She should've given up that sort of thing years ago."

"What sort of thing?" asked Charlie.

"Don't be insolent," Grandmother Bone replied.

Charlie finished his soup and stood up. "I bet you'll leave when my dad comes back," he said.

"Oh, but you're all going to live in that cozy little Diamond Corner." She gave Charlie one of her chilly stares. "But then whale watching can be very danger-ous. He may never . . ."

Charlie didn't wait to hear what his grandmother might say next. "I'm going to see Ben," he cried, rush-ing into the hall and flinging on his jacket.

Maisie called, "Charlie, it's dark, love. Don't pay any attention to Grandma Bone. She didn't mean anything by it."

"She did," muttered Charlie. He left the house, ran

across the road to number twelve, and rang the bell. Filbert Street was always quiet at this time on a Sunday. There were very few cars about, and the street was deserted. And yet Charlie felt a prickling at the back of his neck that told him someone was watching him.

"Come on, come on." Charlie pressed the bell a second time.

Benjamin Brown opened the door. He was a few months younger than Charlie and a lot smaller. His scruffy yellow hair was exactly the same color as the large dog that stood beside him, wagging its tail.

"Can I come in?" asked Charlie. "Grandma Bone's back."

Benjamin understood immediately. "What a disaster. I'm just taking Runner Bean for a walk. Want to come?"

Anything was better than spending the evening in the same house as Grandma Bone. Charlie fell into step beside Benjamin as he headed toward the park. With joyful barks, Runner Bean ran circles around the boys, then darted down the dark street. Benjamin didn't like to lose sight of his dog. He knew he worried unnecessarily. His parents were always telling him to lighten up, but Benjamin couldn't help being the way he was. Besides, a mist was beginning to creep into the street, an unusual, salty sort of mist.

Charlie hunched his shoulders. There it was again. That odd prickling feeling under his collar. He stopped and looked back.

"What is it, Charlie?" asked Benjamin.

Charlie told his friend about the not-quite-humans that he'd seen near Diamond Corner.

"Nothing's normal tonight," Benjamin said shakily. "I never tasted salt in the mist before."

And then they heard the howl; it was very distant, but a howl nevertheless. A sound that was almost human, and yet not quite. For the first time since his parents had left, Charlie wished they hadn't gone whale watching.

Runner Bean came racing back to the boys. His coarse hair was standing up like a hedgehog's.

"It's the howling," said Benjamin. "I've heard it

before. It makes Runner nervous, though he's never usually scared of anything."

It wasn't until much later that Charlie made the connection between the distant howling and the not-quite-humans that seemed to be following him.

As for the salty mist, that was another thing entirely.

STRANGERS FROM THE SEA

Two strangers had entered the city on that chilly Sunday afternoon. They came on the river. Leaving their boat moored beneath a bridge, they climbed the steep bank up to the road. They moved with an odd, swaying motion as though they were balancing on the deck of a ship. A mist accompanied them, a cloying, salty mist that silenced the birds and gave passersby unexpectedly chesty coughs.

The smaller of the two strangers was a boy of eleven with aquamarine eyes, like the color of an iceberg underwater. His shoulder-length hair was a dull, greenish-brown with a slight crinkle. He was tall for his age and very pale, his lips almost bloodless. He lurched across the cobblestones with an expression of grim determination on his thin face.

The boy's father had the same cold eyes, but his long hair was streaked with white. His name was Lord Grimwald.

When they reached the steps up to Bloor's Academy, the boy stopped. His eyes took in the massive gray walls and traveled up the two towers on either side of the entrance. "It's a long way from the sea," he said in a surprisingly tuneful voice.

"You must learn to live without the sea for a while." The man's voice had the echo of a damp cavern.

"Yes." The boy put his hand in his pocket. A restful look came onto his face at the comforting touch of sea gold. In his pocket he carried a golden fish, a sea urchin, and several golden crabs. They were gifts from his dead mother, who had made them from gold found in wrecks beneath the sea. "These sea-gold creatures will help you to survive," she had said.

As the boy began to mount the steps his father said, "Dagbert, remember what I said. Try to restrain yourself."

Dagbert stopped and looked back at his father. "What if I can't?"

"You must. We are here to help."

"YOU are here to help. I am to here learn." Dagbert

turned and leaped up to the top steps. His long legs carried him across the courtyard in a few swaying strides, and then he was pulling a chain that hung beside the tall oak doors. A bell chimed somewhere deep within the building. Dagbert peered at the bronze figures that studded the doors.

"They are older than the house." Lord Grimwald ran his fingers over the figure of a man holding what appeared to be a rod of lightning. "Our ancestor, Dagbert. Remember. We talked about Petrello, the Red King's fifth child."

One of the doors creaked open and a man appeared. He was a burly fellow, completely bald with a square face and small expressionless eyes. "Yes?" he said.

"We're expected," Lord Grimwald announced imperiously.

"Name of Grimwald?" The man's eyes narrowed.

"Were you hoping it might be someone else?"

The man muttered, "Tsk!" and opened the door wider. "Come in, then."

Father and son followed the burly figure down a long stone hall to a door set into one of the oak-paneled walls. "The Music Tower," announced their guide, turning a metal ring. The door swung open, and he ushered the visitors into a dimly lit hallway. At the end of the hall they passed through a circular room and then up a spiral staircase. On reaching the top of the first flight, they turned to their right and entered a thickly carpeted corridor.

"The doctor's study is second on the left," said the bald porter. "As you said, you're expected. The Bloors are there. All three of them."

"Your name?" Lord Grimwald demanded. "I like to know these details."

"Weedon — porter, chauffeur, handyman, gardener. Is that enough for you?" He stomped back down the stairs.

"Insolent fellow." Lord Grimwald's greenish complexion turned a nasty shade of terra-cotta. When he got to the study door he gave it several hard bangs with his fist, instead of the polite knock he might otherwise have used.

"Yes!" answered two voices, one deep and haughty, the other an eager screech.

Lord Grimwald and his son went in. They found themselves in a gloomy book-lined room, where a large man stood behind a desk. To one side of the desk an ancient creature sat in a wheelchair. He was trapped in a wool blanket and wore a round black hat on his bony head. A few white hairs fell to his shoulders like waxy string. Behind him a log fire lent warmth to the room and a welcome touch of color.

"Lord Grimwald." Dr. Bloor walked around his desk and shook his visitor's hand. "It's good to meet you. I am Dr. Bloor, the headmaster. I trust your journey wasn't uncomfortable."

"We came by sea."

"Impossible. We're miles from the sea," said the creature in the wheelchair.

"We came as far as we could, then took a boat up the river." Lord Grimwald shook the clawlike hand that thrust its way out of the wool blanket.

"I'm Mr. Ezekiel," said the ancient man. "I'm a hundred and two. What about that, eh? Don't look it, do I?" Without waiting for a reply he went on, "And this is the boy." He made a grab for Dagbert's hand.

"His name is Dagbert," Lord Grimwald told the old man. "He has many other names, but we have decided on the surname Endless."

"Because my names are as endless as the ocean." Dagbert didn't flinch when his fingers were crushed in the skeletal hand. In fact, he hardly looked at Ezekiel. His gaze was drawn to a figure in the corner; hunched and dark, its face was averted from the visitors, though it gave the impression that it was listening intently to every word. Dagbert was so taken with this sinister form he forgot to restrain himself.

The flames in the grate flickered and died. A damp mist filled the room, and the musty books that lined the walls were bathed in eerie sea light.

"What the dickens?" uttered Ezekiel, drawing his blanket closer.

"It's what he does," Lord Grimwald said impassively. "Soon Dagbert will achieve his full power, and it will be greater than mine."

"Indeed?" Dr. Bloor regarded the boy. "An uncomfortable thought for you, Lord Grimwald."

"Not at all. Dagbert will not disobey. If he does, he will die. He knows this." Lord Grimwald spoke as if his son were not in the room. "I didn't want a child," he went on, "but then this miracle happened" — he indicated Dagbert — "and I found I couldn't be parted from him. Our family is cursed, you see. Every time a boy has achieved full power, he has turned against his father and one of them has died. But we have made a pact, Dagbert and I, to work together always. Haven't we, Dagbert?"

Dagbert gave his father a curt nod.

"Now, Dagbert, CONTROL YOURSELF!"

Dagbert smiled. The sea light faded, and the logs in the grate gave a damp *hiss* and burst into flame.

"Interesting." Dr. Bloor frowned at the boy. "As long as he uses his endowment in the right places."

"Keep an eye on him for me," said Lord Grimwald, "and I'll do what you want."

"We'll put him in Charlie Bone's dorm," Ezekiel said gleefully.

"Please, take a seat, both of you," said Dr. Bloor. "Dagbert, fetch those chairs by the bookshelf."

The boy pulled two chairs up to the desk while Dr. Bloor continued. "Charlie Bone is getting too strong. He needs reining in."

"I can do that, sir." Dagbert took a seat beside his father.

For the first time since the visitors arrived, the figure in the shadows turned his face to the light. Lord Grimwald gave an involuntary gasp, but his son stared at the ruined face of Manfred Bloor with a mixture of awe and fascination. Four great scars ran from the youth's hairline to his chin. His eyelids were puckered with stitches, and his top lip dragged upward in two places, giving the face a permanent grimace.

"Terrible, isn't it?" Ezekiel looked around at his great-grandson. "But we'll get even with them, Manfred."

"How did it happen?" asked Lord Grimwald.

"Cats," said Dr. Bloor.

"Cats?" Lord Grimwald repeated in disbelief.

"Leopards," came a husky croak from the corner.

"They lacerated his throat," said Dr. Bloor in an undertone. "Every word he utters causes him pain."

"Leopards." Dagbert's eyes hadn't left the ravaged face.

"The Red King's leopards," came the dreadful croak.

Dagbert turned to his father. "We're descended from the Red King."

His father nodded. "It's why we're here."

"So you know the story of the Red King?" Ezekiel wheeled himself closer to Dagbert. "You know that when his wife died, the King went to grieve in the forest with only his leopards for company. But did you know that he turned those leopards into cats? Immortal cats, their coats as bright as flames, cats that turn up every generation to keep company with the

27

children who refuse to be controlled." Ezekiel's voice rose to a furious screech. "They did it. Those cats destroyed my grandson."

"Why?" asked Dagbert, undaunted by the old man's fury.

"Charlie Bone," answered the rasping voice in the shadows.

"Indeed, Charlie Bone," said Dr. Bloor. "Granted he was trying to save his father, but to do this . . ." The headmaster flung out his hand toward his son.

"And have you found a way to punish Charlie Bone?" asked Lord Grimwald.

"We're hoping that you can help us." Dr. Bloor gave an exasperated sigh. "Charlie has friends, you see, friends with powerful endowments. They stick together like glue."

"Glue can be dissolved," said Dagbert quietly.

A surprised silence followed this remark. The Bloors regarded Dagbert with renewed interest. But the boy's gaze was held by the scarred eyes that watched him from the shadows, and everyone in the room felt the invisible bond that was instantly formed between Dagbert Endless and Manfred Bloor.

Ezekiel smiled with satisfaction. Many endowed children had studied at Bloor's Academy; some had been gratifyingly evil, but he was certain that none had been as deadly as this northern boy with his ice-berg eyes.

Lord Grimwald got to his feet and began to move about the room in his peculiar swaying walk. "So you will educate my son, and what am I to do for you?"

"Ah, now we come to the crux of the matter," Ezekiel said eagerly. "You can control the oceans, Lord Grimwald. A towering talent if I may say."

Lord Grimwald inclined his head as he continued to swing about the room.

Dr. Bloor said, "Charlie's father, Lyell Bone, is at this moment out on the ocean. He is taking a second honeymoon with his wife, Amy. And they have decided to go whale watching."

"Whale watching!" Ezekiel cackled. "Silly fools. They're going on a little boat, and the waves will rock the little boat from side to side, and then the highest, tallest, widest wave there's ever been will take the little boat to the bottom of the ocean, where Lyell and Amy will rest forever. What do you think about that, Lord Grimwald?"

"I can do that for you." Lord Grimwald stopped pacing and sat down. "But may I ask, apart from punishing Charlie Bone, is there another reason why you want to drown Lyell Bone?"

"The WILL!" said Ezekiel and Dr. Bloor in unison.

"The will?" asked Lord Grimwald.

"It's old, very old, but still legal probably," said Ezekiel. "It was made by my great-grandfather, Septimus Bloor, in 1865, shortly before he died. He left everything: house, garden, the ruined castle in the grounds, priceless treasures, all . . . all to his daughter Maybelle and her heirs. But my great-auntie, Beatrice, was a witch, you see, and hated Maybelle, so she poisoned her and forged another will. This will, the false one, left everything to my grandfather, Bertram. And he left it all to my father, and then to me. Beatrice wanted nothing for herself; she was content to see Maybelle dead and her children become paupers."

"Forgive me for being slow, Mr. Bloor, but where's the problem?" Grimwald spread his hands. "It would appear that the original will no longer exists."

"But it does, it does!" cried Ezekiel. "Someone found it, you see: Rufus Raven, Maybelle's great-grandson. It was given to his wife, Ellen, on her wedding day."

"A will?" questioned Lord Grimwald.

"No, no, not the will, exactly. She was given the box that contained it," explained Dr. Bloor. "The key was lost and she couldn't open it, but Ellen was endowed with an instinct for certain . . . things. She guessed that it contained something of great importance."

"We believe that Rufus gave it to Lyell Bone for safekeeping," said Ezekiel. "They were the best of friends, he and Rufus. We tried to bargain; we tried threats. 'Give us the box,' we said, 'and you'll have half our fortune.' Of course we didn't mean it." A sly smile twisted Ezekiel's meager lips. "But Rufus wouldn't give it up, anyway. So we had to get rid of him and his silly wife. A nasty accident arranged by a car mechanic on my payroll. Their baby survived, but he doesn't know a thing."

"His name's Billy," said Dr. Bloor. "We have him here. He's eight years old and can communicate with animals."

"That's useful," Dagbert said with interest.

Ezekiel giggled. "Billy's endowment hasn't been very helpful to him so far. Take Percy, for instance." He clicked his fingers. "Percy, come here."

An old dog appeared from behind the desk. Its eyes were hidden behind rolls of loose skin; its short legs were barely able to support its heavy body. Dagbert's lips curled in disgust as the creature grunted and dragged its slobbery mouth against Ezekiel's blanket.

"Billy calls him Blessed," said Ezekiel. "Heaven knows why. The dog can understand Billy's gibberish, but he knows nothing of our conversation. We could be talking about butterflies." Ezekiel fluttered his crooked hands in the air above his head. "Or . . . or birthday parties, for all he knows. So he can't tell Billy a thing about our little chat, or his inheritance."

"Are you sure?" Dagbert eyed the dog suspiciously.

"Absolutely," said Dr. Bloor. "The only words that dog knows are his names: Percy or Blessed."

This wasn't strictly true. Blessed might not have been able to comprehend every word that was said, but he understood the current of feeling in the room. He knew they were talking about his friend Billy, and he was aware that the two strangers brought trouble. They smelled of mists and rotting wood. Their skins were cold and slippery, and behind their voices waves could be heard, beating on a stony shore. The boy's eyes glimmered like frozen water and the man's face told of wrecked ships and pitiless drownings. Blessed would describe all this to Billy and Billy would tell Cook. And Cook would give Blessed a large bone, Blessed hoped. The old dog made for the door, wagging his bald tail and slobbering badly as he thought of the longed-for bone.

There came a loud knock on the door and, as it opened, Blessed hurried past Weedon into the hall.

"Cook's put a bit of supper on the table," Weedon announced grumpily.

"Ah!" Dr. Bloor rubbed his hands together. "The dining room is just down the hallway. This way, everyone."

As the two visitors followed Dr. Bloor a small woman emerged from the dining room. Cook was rounder than she had once been and her dark hair was touched with gray, but her rosy face still held traces of her former beauty. When she saw Dr. Bloor and his guests approaching she stood aside to let them pass.

"Thank you, Cook," said Dr. Bloor.

Cook nodded and then gave a small involuntary shudder. She pressed a handkerchief to her face and hastened away. Her heart was pounding so fast that Blessed could hear it as she ran down the stairs behind him.

"Oh, grief. Oh, horrors. It's him. It's him. Oh, Blessed, what am I to do? Why here? Why now?"

Cook burst into the blue cafeteria with Blessed hard on her heels, the handkerchief still pressed to her mouth as though the very air she breathed was poisoned.

"Cook, what's the matter?"

Cook hadn't noticed the white-haired boy sitting at a corner table.

"Oh, Billy, love. I've had a dreadful shock." She pulled out a chair and sat beside him. "A man is here. He . . . he . . ." She shook her head. "Billy, I'll have to tell you. He drowned my parents, swept away my home, and murdered my fiancé, all because I would not marry him."

Billy's wine-colored eyes widened in alarm. "Here? But why?"

"That I couldn't tell you. Something to do with the boy he's brought, I imagine." Cook blew her nose and tucked the handkerchief into her sleeve. "Grimwald's his name. It was forty years ago, and I don't know if he recognized me. But if he did . . ." She closed her eyes against unimaginable horrors. "If he did, I'll have to leave."

"Leave? You can't leave, Cook!" Billy leaped to his feet and flung his arms around Cook's neck. "What will I do without you? You can't leave. Please say you won't. Please, please."

Cook twisted her head from side to side. "I just don't know, Billy. There've been some pretty awful people in this place, but he's the worst. And if the boy is anything like him, then we're in for a rough ride, believe me."

Blessed suddenly put his paws on Cook's lap and, throwing back his head, let out such a mournful howl that Billy had to cover his ears.

"He knows," Billy whispered. "He wants to tell me something, but I'm not sure that I want to hear it."

DAGBERT ENDLESS

On Monday morning a new boy appeared at Bloor's Academy. He wore the compulsory blue cape of a music student. Charlie met him for the first time in assembly. The music students had their own orchestra, and today Charlie's friend Fidelio was lead violin. He waved his bow at Charlie just as the head of music, Dr. Saltweather, came onto the stage.

"Who's that?" said a voice in Charlie's ear.

Charlie looked around to see a boy a few inches taller than himself with long, wet-looking hair and aquamarine eyes.

"Who's who?" asked Charlie.

"The boy with the violin."

"He's called Fidelio Gunn," said Charlie. "He's a friend of mine."

"Is he? And is he a good violinist?"

"Brilliant," said Charlie. "I'm Charlie, by the way."

Dr. Saltweather raised his hand for silence, and the orchestra struck up.

Thirty minutes later the new boy caught up with Charlie as he left assembly. He handed Charlie a letter. Charlie didn't like the look of it. He recognized the Bloors' official stationery. Printed in large, ornate script were the words:

Charlie Bone has been designated official monitor to Dagbert Endless. He will show him all locations relevant to a music student in the second year. He will also acquaint Dagbert with the rules and regulations of this academy, and impart to him any information regarding compulsory attire and equipment. If Dagbert Endless infringes upon any academy rule, Charlie Bone will be held responsible.

Charlie swallowed hard.

"That's me," said the boy, pointing to his name on the letter. "Dagbert Endless."

Charlie was baffled. "I wonder why they've chosen me."

"Because you're endowed," Dagbert told him. "So am I. Don't know a thing about music. Wouldn't mind having a go at the drums, though. What about you?"

"Me? Oh, I play the trumpet," Charlie replied. He wondered why the boy had arrived so late in the school year. They were almost halfway through the second term.

"I come from the North," Dagbert informed him. "The far, far North. I was at Loth's Academy but they expelled me."

Charlie was instantly intrigued. "What for?"

"There was a drowning," the boy said airily. "Not my fault, of course, but you know how parents are. They wanted retribution and someone gave them my name." Dagbert lowered his voice. "He didn't last long, I can assure you."

"Who?"

"The snitcher."

They had reached the hall and Charlie was so keen to hear the gruesome details of the drowning, he quite forgot the rules. "So what happened then?"

"Silence in the hall, Charlie Bone," called one of the prefects, a cheerful girl who rarely gave detention.

"This way," Charlie whispered, nudging Dagbert's arm.

They walked to a door beneath a carving of crossed trumpets. Once through the door Charlie said, "I'm glad Fiona's on duty and not Manfred Bloor."

"What's wrong with Manfred?" asked Dagbert.

Charlie didn't like the look that Dagbert shot at him. "Never mind." Quickly changing the subject, Charlie explained that they were in the blue coatroom of the music students. "Drama students wear purple capes — their coatroom door is under two masks — and crossed paintbrushes show where the art students go. They wear green. We have our own cafeterias, too. But we all work together, except when we do music, art, or drama."

Children began to crowd around Dagbert. Where

did he come from? Why was he here? Did he live in the city?

Charlie noticed Billy Raven sitting in a corner. As soon as he saw Dagbert he gave Charlie one of his worried looks and ran out. Dagbert glanced at the small white-haired boy before talking to the others. He told none of them what he had told Charlie. He would only say that he lived above a fish shop.

"I like fish, you see." He gave Charlie a private smile.

"He's an odd fish," Fidelio Gunn whispered in Charlie's ear.

Charlie grinned. Dagbert saw Fidelio's head close to Charlie's and the smile left his face. His eyes suddenly became so icy they sent a shiver down Charlie's spine.

"It's English next," Charlie said. "We'd better get to Mr. Carp's room."

"You should enjoy that, eh, Dagbert?" said Fidelio. "A carp is a very fine fish."

Dagbert was not amused. "Show me the way," he commanded.

They left the blue coatroom and made their way through groups of children in blue, green, or purple capes, all heading in different directions.

Mr. Carp was stout and red-faced. He was always dressed very neatly in a striped vest and smart gray suit. He found Charlie Bone irritating, partly because of his messy hair and partly because his mind always seemed to be elsewhere. He didn't pay attention and sometimes gave silly answers that made the class laugh.

"You, boy, sit there," he told Dagbert. "That's right, next to Charlie Bone. He is to be your monitor, I'm told. Though he needs one himself, if you ask me." Mr. Carp laughed at his own joke while the rest of the class remained silent.

Dagbert took the desk next to Charlie. On the other side of Charlie, Fidelio raised an eyebrow. With a scraping of chairs the class sat down and a lesson on punctuation began.

For the rest of the day Dagbert stuck to Charlie like a limpet. It wasn't Dagbert's fault, Charlie reasoned, but he was beginning to seriously affect Charlie's social life. His friends Emma and Olivia approached during break, but things took a bad turn when Olivia suggested that Dagbert smelled fishy. Charlie had assumed that the smell was wafting up from the kitchens but now he realized that Olivia was right.

Dagbert's response caught Charlie off guard. "We think you stink of cheap perfume, don't we, Charlie?" He winked at Charlie, who opened his mouth to protest when Dagbert continued. "And we think you both look a mess. Those ridiculous hairdos, for one thing."

"I . . . didn't . . . ," Charlie stuttered.

Emma stared at him in dismay, while Olivia said, "I see. Well, we know where we stand, don't we?" She grabbed Emma's arm and dragged her away. They'd only gone a few steps when Olivia turned back and called, "I always knew you were a fraud, Charlie Bone. A fraud and a liar."

Charlie would have run after the girls, but Olivia's hurtful words stopped him in his tracks. Had she always thought him a fraud? He watched the two girls walk across the grounds. In her purple cape, red coat, and black tights, Olivia looked anything but a mess. Her brown hair was streaked with black and gold and topped with a small black velvet beret. Charlie had been about to compliment her when Dagbert made his fatal remark. Even Emma looked elegant today, with her blond hair piled on top of her head.

"Let them go," said Dagbert. "We know their type. Airheads."

"Stop saying 'we,'" Charlie said irritably. "We don't have the same opinions at all. And those girls aren't airheads."

Dagbert ignored this. "You promised to show me the Red Castle. I can see the walls from here. Come on."

At the far end of the grounds, the deep red walls of a castle could be glimpsed between the trees. Now a ruin, it was difficult to believe that the Red King had once held court there. At times, Charlie had found the ruin a refuge, but always there was a feeling of unease behind the great walls, a hint of the castle's troubled past when the king's children had turned against one another.

"You go ahead," Charlie told Dagbert. "I want to talk to someone." He had seen his friend Gabriel Silk wandering toward them.

As Gabriel got closer, Dagbert said loudly, "You're right, Charlie. What a loser."

It was unfortunate that Gabriel happened to be passing Bragger Braine, the worst bully in the second year. Bragger and the group of boys surrounding him took one look at Gabriel's long, sad face and burst into malicious laughter.

"Gabe!" Charlie shouted.

But Gabriel had fled. Charlie scanned the grounds and eventually saw Gabriel running for the garden door.

"Dagbert, why did you say that?" Charlie demanded angrily. "Gabriel's very sensitive. I don't know how I'm going to explain things to him."

"I wouldn't bother," Dagbert said casually. "Who

wants a friend like that? I heard he can't even wear old clothes."

"He can't help it. He gets all the feelings of the people who've worn the clothes before him." Charlie stamped his foot. "And if you want to see the ruin, go by yourself."

Furious, Charlie stormed away from Dagbert and made for the school. The smell of fish suddenly became so overpowering he almost retched. It was a relief to get inside the hall and close the door against the choking odor. Charlie ran along to the blue coatroom where Gabriel often took refuge when things weren't going well. But instead of Gabriel, he found Billy Raven, huddled at the end of a bench.

"Billy, have you seen Gabriel?" Charlie asked.

Billy shook his head. He looked very troubled.

"What is it?" Charlie sat beside the smaller boy.

"You need to know some things," said Billy, "about that boy Dagbert. Blessed told me —"

"There you are!" Dagbert stood in the doorway, his face blank and the fish smell under control. It seemed to be something he could send out or stop at will. "You've got some freaky friends, Charlie Bone."

"Look," said Charlie, trying hard to keep his temper. "I don't mind being your monitor but leave my friends alone or . . ."

"Or what?" Dagbert's expression hardened.

Charlie couldn't think of a reply.

"Or nothing," Dagbert answered for him. "You're powerless, Charlie Bone. So you might as well make the best of things."

Charlie was thinking, *He's seen off three of my friends. But there's always Tancred and Lysander.* He stared at Dagbert, but whatever the fish boy was, he didn't appear to be a mind reader.

After supper, while other students went to their classrooms, Charlie led Dagbert up to the King's room.

"What is the King's room?" asked Dagbert as they climbed the narrow staircase at the far end of the building.

"It's where the Red King's portrait hangs. All

endowed children have to do their homework there. Because we're the Red King's descendants."

"So now I'll get to meet the rest of you." Dagbert leaped ahead of Charlie. By the time Charlie reached the tall black doors of the King's room, Dagbert was already inside. Charlie found him gazing at the shelves of books that lined the curving walls.

"A round room," Dagbert observed with satisfaction, "and a round table. How Arthurian."

Four children came in: Joshua Tilpin, Dorcas Loom, and the twins, Inez and Idith Branko.

"Now let me see." Dagbert stared at Joshua. "Magnetism?"

Joshua beamed.

"Good, good." Dagbert turned to Dorcas, who was setting her books in order on the table. "And you can bewitch clothing?"

"How can you tell?" asked Dorcas, a large girl with a puffy face and tangled, yellow hair.

"I can't," Dagbert admitted. "Someone told me."

"And we are telekinetic," one of the twins announced. No one could tell them apart. They both had pale, doll-like faces and shiny black hair. Their bangs ended in a sharp line just above their eyes, dark eyes that never showed a trace of emotion. "Who are you?" the same twin asked.

"I am a boy whose name is as endless as the ocean." Dagbert smiled at them. "My name is Dagbert."

The twins gaped at him. Neither of them asked any more questions.

Charlie felt uncomfortable alone in the room with four children who had made no secret of being his enemies, and a fifth who certainly couldn't be described as a friend. He heaved a sigh of relief when Tancred and Lysander appeared.

Tancred was in a particularly boisterous mood; his green cape billowed around him like a cloud, his blond hair stood up in spikes, and books kept fluttering out of his hands. As he placed his homework on the table, a gust of wind whistled around the room carrying loose paper into the air and rolling pens and pencils across the table.

"For goodness' sake, can't you learn to control yourself, Tancred Torsson?" Dorcas grumbled as she bent to retrieve a book.

Before Tancred could reply, Dagbert cried, "A storm boy! Good to meet you. I'm Dagbert Endless." He walked over to the two older boys and shook their hands. "And you must be Lysander Sage, the spirit-caller."

Lysander, who had African ancestors, gave Dagbert a cool smile.

Dagbert ignored the last three children to arrive. Avoiding Charlie, Emma took a seat close to Tancred, and Gabriel sat on his other side. Only Billy chose to sit beside Charlie. For this he received one of the new boy's chilly stares.

There should have been a twelfth member of the group, but Asa Pike had not been seen for several weeks. Charlie found that he missed the weedy sixth year with his wispy red hair and the wolfish yellow eyes that gave away his terrible endowment.

Lysander was now the oldest member of the endowed, and so he had been put in charge of the home-work room. He had inherited a natural air of authority from his father, the famous Judge Sage. Joshua, Dorcas, and the twins might try to test Lysander's position, but they were a little in awe of the tall spirit-caller and, so far, no one had openly defied him.

"Where's our number twelve?" asked Dagbert. "I was told there is a wolf boy."

"Was," said Lysander quietly. "He's no longer with us. Get on with your work now."

Dagbert meekly opened one of his books and began to read.

Charlie couldn't concentrate. He gazed up at the Red King's portrait and then at the clock on the wall. When Manfred had presided over the King's room, he would command Charlie to look away from the painting and concentrate on his homework.

Charlie had always longed to travel into the painting to talk to the king, but it was impossible. Behind the king stood Harken the Enchanter, a shadowy figure who blocked Charlie's every attempt to reach his ancestor.

Once, the shadow had escaped, but now he was trapped again, an angry, brooding presence whom Charlie could almost feel watching him. *But I don't need to reach the king anymore,* he silently told the shadow, *because I've found my father and there's nothing you can do about it.*

Someone else was watching Charlie. Dagbert's aquamarine eyes were fixed on him. Charlie quickly dropped his gaze and tried to concentrate on his homework.

At eight o'clock everyone closed their books and began to file out of the King's room.

Before Dagbert could catch up with them, Charlie whispered to Billy, "Want to come home with me this weekend?"

"Yes, please," said Billy. "I've got so much to . . ."

"Hey! Wait for me!" Dagbert's voice came ringing after them. "You're supposed to show me the dorms, Charlie Bone."

"I thought Matron would have shown you," said Charlie.

"She did, but I've forgotten." Dagbert grinned as he came up to Charlie with his peculiar lurching and pitching motion.

Billy Raven slipped away.

"That boy gives me the creeps." Dagbert remarked as he watched the retreating student.

"You probably do the same to him," said Charlie.

"Why?" Dagbert looked genuinely surprised.

Charlie hurried on without answering. He wondered where Dagbert would be sleeping. Every bed in his own dormitory was occupied. So there was no danger of the new boy moving in. Or was there? Ahead of him, he could see Gabriel Silk standing in the hall. He looked distraught. Charlie called out to him, but he turned away and went through a door farther down the hallway.

"What's going on?" Charlie walked into his dormitory, Dagbert dogging his steps.

Fidelio was sitting on the bed next to Charlie's. "They've moved Gabriel," he said. "Poor old Gabe. It's not fair. They've put him in with Damian Smerk."

Charlie gasped. "His worst enemy."

Dagbert made his way over to the bed that had once been Gabriel's.

"Now we know the reason for Gabriel's banishment," Fidelio muttered, turning his head in Dagbert's direction.

Charlie lowered his voice. "I'm supposed to be looking after him. I guess that's why Matron put him in here."

Other boys began to arrive. Three first years and five second years led by Bragger Braine and his devoted slave Rupe Small. Dagbert ignored them. This was surprising, considering that he had gone out of his way to make friends with most of the endowed. *Perhaps he considered these ordinary boys not worth the effort,* thought Charlie.

Bragger Braine stopped at the end of Dagbert's bed and commanded the new boy to introduce himself. Dagbert continued to transfer clothes from his bag into the cabinet beside his bed.

"I'm talking to you, boy," Bragger shouted, his wide puglike face reddening.

"Answer!" squeaked Rupe Small.

"Answer, answer, answer!" chanted the others.

Charlie suddenly realized he would have to defend the new boy. "Leave him alone," he said.

"Who asked you, Charlie Bone?" snarled the beefy second year.

"I'm responsible for him," Charlie said in a reasonable tone. "His name is Dagbert Endless."

"I suppose he's one of you peculiar 'endowed' people," Rupe piped up with a giggle.

Charlie found Rupe even more annoying than Bragger. He had such a whiny, high-pitched voice. He followed Bragger's every move with his big doggy eyes, and never said a word unless he was quite sure that Bragger would approve.

"They're not peculiar," Fidelio said evenly.

"OK, so what do you do, new boy?" Bragger climbed onto the rail at the foot of Dagbert's bed. "Forgive me for saying so, but Endless isn't a name."

All at once Dagbert straightened up. He fixed Bragger with his aquamarine eyes and said, "My name is as endless as the ocean and I drown people."

Bragger's feet slipped off the rail and he landed on his back on the floor.

Nobody laughed.

THE HOWLING

It was one of the other boys who passed on the news about Dagbert. It certainly wasn't Bragger. Falling on your back in terror is nothing to brag about.

Word spread fast. Soon even the most clueless first years had heard the rumor: Dagbert Endless drowned people.

But how? That was the question on everyone's mind. On bath night it was noticeable how shallow the bathwater was in every bath. Some of the children decided against bathing altogether and opted for a cold shower in the unheated changing rooms. In February. That's how worried they were.

"What's the matter with you all?" grumbled the matron. "You usually complain that you can't get enough water. Now, all at once, you don't want any. You've barely got enough to clean your knees."

People began to avoid Charlie because Dagbert was always at his side. In team games Charlie was always the last to be picked, as though the new boy was permanently attached to him, and if you got Charlie, you were saddled with Dagbert-the-drowner as well.

There were exceptions, of course. You couldn't keep Joshua, Dorcas, and the twins away from Dagbert. So Charlie had to put up with their company as well. He found it exhausting, listening to them boasting about their peculiar talents. However, he did manage to learn something very interesting.

They were sitting in the King's room, waiting for homework to begin. Lysander and Tancred hadn't arrived. Billy was searching for a reference book, Emma was late, and Gabriel was in the infirmary with a virus.

Charlie had opened his history book and was pretending to take notes on the American War of Independence. The conversation on the other side of the table was being conducted in harsh whispers, with the occasional giggle thrown in by Dorcas. And then, all at once, Charlie caught the phrase:

"She taught me everything I know about bewitching clothes."

Dorcas was talking about Charlie's great-aunt Venetia. He lowered his head and opened his ears.

"Anyway, she told me about this man," Dorcas went on. "She wanted to marry him because, for one thing, he's rich, and for another his little boy is endowed — at least Venetia thinks he is . . ." She stopped and Charlie felt her eyes on him. He kept his head down, but Dorcas continued in such a soft whisper he could only catch the odd words. Words like Archie Shellhorn, poison, beads, heart failure . . . herbs of infatuation . . . wedding. . . .

It was easy enough to guess the rest, and it didn't take Charlie long to work out what his great-aunt had done. Uncle Paton had warned him that Venetia wasn't above murder, and he was right. She had poisoned Archie Shellhorn's wife with a string of beads that stopped her heart, then soaked Archie's coat in a brew of infatuating herbs. And poor, deluded Archie, desperately in love, had begged Venetia to marry him.

At this point Lysander and Tancred breezed in, the latter looking even more blown about than usual.

"Sorry we're late," said Lysander. "We were in a meeting. Glad to see you're all getting on with your work. Where's Emma?"

"Here. I'm here." Emma came in behind them.

Silence fell. Everyone bent their heads toward their books. Homework began.

Charlie stared at the pages of his history book without seeing them. His mind roamed elsewhere. He was trying to imagine what it would be like to have a stepmother like Great-aunt Venetia: poisoner, bewitcher, murderer. He could hardly wait to see Uncle Paton. *One more night to go,* he thought, and then he'd be free of Dagbert Endless. He would be sitting at home, eating one of Maisie's delicious suppers.

It was not to be.

On Thursday night, only five minutes after lights-out, Dagbert decided to tell a bedtime story.

"It's against the rules to talk after lights-out." Charlie's whispered warning made no impression on

Dagbert, so he raised his whisper another notch. "You'll get detention."

"Who says?" asked Dagbert.

"Let him tell the story," said Bragger, eager to keep on the right side of Dagbert.

"Yes, let him," squeaked Rupe. "You're a spoilsport, Charlie Bone."

Fidelio muttered, "You won't be seeing your fish shop on Friday night."

"Want to bet," Dagbert sneered.

Fidelio turned over and punched his pillow into shape.

In a loud voice Dagbert continued his story. It was boring and badly told. It certainly wasn't funny, even though Bragger and Rupe kept giggling. Stories about mermaids always made Charlie yawn. He yawned and closed his eyes.

Two seconds later the door opened and Matron marched into the room. She turned on the light. Charlie opened his eyes and blinked.

"Who was talking?" Matron demanded.

"I was," Dagbert said cheerfully. "I was telling a story."

"You're breaking the rules," said Matron.

"Am I?" Dagbert sounded incredulous. "I'm really sorry. I didn't know."

Matron gave a sigh of annoyance. "Charlie, you're responsible for the new boy. You're supposed to tell him the rules."

"Yes, well I . . . ," Charlie began.

"Detention for you," snapped his great-aunt. "You won't be going home until Saturday."

"But I did tell him," Charlie protested.

Matron switched off the light and marched out, slamming the door behind her.

The silence that followed was broken by a snort from Bragger and a snigger from Rupe.

Charlie lay on his back, staring into the darkness. He told himself that he didn't care. What was one more day after all? He lay awake long past midnight and then, just as he was drifting off to sleep, a sound came stealing through the night. A far, far distant howl.

There was a rustle of sheets, and Charlie saw the rounded shape of Billy Raven's white head. He was sitting up — listening. *He knows what the howl means,* thought Charlie, *and soon he'll tell me.*

The last thing Charlie expected was an apology, but at breakfast the next morning, he got one.

"Sorry about last night," said Dagbert, swallowing a spoonful of cornflakes. "I couldn't afford to get detention. The people I live with won't understand if I don't turn up tonight."

"You didn't have to talk after lights-out, though, did you?" said Fidelio. "Charlie warned you."

Dagbert frowned. "It's hard to keep stories to yourself," he murmured.

Charlie almost felt sorry for him. "Well, you won't get away with it a second time. Matron's told you now, so you'll have to keep your stories bottled up."

"Yes, I will," Dagbert said pensively. "Imagine. Stories in a bottle."

Not for the first time Charlie wondered what was going on in Dagbert's head.

Charlie spent the rest of the day in a state of suspense. All he wanted was to hear what Billy had to tell him.

At four o'clock Weedon unlocked the main doors, and children piled out of the academy. From their dormitory, Charlie and Billy could hear the shouts that began immediately as pupils were released from the gloomy hall. Charlie peered out of the window overlooking the courtyard. He saw Dagbert Endless following the crowd. He was the only one who didn't look happy. His expression was solemn, almost apprehensive. He was the last to leave the courtyard.

Charlie turned from the window. "They're all gone, Billy."

Billy was sitting on his bed with his knees drawn up to his chin.

"Before we talk about Dagbert I want to know what you heard last night," said Charlie.

"A howl," Billy replied.

"I heard it, too. You know what it meant, don't you?"

Billy nodded. He hunched his shoulders and hugged himself. "It was a call for help. It was frightened and lonely."

Charlie looked into Billy's wine-dark eyes, magnified by the round lenses of his glasses. "Do you know where the voice — the howl — came from?"

"Not exactly. It's far, far away, maybe underground. It says it's trapped."

"Trapped?" said Charlie. "Who's trapped it, I wonder?"

Billy shrugged. "Charlie, I want to tell you about Dagbert," he said. "I've been trying all week, but he's always there, right behind you. He calls me a freak."

"And Gabriel a loser, and he told Olivia and Emma they looked a mess. An absolute lie."

Billy leaned forward. "Cook knew Dagbert's father. He drowned her parents, swept away her home, and murdered her fiancé. All because she wouldn't marry him."

"Wait a minute!" Charlie exclaimed. "I remember. Cook told me. His name is Grimwald."

"Lord Grimwald," said Billy. "Blessed says he smells of rust and seaweed and shipwrecks and drownings. And there's a cold pearl in his heart, trapped like sand in an oyster shell. Cook's going to leave. She's frightened."

Charlie slid to the floor. "Cook, leave? She can't. She keeps the balance here. She's the lodestone of the house. Why should she leave? No one knows who she really is."

"Dagbert might find out," Billy said gravely.

Charlie resolved to change Cook's mind. He would see her at supper and convince her that she must stay. Otherwise, who would care for Billy during the long school holidays? He had no home, no parents, no one else in the world to turn to. The Bloors kept promising him that he would be adopted but it had never happened, unless you counted the de Greys, who had treated Billy like a servant and kept him locked up.

Students in detention could usually expect a cold supper in the cafeteria. But when Billy and Charlie went downstairs at six o'clock, the blue cafeteria was deserted. Chairs had been piled onto tables and a blue checkered cloth covered the counter.

Charlie opened the door into the kitchen and looked around. There wasn't a soul in sight. The heavy saucepans were all hanging in place, the ovens were closed and cold, and there wasn't even a whisper of steam.

"What are you doing?" said a voice.

Charlie swung around. He came face to face with Weedon's wife. Mrs. Weedon was a wide, grim faced, and goggle-eyed woman who was usually in charge of the green cafeteria.

"I'm looking for Cook," said Charlie.

"Cook's out." Mrs. Weedon's bloodred lips smacked unpleasantly.

"We wanted some supper." Charlie looked at Billy, standing hopefully beside a cloth-covered table.

Mrs. Weedon glanced at Billy. "And I suppose you've got detention, Charlie Bone?"

"That doesn't mean I'm not to be fed," Charlie said defiantly.

"Tsk!" Mrs. Weedon turned her back and walked out. "You'd better come with me," she called back to them.

The green cafeteria was in the same state as the blue: chairs on tables, counter covered in a cloth — a green one this time.

"Baked beans is all I've got." Mrs. Weedon snorted. "You can sit there." She pointed to a table. "I'm not supposed to be on duty but Cook rushed off, goodness knows where, and the Bloors want their supper, which I've got to carry all the way over to the west wing, if you please."

Charlie had never known Mrs. Weedon to say much. "Cook hasn't left, has she?" he asked tentatively.

"Left? Of course not." Mrs. Weedon's goggle eyes tightened a fraction. "Why? What makes you think she's left?"

"I don't. It's just . . . well, we just wondered."

Mrs. Weedon frowned and shook her head. "You

wonder more than is good for you." She stomped through the door into the kitchen.

Charlie and Billy removed two chairs from the table Mrs. Weedon had indicated and sat down.

The beans, when they arrived, were barely warm. The toast was burnt and there wasn't a smidgen of butter. Charlie decided to try for a second helping. Telling Billy to follow him, he went to the door of the green kitchen and looked in. There was no sign of Mrs. Weedon.

"Come on," Charlie whispered. "Let's look for some food. I'm starving."

They crept into the kitchen. A row of jars drew Charlie's eye. Sure enough they contained cookies — chocolate truffles and garibaldis. The boys took two of each, stuffing them into their mouths as they moved farther into the room. Billy found a box of shortbread and slipped a piece into his pocket. Charlie found some gingerbread and broke off a chunk. He was beginning to feel better already. They reached the door at the back of the kitchen and stepped into a yard where a narrow flight of stone steps led up to the road.

"You know we could get out this way," said Charlie. "We could go into the city and find a nice café and . . ."

Billy's elbow dug into Charlie's ribs. "Look!" Billy whispered.

At the far end of the yard two people squatted in a dark corner. Really, they were not quite people. They had the shining eyes of a predatory animal and their faces were dotted with patches of hair. For a few seconds they were so still they could almost have been taken for statues, but all at once, they emitted a faint whimper and scuttled toward the steps. They climbed the flight of steps on all fours, bounding to the top as fast as cats. The iron gate onto the street gave a light clang as the two figures pushed it open and disappeared.

Billy gripped Charlie's arm. "What were they?"

"I don't know," said Charlie. "But they've been following me." He noticed something in the corner where the strangers had been squatting. Could it be a bowl? He walked over to it.

"Look!" he called. "This bowl's half full of cereal-type stuff. Nuts and oats and bananas and things. It looks as if someone's been feeding them. Come and see."

Before Billy could move, a hand shot out of the doorway behind him.

Mrs. Weedon grabbed the back of Billy's collar, almost choking him. "Now what have you done?" She glared at Charlie.

"We were hungry," he said.

"That's no excuse for snooping." Mrs. Weedon released Billy and gave him a little push. "Did you see anyone here?"

"We . . . ," Billy began, but Charlie quickly cut him off with a loud, "No. No one."

"Hmmm." She regarded Charlie with her suspicious, bulging eyes. "Get inside."

They meekly obeyed.

"I shall tell Dr. Bloor about this," said Mrs. Weedon

as she followed them through the cafeteria. "You'd better go straight to bed."

"We haven't done anything wrong," Charlie protested.

"I've only got your word for that." She grunted.

They heard the lock click as they walked away from the cafeteria door. Charlie felt for the ginger-bread in his pocket, glad that he'd managed to grab something before he was caught.

Matron looked in on the boys when she came to turn off the light. "Your uncle will pick you up tomor-row," she said coldly. "What a nuisance you are, Charlie Bone."

"Billy's coming home with me," said Charlie.

The matron pursed her lips but she didn't argue. Uncle Paton had forced the Bloors to sign a docu-ment, promising that Billy could spend the weekend with anyone he wished.

It was a bitterly cold night and they huddled under the blankets to eat the food they'd taken from the kitchen. Charlie soon fell asleep. He dreamed of his parents, riding the waves in their sturdy boat, while whales sang in the ocean. "They do sing, you know," his mother had said. "Are you sure you don't want to come?"

Charlie had found himself shaking his head. His parents needed their time alone. They had lost ten years of being together; besides, instinct warned Charlie that he must remain in the city, the place where so many people had wanted his father "out of the way," where plots were hatched and where Charlie's friends were constantly in danger.

In Charlie's dream the whales' song gradually changed into a sad lament, and as he listened to it, he became aware that he was awake and listening to the distant, desperate howl again.

"Billy, can you hear it?" Charlie whispered.

"Yes," said Billy. "It keeps repeating the same words, over and over. 'Help me!' It kind of knocks against my heart, Charlie. What are we going to do?"

"Help it," Charlie replied, though he had no idea how.

THE ALTERING BUGS

On Saturday morning, rain, occasionally turning to sleet, drifted down the windowpanes. The sky was a dismal, leaden gray and the temperature freezing.

There was still no sign of Cook so Charlie and Billy ate a miserable breakfast in the green cafeteria: burnt toast again, no butter, and no cereal. They thought they would have to go without a drink until Mrs. Weedon plunked down a jug of water and two mugs on the table.

"I suppose we couldn't have a bit of butter?" Charlie asked cautiously.

"You suppose right," said Mrs. Weedon.

"Jam?" suggested Billy.

Mrs. Weedon ignored him and marched out, returning two minutes later with a pot of white stuff. "Dripping," she told them. "It's good for you."

The boys eyed the dripping doubtfully. As soon as Mrs. Weedon had gone, Charlie stuck his knife into the pot and brought it out, smeared with dripping. He licked the knife. "Uuurrrghh! It tastes disgusting."

Billy was of a different opinion. "I quite like it," he said, spreading the dripping thickly onto his toast. "The burnt bits don't taste so bad with this on top."

After breakfast they wandered up to the King's room. There was no one around to tell them what to do. If Manfred Bloor had been there, he would probably have ordered them outside onto the grounds. He had been very keen on getting students outside, especially when it was cold or wet. Where WAS Manfred?

"I heard he looked like a monster." Billy glanced around the room, half-expecting Manfred to appear from behind a bookcase. "He's all bent and lame."

"I'm surprised he's alive," said Charlie in a low voice. "Not many people could survive a leopard attack."

"Leopards." A note of awe crept into Billy's voice. "And they look like ordinary cats, except for their color."

"Mmmm." Charlie had never ceased to wonder how three cats had, for a few vital minutes, become leopards, capable of tearing a human being to shreds. Well, not shreds, perhaps, but near enough.

At noon the boys decided to look for Cook. After such a meager breakfast their stomachs were already rumbling. As they descended the main staircase they saw a figure making its way across the hall. A dark cape covered most of the body. Only the feet, clad in black boots, could be seen from below pants that hung in folds around the ankles. A hood was thrown over the head which jutted forward from the hunched shoulders in an odd, uncomfortable way.

The boys froze as the hooded figure limped over to the door in the west wing. There was something desperate in the way it rattled and shook the ringed handle, seemingly unable to turn it. But at last the door opened and it was then that the figure turned toward the boys.

They expected to see a frowning face, an expression of annoyance at being watched. But the hooded man had no face. Charlie and Billy found themselves looking at a white mask with slanting, silver-rimmed eyeholes and a gaping, boat-shaped mouth. And then it was gone, slipping through the small door with surprising speed, leaving the boys agape on the stairs.

"Manfred," Billy whispered.

Charlie nodded. "Must be."

"I feel all peculiar," said Billy. "I'm trying to imagine what sort of face he's got."

"Don't," said Charlie.

They found Cook, at last, at the far end of her kitchen. She was muttering out loud to herself as she threw chopped onions into a sizzling pan. Charlie called her name and, receiving no reply, gently touched her arms. Cook screamed and her wooden spoon went flying through the air.

"Why did you do that?" she screeched.

"You couldn't hear me, Cook. You were talking to yourself."

"Was I? Well, what of it?" Cook straightened her apron and turned down the gas.

When she heard about the food the boys had been forced to endure, Cook calmed down a little and promised them some minestrone soup for lunch. "With a bit of apple crumble to follow," she added. "I've got some in the oven for the Bloors."

"Where've you been, Cook?" Billy asked. "You're always here at breakfast time."

"I was staying with a friend. I nearly didn't come back, I can tell you. But my friend convinced me that I must. She's such a sensible person." Cook lifted the lid on her saucepan and threw in a handful of herbs.

"Mmmm!" Charlie closed his eyes. The smell coming from the saucepan was so delicious he could almost taste it.

"It's not ready yet." Cook shooed the boys back into the cafeteria. A few minutes later she appeared with two bowls of steaming minestrone.

"You wouldn't really leave Bloor's, would you?" Charlie asked Cook.

She grimaced. "Has Billy told you about that boy Dagbert?"

"I know all about Dagbert." Charlie sighed. "And Lord Grimwald and what he did to you. It's horrible,

Cook, but Dagbert doesn't know who you are. Why should you be afraid of him?"

"I can't help it, Charlie. It churns my stomach, just thinking about that family. By the way, Billy, your rat has been moved."

"Rembrandt? Why? Why can't he stay in the Pets' Café?"

"He's disgraced himself," said Cook. "Been stealing treats. It's all very upsetting. You know how Mrs. Onimous loves him. She didn't want him to go, of course, but Mr. Onimous insisted. I hear the poor snake misses him terribly, quite lost its color. But there we are."

"But where's Rembrandt now?" Billy asked in a desperate voice. "Is he happy? Does he like his new place?"

"He's in the Kettle Shop," Cook informed them. "Can't steal anything there, except tea, of course. And he's not very fond of that, by all accounts." She turned away.

"Where is the Kettle Shop?" asked Billy.

Cook hesitated. Her mind seemed to be elsewhere. "The Kettle Shop," she said absently, "is on Piminy Street. Ask for Mrs. Kettle — a very good friend of mine. Enjoy your soup."

When Cook walked back into the kitchen, Charlie noticed that the spring had left her step. She was usually such a positive and cheerful person; it worried him to see her so dejected.

The promised apple crumble soon followed the minestrone soup and, leaving Cook still talking to herself, Charlie and Billy made their way back to the King's room. With no one in charge, it was difficult to apply themselves to work.

"If Olivia was here she'd make us explore," said Billy wistfully.

But Olivia wasn't there and the very mention of her name made Charlie angry. He couldn't forget the way she had flounced off, telling him he was a liar and a fraud.

"Oh, come on, let's explore," Billy pleaded.

Charlie groaned and put down his book, which had suddenly started to get interesting. "OK."

Where to explore? Billy didn't have an answer. Not in the attics where Mr. Ezekiel lived among his grisly experiments. And not in the basement, where Dr. Bloor kept ancient instruments of torture, among other gruesome objects. And certainly not on the grounds, where sleet had turned to a white mist of hail.

They eventually decided on the art room. Paintings were always entertaining, even if they weren't beautiful. And the sculpture room held some very impressive works. Lysander was a particularly fine sculptor, and Tancred's statues could be interesting, never mind that you couldn't always tell what they were.

The art room lay just beyond the boys' dormitory and overlooked the garden. Today the long windows showed only a moving sheet of snow and hail. It cast an eerie light over the forest of easels and drawing boards.

"Let's go and see Lysander's statue," Billy suggested.

A wrought-iron spiral staircase led down to the sculpture room. As they descended, an unexpected sound came drifting up to them. Singing. Or was it chanting? Who could it be? As far as they knew no one else had been given detention that weekend.

When they reached the sculpture studio, they tiptoed around blocks of wood and plaster and odd-shaped statues. In the center of the room stood Lysander's masterpiece, a very lifelike carving of his mother, Jessamine Sage, and her new baby.

The chanting grew louder as they moved through the long room. When they got to the other side, there was no doubt that the voice was coming from the room beyond. A room used for dressmaking classes and first years' drawing lessons.

Charlie put his hand on the doorknob.

"Go on," whispered Billy. "Let's see who it is."

Charlie flung open the door.

There was a shriek, a flurry of paper, pins, and

fabric, and the boys found themselves staring at Dorcas Loom. On the wide worktable in front of her lay the biggest pair of scissors Charlie had ever seen. And he didn't fail to notice the pots and boxes, the small cans, and bunches of herbs that sat in neat rows beside the scissors. His great-aunt Venetia had something to do with this.

"Snoops!" cried Dorcas.

Charlie ignored her accusing glare. "What are you doing in school?"

"What are YOU doing in here?" she retorted, hastily pulling a sheet of tissue paper over something blue.

Charlie had seen what it was. "I've got detention," he said airily. "What's your excuse?"

Recovering her composure, Dorcas said haughtily, "I don't need an excuse. I'm working on something for your aunt Venetia."

"I can see you've got all the right stuff." Charlie picked up one of the cans and read the label. "Altering Bugs. Is that to . . ."

"Give it to me!" Dorcas interrupted. She grabbed

the end of the can while Charlie still held firmly to the lid. It was inevitable that the two parts should separate.

A cloud of orange bugs poured onto the table, covering scissors, pins, and cotton reels.

"Fiends!" yelled Dorcas, frantically pulling things out of the way of the bugs. "Get out of here. GET OUT!"

Charlie and Billy didn't move. Before their very eyes, the bug-covered items were slowly changing shape; they were growing longer, thinner, smoother.

"Wh-what are you doing, Dorcas?" Billy asked shakily.

"Mind your own business," she bellowed. "GET OUT. GO AWAY!"

She was drowned out by a roar from the doorway.

"Are you deaf, Charlie Bone?" shouted Weedon. "I've been searching the entire school for you. It's time to go home. Unless you plan to spend another night here."

"NO, no," said Charlie. "I didn't realize. Is Uncle Paton . . ."

"Won't come in. Keeps phoning me from that wretched cell phone of his. Blasted gadgets. Should never have been invented. Instruments of the devil, if you ask me."

Charlie rushed past Weedon with Billy close behind him. They tore up to the dormitory to fetch their bags and were back in the hall in three minutes flat. Weedon came lumbering downstairs after them.

"You don't deserve a vacation," he grumbled, unlocking the heavy door.

Charlie didn't bother to point out that one day away from school wasn't exactly a vacation. The sleet had died away at last, but it had been replaced by an icy fog. They could barely make out Uncle Paton's car parked across the square. As usual his head was bent over a book. Unusually, he wasn't wearing his dark glasses.

"Can hardly see a thing in this fog," Uncle Paton remarked as the boys scrambled into the backseat. "So I doubt that anyone can see me."

They drove cautiously out of the square. It was

already getting dark and the streetlights appeared as soft halos of light, hanging in the fog.

"Extraordinary fog," said Uncle Paton as he peered ahead. "It tastes of salt. Must have blown in from the sea, though goodness knows it's miles away."

"The sea." Charlie was beginning to make a connection. "Uncle P., there's a new boy at school. His endowment, he says, is drowning."

Uncle Paton chuckled. "Drowning? A ghostly shipwreck of a person, then?"

"It's serious, Mr. Yewbeam," said Billy earnestly. "He drowns OTHER people."

Charlie added, "His father is Lord Grimwald. The man who . . ."

"Good heavens! I know who you mean, Charlie. A wrecker if ever there was one. He's been keeping quiet lately. I thought he was dead and buried. Mind you" — Uncle Paton honked at a car that loomed out of the fog, dangerously close — "there have been a few drownings in his area lately. Fishermen mostly.

They put it down to the weather, but you never know."

"Where is his area?" asked Charlie.

"North." Uncle Paton waved a hand in no particular direction. "One of the islands. No one knows the precise location. They're a curious bunch, the Grimwalds. Legend has it that when a son of that family reaches twelve years, his father dies — or he does. The two cannot both survive beyond the son's thirteenth year. A family tragedy, you might say. On the other hand, one drowner is better than two."

Charlie had lost a father when he was too young to remember him. But now that father was found, how terrible it would be to lose him again, when he was twelve. A twinge of fear caused him to shiver as he thought of his parents surrounded by the sea. He could even taste the salt on his lips.

The car jerked to a halt as Paton suddenly realized they were outside number nine. When they got out of the car, the fog wrapped itself around them like an icy blanket.

Billy coughed and clutched his chest. "It goes right down your throat," he spluttered. "Like swallowing cotton wool."

As they climbed the steps the muffled sound of church bells stole through the misty air, and Paton said, "Ah, that reminds me, your great-aunt Venetia was married today, Charlie." He opened the front door.

"What a horrible day for a wedding." Charlie remarked as he stepped inside. "Bad luck, I expect."

His uncle wiped his feet on the doormat. "I wasn't invited, naturally."

The boys were very glad to find that Maisie hadn't been invited either. They were able to sit down to a delicious tea without Grandma Bone's sour face looming across the table.

"You should have seen your grandma," Maisie said. "She decided to go to the wedding after all. Disapproval all over her face, but she couldn't miss it. She was purple from head to foot. Yes, even purple shoes with big bows on them, and what a hat! Grapes galore. Looked like a fruit salad."

The image of Grandma Bone's long face beneath bunches of purple grapes caused Charlie to choke on his snack, and then the whole table was laughing, Uncle Paton loudest of all.

Charlie thought of visiting Benjamin after tea, but the view from the kitchen window wasn't encouraging. The houses across the street were buried in darkness and fog. All that could be seen were tiny pinpricks of light from the cars making their way slowly down the street.

Billy peered wistfully through the window. He longed to fetch his pet rat but didn't dare to suggest it on such an unfriendly night.

"We'll get Rembrandt first thing tomorrow," Charlie promised. "And we'll take Benjamin and Runner Bean with us."

Sometime during the night, the fog slowly rolled away. A full moon appeared high in the sky, and a hard frost covered the city. Every roof glittered as though it were dusted with silver. In the wilderness across the river, a captive creature began its melancholy howl.

Sunday morning greeted the boys with bright sunshine and an icy blue sky. They made their own breakfast — cereal, toast, and milk — before anyone else was up. But Maisie struggled downstairs in her curlers and pink bathrobe, just as they were finishing.

"You make sure you're back by lunchtime or I'll come after you," she said. "Piminy Street is right behind the cathedral, near Ingledew's bookstore. If you want to stop at the shop for lunch, give me a ring."

"We won't be going there," Charlie said awkwardly.

Maisie tilted her head to one side. "Had a fight with one of your girlfriends?"

"I don't have a girlfriend," Charlie said heatedly, "and I haven't had a fight with anyone."

On their way out, the boys noticed a very large,

colorful hat sitting on the hall chair. It did look like a fruit salad. The sight gave Billy a fit of the giggles, and Charlie immediately felt better.

Benjamin was always ready for an expedition, and Runner Bean was beside himself with joy when his leash was taken from its hook in the hall.

Benjamin's parents were already hard at work when the three boys left number twelve. Being private detectives meant that weekends could be just as busy as weekdays. Today they weren't actually out on a case, they were in the kitchen devising yet another set of cunning disguises. They had to renew their disguises frequently when they were "shadowing a subject," as they put it. Sometimes, even Benjamin failed to recognize them. They were always very pleased when this happened, although Benjamin wasn't.

"Can I have lunch at your place?" Benjamin asked as they headed toward the cathedral.

Charlie was aware that Mr. and Mrs. Brown relied on Maisie to give their son good, wholesome meals on the weekends. "'Course you can," he said.

"And shall we go to the Pets' Café for a snack when Billy's got Rembrandt?" Benjamin said eagerly.

"No," said Charlie rather quickly.

Benjamin came to a halt. "Why not?"

"Let's just say that Emma and Olivia might be there, and they might not be too happy to see me."

"Why?" asked Benjamin.

Charlie told him about Dagbert.

"But you've got to put it right between you," Benjamin insisted. "You can tell them it was all a terrible mistake."

"It's not that easy," said Billy as Charlie strode ahead. "You see, Dagbert has made us all on edge. He called me a freak."

Runner Bean dragged Benjamin after Charlie. Benjamin panted, "I think you should make up with them."

"Well, I don't." Charlie walked even faster. "And that's that."

It wasn't true. Charlie did want to make it up with Emma and Olivia. He just couldn't think of a way to do it. He hadn't realized that he would have to pass the end of Cathedral Close on the way to Piminy Street.

Ingledew's bookstore lay in Cathedral Close. It stood in a row of old half-timbered houses in the shadow of the great cathedral. Charlie glanced up the cobblestone alley that led to the bookstore and hurried on to Piminy Street. He wondered if Olivia was in the bookstore with Emma. What would they be doing? Helping Emma's aunt, Miss Ingledew, no doubt. They would be sorting books, brushing the soft leather bindings, and dusting the gold leaf that edged the delicate pages. Or would they be dreaming up some scheme to punish him for words he'd never uttered?

Charlie was correct in one respect. Emma and Olivia were in the bookstore, dreaming up a scheme, or rather Olivia was. But it had nothing to do with Charlie. It was more in the way of an experiment.

Olivia's endowment had been kept secret from the Bloors. Only her closest friends knew that she was an illusionist. Some of these friends, Charlie included, thought that it was only a matter of time before her talent was discovered, for Olivia was an actress. She loved to entertain, and the temptation to use her talent for fun sometimes got the better of her.

It was Emma's obsession with birds that led Olivia to have one of her more dangerous ideas. Emma could fly, but first she had to become a bird. She drew birds, she collected feathers, she pored over illustrations of birds that had long become extinct. Only that morning she had come upon a bird that she had never heard of. It was in one of her aunt's oldest and most precious books.

Emma took the book into the back room and laid it open on her knees. "Just imagine, Liv! To be a bird like that, your beak so long and your feet so big, but your wings so small they can hardly get you off the ground."

Olivia lay sprawled on Miss Ingledew's comfy sofa. She folded her arms behind her head and closed her eyes. "I can see a fabulous bird," she said with a smile.

"How about I create a bird for you, Em? And you become that bird. So then there'd be two, and we could get your aunt to make a guess. Which is Emma and which is the illusion?" She opened her eyes and sat up, clapping her hands. "Yes. Let's do it."

Emma regarded her friend with an anxious frown. "I don't think so, Liv. It wouldn't be right."

"Why not? Oh, come on, Em!"

"We shouldn't — you know — use our endowments just for fun."

"Why? Who says?"

"It's something one just knows," Emma said firmly.

Olivia flung herself back onto the cushions. "Well, I'm going to do it."

"NO, Liv. Please don't. You might . . ."

But the fabulous bird was already taking shape. As Olivia looked over her shoulder, a cloud of multi-colored feathers materialized in the air behind her head. And Emma watched helplessly as the feathers began to find their places within the form of a beautiful creature. It had wide wings, a graceful sweeping fan for a tail, eyes like bright jewels, and a sharp orange beak.

Not content with the shape of the bird, Olivia made it utter a long cooing sound as it swept through the curtained doorway and into the shop beyond.

At the very same moment the shop bell tinkled, the door opened, and a tall woman appeared on the threshold.

Miss Ingledew, labeling books on the counter, looked up from her task in confusion. Two things struck her. One, that she had forgotten to lock the shop door on a Sunday and two, that an extraordinary bird had escaped from the zoo and found its way into her shop. The situation was made even more confusing when Emma ran into the room, crying, "Oh, no!" Upon which, the bird vanished into thin air.

"Ah," said the stranger. "An illusion. How very interesting."

There was no mistaking the unwelcome visitor. With her jet-black hair and high, arched eyebrows, Emma would have known Charlie's great-aunt Venetia anywhere. But what a change had come over her. Gone were the dirty skirt and ill-fitting coat that she'd been wearing recently. This woman was dressed in a smart lilac-colored suit with a fur collar and matching fur-cuffed boots.

"I am recently married," said the woman, descending the three steps into the shop. "I am now Mrs. Venetia Shellhorn. I am about to take a honeymoon."

"Yes?" said Miss Ingledew, not in the least enlightened.

"Yes. And I have brought my . . ." Venetia looked over her shoulder. "Where are they?" she said irritably.

The door opened very slowly.

"My children." Venetia waved her gloved hand at the door.

Standing on the top step were two of the most pathetic-looking children Emma had ever seen.

FEROMEL'S KETTLE

Venetia beckoned the children and they shuffled forward, the girl leading the way, the boy hardly moving at all.

"This is Miranda." Venetia grabbed the girl's hand and pulled her to her side. "She's small for seven, isn't she? But Eric, well, my goodness, look at him. You'd never think he was six, would you?" She lunged at the boy and tried to grasp his hand, but he backed away and stood against the bookshelves.

"Have it your way, silly boy," Venetia said testily. She turned to Miss Ingledew. "I'm told that my great-nephew calls here on Sundays."

Miss Ingledew said sharply, "Not always."

"No matter." Venetia looked at Emma. "I expect you'll be seeing him today, won't you, Ella — or whatever your name is?"

"Well . . . ," Emma began.

"You can pass them over when you see him," Venetia told her.

"Pass them . . . " Emma hesitated. "Do you mean your children?"

"Well, of course. Who do you think?" Venetia gave Miranda a little push toward Emma.

"You can't leave them here," Miss Ingledew said indignantly.

Venetia marched up the steps, the tap of her high-heeled boots resounding like gunshots. "There was no one at number nine. Paton was probably in, but he never answers the door. So I'll have to leave the children here. My sister Eustacia will pick them up at five. I'm told you make very good sandwiches, Miss Ingledew."

"This is a bookstore, not a nursery." Miss Ingledew was so annoyed she slammed a very valuable book onto the counter.

"I can't take them on my honeymoon, can I?" Venetia sang as she sailed out into the street. "Toodle-oo kids, be good."

The door tinkled shut, leaving Miss Ingledew with a stunned expression, staring over Miranda's head at Emma.

"Well!" Miss Ingledew said at last. She would like to have said a great deal more, but the two children looked so woebegone, she realized it would only make things worse if she were to complain. Venetia had relied on her good nature.

The two children had moved together now. They stood holding hands in the center of the shop, staring helplessly, first at Emma, then at Miss Ingledew. They were, indeed, very small for their ages. Miranda had long, mouse-brown hair and gray eyes. She wore jeans and a red coat that appeared to have shrunk several sizes. The cuffs didn't even cover her bird-thin wrists. Eric's tangled hair was darker. It obviously hadn't been cut for some time and straggled to his shoulders in untidy wisps. He wore green corduroy trousers, very dirty at the knees, and a black jacket missing several buttons.

Emma's heart went out to them. She couldn't bear

to see anything small in distress. "Come and meet my friend." She held out her hand. "We're drawing birds. Do you like drawing? I'm Emma, by the way."

Miranda said, "Can we get our dog?"

"Dog?" Miss Ingledew frowned. "Where is it?"

"We had to leave her in the house. She's all alone. She hates being alone." Miranda's eyes began to fill with tears.

Olivia chose that moment to pop her head around the curtain. "Oh!" she squeaked, seeing the children. "I didn't know anyone was here. I was lying low, in case someone saw the bird."

"What bird?" Eric brightened up.

"Oh, just a bird," Olivia said casually. "Who are you?"

The children stared at Olivia, saying nothing.

"This is Miranda and Eric," Emma said in an overly cheerful voice. "They're Charlie Bone's new, er, step-cousins, I suppose."

Olivia rolled her eyes. "You poor things. I wouldn't like to be connected to THAT family. I'm Olivia."

"Olivia!" Miss Ingledew said sharply. "Please don't speak of Charlie's family like that."

"Oops." Olivia withdrew her head.

"Please can we get our dog?" Miranda persisted.

Miss Ingledew rubbed her head. "I don't know, dear. I mean, how will you get into the house. Did your stepmother leave you a key?"

Miranda shook her head.

Miss Ingledew sighed. "Give me a moment. I'll have to call a friend for advice." She took her phone from a pocket and began to dial a number.

Emma coaxed the two children into the back room while her aunt phoned Paton Yewbeam. Miranda and Eric gazed doubtfully around the book-filled room and eventually chose to sit, side by side, on the sofa.

"Will your aunt be long?" asked Miranda. "Chattypatra will whine and whine until we get back to her."

"Great name," Olivia remarked. "Where did it come from?"

"It was really Cleopatra," Miranda told her. "But

she chats so much. You know, barks and growls and stuff. So Mom . . . " She stopped and looked at Eric. He drew in his lower lip but didn't cry. "So Mom," Miranda continued, "Mom called her Chattypatra."

"Brilliant," Olivia said approvingly.

Miss Ingledew looked into the room and told them that when Mr. Yewbeam had found a key to Venetia's house, he would send Charlie over to the bookstore with it.

"Will it take a long time?" Miranda's red-rimmed eyes looked imploringly at Miss Ingledew.

"I shouldn't think so, dear. Now, would you like to help Emma make some sandwiches?"

"Of course you would," said Olivia. "Come on, let's make some honey and banana, or how about cheese and raisins, or grapefruit and peanut butter, or we could do sausage and orange?"

To Miss Ingledew's relief, Miranda, wearing a dazed expression, followed Olivia into the kitchen, with Eric only a few steps behind.

As soon as Miss Ingledew had returned to the

shop, Paton Yewbeam called with the news that Grandma Bone had gone out, locking her door behind her, and now there was no possibility of searching her room for a key.

"Oh, Paton, I don't know what I'm going to do," said Miss Ingledew. "Those poor children. They look so miserable. I thought the dog might cheer them up."

"What was my ghastly sister thinking of," said Paton, "leaving them in your shop? Look, Julia, I don't know if it will help, but I'm pretty sure Venetia leaves her door key under a gruesome-looking troll on her top step."

"A troll?" said Miss Ingledew, never having visited Venetia's house.

"Awful-looking creature. Stone. Big ears. Long nose. Beard. Squat thing. Huge feet."

"I know what a troll is," Miss Ingledew said quickly. "I was just questioning the wisdom of leaving one's door key underneath one."

"It's not alive, Julia, dearest."

"I know it's not alive." Julia gave a huge sigh.

Sometimes it seemed that Paton didn't live in the same world as everyone else. "I just mean that someone could find the key and break in."

"Who on earth would want to break in?" said Paton. "Venetia's only valuables consist of large amounts of bewitching ingredients that only she would know how to use."

Miss Ingledew gave up. "Thank you, Paton. We'll think about it."

For his part, Paton wondered what Julia was going to think about. He loved her dearly but there were times when they just didn't seem to be on the same wavelength. As soon as Charlie and his friends got home, he would tell them to run up to Venetia's house to see if there was a key under the troll. "No, on second thought, I'd better let them have their lunch first," Paton said to himself.

Charlie, Billy, and Benjamin were walking slowly down Piminy Street. They still hadn't found the Kettle Shop and were beginning to think it didn't exist. Piminy

Street was full of odd little shops, all closed, of course, it being Sunday. There were cheesemakers, candle-makers, shoemakers, carpenters, several bakeries, flower shops, and even a stone shop.

"The Stone Shop," murmured Charlie, peering into the dark window. "What does THAT mean?"

"They sell things made of stone?" Benjamin suggested.

Charlie suddenly became aware of a tall figure, just inside the window. He looked closer. "A statue," he said. As his eyes grew accustomed to the dark, the interior of the shop gradually came into focus. Now he could see other figures: There was a group of life-size statues of Roman soldiers; beside them stood three fierce-looking women carrying clubs and axes and, farther back, a man that looked more ogre than human. At the far end, beneath a skylight, there was a mounted knight, wielding a lance. The knight's horse wore a feathered headdress, and beneath the saddle its body was covered in a kind of blanket patterned with leaves.

"He's jousting," said Benjamin knowledgeably.

"Imagine if they were alive," Billy said, almost in a whisper.

Charlie took a step back from the window. It was quite possible that there were people in the city who could bring statues to life.

"I smell fish," said Benjamin. "So does Runner."

Runner Bean had reached a shop farther down the road. He was standing in the middle of the sidewalk, barking furiously.

"Is he doing that because he likes fish?" asked Charlie, as they ran toward the yellow dog.

"Hates it," panted Benjamin, grabbing Runner Bean's collar.

But the window his dog was barking at was completely empty. A sign above the window said, "FISH." It had been printed on a white background in untidy blue letters and looked as if it had been hurriedly painted over something else. In fact, if you looked closer, you could just make out the word "BUTCHER" beneath the white paint.

"Do you know what it smells like to me?" said Billy.

"Dagbert," said Charlie.

They stared at the empty shop and then at the window above it, wondering if it could be the very place where Dagbert was staying. And if it was, what sort of people owned a shop that was empty and hurriedly painted?

"Very odd people, indeed," said someone who seemed to have read their minds.

They turned to see a woman standing outside a house three doors away. Her copper-colored hair was so smooth it looked like a helmet, and her padded black coat so shiny it could have been made of steel. She was very wide and her broad shoulders gave the impression of immense strength.

"I've been waiting for you, my dears," said the woman. "I'm Mrs. Kettle, Cook's friend. Got a little animal just dying to see you."

"Rembrandt!" cried Billy, rushing up to her.

"You're Billy, aren't you?" said Mrs. Kettle. "And

you must be Benjamin, because of the dog, and you're Charlie. Come in my dears, it's perishing cold out here." Mrs. Kettle went into her shop, which couldn't have been more different from the deserted fish shop down the road.

Everything in Mrs. Kettle's shop appeared to shine. It was only when Charlie's eyes had become accustomed to the bright twinkling all about him that he realized every item was a kettle. They came in all shapes and sizes and every color. They jostled together on shelves, displayed themselves on tables, or sat singly and proudly on pedestals. The pride of the place was the biggest copper kettle Charlie had ever seen. It stood in the center of the window, surrounded by other, lesser kettles, and you could see a strange, slanting copper-tinted version of the whole shop reflected in its bright, shiny side.

"That's just for show, my dear," said Mrs. Kettle, following Charlie's gaze. "My best kettle is behind the scenes. Come with me." She went through an archway at the back of the shop and beckoned them into yet another kettle-filled room, only this one had a few more spaces in it. Four chairs with cushions, not kettles, on their seats, clustered around a small table.

Billy wasn't interested in any of it. Unable to contain his impatience, he burst out, "Where is he? Where's my rat?"

"Well, now, I wonder," teased Mrs. Kettle. "Did you think I'd forgotten, my dear?"

"No. Yes," Billy blurted. "No. Please, is he here?"

"Of course he is!" Mrs. Kettle plunged her hand into one of her kettles and brought out a glossy black rat.

Billy snatched the rat from her, crying, "Rembrandt!"

Rembrandt, equally pleased to see Billy, squeaked delightedly.

"He loves that kettle," said Mrs. Kettle. "He's tried them all, but that's his favorite."

Benjamin looked worried. "Um, do you sell your kettles?"

"Don't worry, my dear," said Mrs. Kettle. "I wash

them inside out. Rats can be untidy creatures, can't they?"

Charlie became aware of a drumming sound coming from somewhere behind him. Runner Bean was so excited to see Rembrandt, his big, happy tail was beating a rhythm on two enamel kettles.

"Rembrandt doesn't want to play," said Billy, holding his rat very close.

At a command from Benjamin, Runner Bean reluctantly stopped wagging, but the drumming was immediately replaced by a fierce whistle that came from a kettle on the stove.

Mrs. Kettle took off her coat and told the boys to do the same. The temperature seemed to have risen by twenty degrees at least, and Charlie took off his sweater as well as his jacket.

The boys sat down and Mrs. Kettle poured four cups of rather strong tea. Benjamin didn't like tea but he realized that he was unlikely to get anything else in a place full of kettles. As a matter of fact it was very good tea indeed and, after a few sips, they felt very buoyant, even Benjamin. It was like gulping down air that made you feel exceptionally lightweight and bouncy.

While they drank their tea Mrs. Kettle told them about the fish shop up the street, even though they hadn't gotten around to asking her.

"There was a butcher there," said Mrs. Kettle. "A very nice man — gave me lots of free cuts. Well, he just upped and went, overnight. Never said a thing about moving."

"Perhaps he had an offer he couldn't refuse," Charlie suggested.

"Must've," agreed Mrs. Kettle. "But you'd think someone who'd paid over the odds for a place would put something in it. And I've never seen so much as a fin in that window."

"But there is a smell of fish," Benjamin pointed out.

"Exactly." Mrs. Kettle leaned forward. "And do you know what? I think they wrote 'FISH' over the shop window, just to explain the smell of it, if you get me. And not because they're selling the stuff."

"Oh," said Charlie, when he'd grasped what Mrs. Kettle had implied. "If you mean that someone in there smells of fish, we might know who it is."

"Really?" Mrs. Kettle's coppery eyes became as round as oranges.

"He's called Dagbert Endless," Charlie told her. "Wherever he goes, the smell of fish follows him. He says he drowns people. His father is Lord Grimwald, and . . ."

"We knew it!" Mrs. Kettle exclaimed. "Or rather we guessed it. Cook suspected, but she wasn't sure. Oh, my poor friend, I hope she's not in trouble. I've already warned her not to come here again, and we're such good friends."

Charlie said, "But it was such a long time ago when Lord Grimwald did those terrible things . . ."

"And he must have married someone else," Billy added, "so he won't be bothering Cook again."

"All the same." Mrs. Kettle drained her cup. The tea didn't appear to have had a bouncy effect on her at all. In fact, she looked quite dejected. "Cook's such a good friend," she repeated, shaking her head.

To cheer her up, Benjamin asked if she had any electric kettles.

Mrs. Kettle looked quite indignant. "Do you call them kettles? I certainly don't. A kettle boils when a hot stove tells it to, not when a button is pressed."

Benjamin gave an apologetic smile. "Sorry."

Charlie decided it was time to leave. They had come for Rembrandt and they had got him. He stood up and thanked Mrs. Kettle for the tea.

"You're very welcome, Charlie Bone," said Mrs. Kettle. "You'll come again, won't you?"

Charlie said, "Yes, of course."

Mrs. Kettle led the way back into the shop but, just as he was about to pass through the archway, Charlie stopped. He felt something to the left of him, tugging in an extraordinary way. He had to steady himself against the wall, and an odd tickle in his

114

throat made him cough. He turned his head, very slowly, and saw on a round shadowy table, a dark, lumpish thing. Looking closer, he saw that it was an ancient kettle, blackened by smoke.

"I told you my best kettle was behind the scenes," Mrs. Kettle said softly.

"THAT'S your best kettle?" Charlie moved closer to the blackened thing.

"Oh, yes, by far." Mrs. Kettle spoke so quietly Charlie could barely hear her, and yet he sensed her excitement. "It was made by my ancestor Feromel more than five hundred years ago. Feromel was a blacksmith and a magician. He made many magical iron pots. Goodness knows where they are now." She came and stood directly behind Charlie. "You're a traveler, aren't you, Charlie? I wondered if you would feel it."

"Feel it?" Charlie ran his hand over the charred, rusty-looking handle. The lid had a round polished knob in the center. Charlie gently lifted it. He gazed into a circle of dark liquid. "It's full," he said.

"It's always full," said Mrs. Kettle. "Always. It can't be emptied. It can only boil dry. But the day when that happens will be the end . . ."

Billy crept up to them. "The end of what?"

"The world?" Charlie's gaze was held by the smooth black water.

"The end of a life," said Mrs. Kettle. "Put the lid back, Charlie, and take it with you."

"Me?" Charlie quickly replaced the lid. "It's yours, Mrs. Kettle. I can't take it."

"Just for a while," she said gently. "You must, Charlie. Feromel would want you to."

"But why?" Charlie stared at the round, black thing, his hands at his sides, his fingers twitching anxiously. He didn't want the ancient kettle with its ability to foretell a death. How many lives had been lost, he wondered, while it boiled away, merrily, in dark, smokey places, poisoning the air with its sinister steam.

"It's not a bad thing, Charlie." Mrs. Kettle lifted her

precious heirloom and held it out to Charlie. And then his tingling fingers had closed around the handle.

"I hope it will never boil dry for you, Charlie," said Mrs. Kettle. "These are dangerous times for people like you, especially with that fish boy around, so it's bound to get warm. It has no need of a stove. It will sit wherever you want. If there is a hint of danger in the air it will heat up. The hotter it gets, the more you will need to look out for yourself." She smiled at everyone. "Now get along with you, my dears. And I'll keep an eye on the fish shop."

They thanked Mrs. Kettle for the tea and, a few moments later, Charlie found himself walking down Piminy Street with a black kettle swinging from his hand.

At the end of the street, they turned a corner and ran straight into Emma and Olivia, with two very small children.

"Oh, no, not Charlie Bone," said Olivia, and she ran off in the direction of High Street.

A STONE TROLL

Olivia was starting to annoy Charlie. "Why did she flounce off like that?" he said.

Emma gave him a sulky look. "Why do you think?"

Charlie was exasperated. "She can't believe I said those things about her. Dagbert made it up. He lied. YOU didn't believe him, did you, Emma?"

"Well . . . ," she said awkwardly. "I always believe it when people say I . . . don't look nice, or I'm stupid, or . . ."

"You shouldn't, you stu —" Charlie stopped himself. "I mean you mustn't."

"Dagbert lies all the time," said Billy.

"He called Billy a freak," added Benjamin.

"And Billy wasn't upset," said Charlie.

"I was," muttered Billy.

Charlie pretended he hadn't heard. "And I really like the way you're doing your hair, Em."

Emma looked more cheerful. She almost smiled. "I'll explain it all to Liv. She's very sensitive about her appearance. But, to tell the truth, I think she enjoys a bit of drama. She'll soon get bored with being angry, and then she'll act like it never happened."

"I hope it's soon," said Charlie.

The small boy by Emma's side had been staring at the black kettle. He suddenly said, "What's that?"

"This?" Charlie swung the kettle self-consciously. "It's just an old kettle I'm borrowing."

"Very, very, very old," the boy observed.

Emma cried, "I'm sorry, I forgot! These are your cousins, Charlie."

"You mean Great-aunt Venetia's . . . children?" Charlie began to take an interest in the waiflike pair. "I'm Charlie." He grinned at them. "So — my great-aunt is your new mother."

"We know," said the girl. "I'm Miranda and this is Eric. We're going to get our dog."

"You wouldn't come with us, would you, Charlie?" Emma smiled persuasively. "I don't like Darkly Wynd, and now Olivia's gone . . ." She hugged herself and shivered.

"Of course we'll come," said Charlie.

Darkly Wynd was not the sort of place people liked to visit on their own. A dark, narrow alley led into a courtyard where tall, gray buildings gathered around a square of rough cobblestones. Most of the houses were boarded up, their doors nailed shut and their windows barred.

At the end of the courtyard a block of buildings stood facing the alley. They had tall pointed turrets, iron-framed balconies, and long windows, their pediments adorned with strange stone figures: trolls, goblins, dwarves, demons, and unlikely beasts.

Aunt Venetia's house, on the right, had a shiny new roof; it looked a lot cleaner than Aunt Eustacia's house, in the middle, or Lucretia's, on the left.

"Great-aunt Venetia's had her house done up," Charlie remarked. "It looked awful after the fire."

"Fire?" Miranda's small face puckered with fear. "How did it happen?"

"Oh, er, just an accident," Charlie replied evasively.

Emma gave him a look that said "thank you for not going into detail."

Three sets of steps led up to three black doors, and a number thirteen, in polished bronze, was fixed to the center of each door.

"Three thirteens," Billy whispered. (It was the sort of place that made you speak very softly.) "Doesn't the mailman get confused?"

"Probably," said Charlie.

A sudden, frantic whining came from inside the third number thirteen, and Miranda cried, "It's Chattypatra! You can hear her."

They ran across the courtyard and stopped at the foot of the steps. Runner Bean began to bark excitedly. His tail wagged so fast you could hardly see it.

"Your uncle said the key was under the troll," Emma told Charlie.

"What troll?" And then Charlie saw it. A squat, evil-looking lump of stone standing in a dark corner of the porch.

"We're coming, Chattypatra," called Miranda. "We're coming."

The whining increased. It grew into a stream of delirious barks, while Runner Bean joined in with his own special brand of yelping.

"SHUT UP!" cried Charlie, glaring at the big dog.

Benjamin clamped his hand around Runner Bean's nose. "You don't have to talk to him like that," he said in an offended tone.

"Sorry, but I just can't think." Charlie stared at the troll.

"What's there to think about? The key's under the troll." Emma began to mount the steps.

"No, Em." Charlie grabbed her arm. "Take this." He handed her the kettle.

"Wow, it's heavy." She touched the blackened side. "And it's warm."

"I know." Charlie had noticed the kettle getting warmer. Did it have something to do with Great-aunt Venetia's house? He climbed the steps while the others remained on the sidewalk, watching him silently.

He bent toward the troll and stopped. The troll had blinked. Could it have been a trick of the light? Charlie's own shadow passing over the stone? No. He was quite certain that one of the troll's stone eyelids had closed over its round, malevolent eye. It had happened so fast, Charlie barely had time to register it. But it HAD moved.

Charlie turned to the group behind him, all looking up expectantly, except for Eric who was gazing at the troll with an odd, distant expression.

Charlie took a breath, bent down very quickly, and pushed the troll backward. And there was Great-aunt Venetia's front door key. He picked it up and flourished it at the others.

Everyone cried, "Hooray!" and rushed up the steps.

Charlie fitted the key into the lock, turned it, and the door swung open without so much as a squeak, let alone the sinister creak that he expected.

A small, white dog shot out of the house and leaped into Miranda's arms.

"Oh, Chatty, Chatty!" Miranda's eyes were in danger of overflowing.

Eric merely smiled in an offhand way.

Runner Bean was beside himself with joy. He tore away from Benjamin and leaped at Miranda, nuzzling the dog in her arms. Chattypatra had no objection; in fact, she nuzzled him back and yapped very sedately into one of his ears.

"A marriage made in heaven." Benjamin sighed contentedly. "I knew Runner would find a girlfriend one day."

Miranda gave him a serious look.

Charlie replaced the key and they left Darkly Wynd as quickly as possible. Charlie felt sorry for the two children who would have to return to the company of his awful aunt Eustacia later. He wondered if he should ask them to stay at number nine, but something stopped him — perhaps it was the cool look in Eric's eyes and the way the small boy kept glancing at the kettle.

"Here!" Emma passed the kettle back to Charlie.

"That has to be the weirdest kettle ever. It's gone cold now."

Charlie's fingers closed over the freezing handle. He didn't mention the kettle's strange history.

The two groups of children parted when they reached High Street. Charlie, Benjamin, and Billy turned left toward Filbert Street, while the others headed back to the cathedral.

Benjamin needed Charlie's help to drag Runner Bean away from his girlfriend, and Chattypatra, now walking obediently beside Miranda, kept stopping to look wistfully in Runner Bean's direction.

"It doesn't seem fair," said Billy. "Those dogs would much rather be together than with us."

"Are you going to tell us what they were saying?" asked Charlie.

Billy went pink. "Oh, just love stuff."

Benjamin raised his eyebrows and looked at his dog. "Like what?"

Billy cleared his throat. "Like, er, you're the best thing I've seen since breakfast."

"BREAKFAST?" questioned Charlie. "Do you call that 'love stuff'?"

"It was his favorite," Benjamin said thoughtfully. "Leftover steak."

Charlie didn't ask what Chattypatra had said. He thought he'd probably be disappointed. He reckoned Billy was keeping a whole lot to himself. He would be too embarrassed to repeat anything very lovey-dovey.

They reached number nine and Benjamin was invited in to lunch. Billy looked anxious. As soon as they were inside he carried Rembrandt up to Charlie's room. He didn't want Runner Bean chasing his rat all around the house.

Maisie had prepared one of her usual, mammoth lunches. "You got into number thirteen, then?" she said as the boys dug into their roast beef. "Paton told me all about it."

"We found the dog and Runner fell for her." Benjamin glanced fondly at his dog, who was sitting in a corner not even touching the bone that Maisie had put down for him.

"He has got it badly," Maisie observed. "That's a real lovelorn look." She suddenly noticed the black kettle on the floor beside Charlie's foot. "And what's that, may I ask?"

"It's, um, a kettle," said Charlie. "I got it at the shop on Piminy Street."

"Whatever do you want an old thing like that for?" asked Maisie. "Isn't my nice electric kettle good enough?"

"That one's special," said Billy.

"Oh!" Understanding dawned in Maisie. "I suppose Mrs. Kettle is one of those Red King people."

"Her ancestor was a kind of magician-blacksmith," Charlie told her. "He made the kettle and — well, it might be helpful to me."

"Hmph." Maisie was proud of Charlie's endowment, but there were times when she considered it a terrible misfortune. So often it had led him into danger, into situations that he'd been lucky to survive.

The front door slammed, and heavy footsteps could be heard marching across the tiled hall. Charlie tried to move the kettle farther under the table with his foot. But he was too late. The next minute the door flew open and Grandma Bone stood there glaring at them. Her eyes immediately fell on the black kettle. It was uncanny how she always noticed the things that Charlie didn't want her to.

"What's that?" she demanded.

"Nothing, Grandma," said Charlie foolishly.

"Don't be stupid. I can see it isn't nothing. It's a filthy old kettle. Take it out. I don't want it in my house."

Maisie pulled back a chair, saying, "Do you want some lunch, Grizelda?"

Without raising her eyes from the kettle, Grandma Bone said, "I've had lunch, and don't try and distract me."

Charlie was suddenly inspired. "It's for school,

Grandma. We were told to find ancient artifacts for history. I feel rather proud of myself."

Grandma Bone's face softened a little. School work was a priority in her book. She wasn't entirely put off the scent, though. "Why did you say it was nothing if it's for school?"

Charlie was stumped. He looked at Billy and Benjamin, hoping for assistance. They stared back, in helpless silence.

Charlie was saved by Runner Bean. The big dog hated Grandma Bone. The very smell of her was enough to bring a great, grumbling growl out of him.

"I thought I told you not to bring that dog in here." Grandma Bone turned her attention to Benjamin.

"Yes, Mrs. Bone," said Benjamin, almost inaudibly.

Maisie couldn't stand having one of her meals interrupted in this way. "For goodness' sake, Grizelda." She banged down the empty chair. "If you don't want to eat, leave us in peace. These boys are cold and hungry and I won't have you putting them off their nice hot meal. The dog's not doing any harm."

"You watch it, Maisie Jones." Grandma Bone was enjoying her very bad mood. You could tell by the nasty smile on her face. "If you keep defying me," she continued, "you'll be out on your ear. This is my house and you're only here on sufferance."

A voice from behind her said, "OUR house, Grizelda."

Grandma Bone nearly jumped out of her skin. She hadn't heard Uncle Paton creep up behind her.

"Stop talking nonsense and let us eat in peace." Uncle Paton seized his sister's shoulders.

She wriggled out of his grasp, muttering under her breath, then rushed upstairs.

Uncle Paton walked into the kitchen and took his place at the end of the table. "Sorry I'm late," he said as though nothing at all had happened.

The boys felt like cheering, but restrained themselves in case Grandma Bone found a nasty way to get back at them. Benjamin already had indigestion. It was the only drawback to visiting Charlie, the gut-churning scenes with Grandma Bone.

The rest of the meal passed very pleasantly. By the time they'd reached the plum pudding, Charlie had told his uncle all about the visit to Mrs. Kettle and the rescue of Chattypatra.

"Let's have a look at this kettle," said Uncle Paton, when the last bit of plum pudding had gone.

Charlie lifted the kettle onto the table.

"Dirty thing," grumbled Maisie, stacking the empty plates.

Uncle Paton put on his glasses and pulled the kettle toward him. He lifted the lid. "Mmmm." He sniffed the dark liquid. "Smells of nothing at all," he remarked, "but this is certainly very, very old." He tapped the side. "Iron. Yes. Quite cold."

"That's because there's no danger," said Billy.

"I bet it was hot a moment ago," said Benjamin, looking at the spot where Grandma Bone had been standing.

"She's not dangerous," said Charlie. "She's just mean. But something in Aunt Venetia's house was dangerous, unless . . ." He hesitated.

"Unless what, Charlie?" Uncle Paton looked over the top of his half-moon glasses.

"Nothing." Charlie didn't know how to explain the troll's blink. After all, it could have been his imagination.

Uncle Paton told him to keep the kettle in his room. "Somewhere out of sight, if I were you, Charlie," his uncle added. "You don't want to lose it."

Ordinarily, Charlie would have gone to the Pets' Café on a Sunday afternoon. But today didn't feel ordinary. He didn't want to meet up with Olivia again, and the word was out that Tancred and Lysander would be with their girlfriends. Somehow, Charlie didn't see the Pets' Café as a likely place to take one's girlfriend. The atmosphere was hardly what you would call romantic.

So the boys watched TV in the kitchen, until the light left the sky, and a night full of stars covered the city.

When Benjamin went home, Runner Bean still had a yearning look in his big brown eyes.

"I'll have to take him back to see Chattypatra," Benjamin called across the street. "Next weekend, maybe."

"Maybe," said Charlie. He thought of the two small children in Darkly Wynd. He hoped Chattypatra would be allowed to sleep with them.

Charlie watched Benjamin go through his front door and turned to climb the steps of number nine. A movement down the street caught his eye. Something bobbed behind a tree, a low, shapeless thing. He quickly stepped inside and closed the door.

It was time for candles. Maisie switched off the kitchen lamp and Charlie turned out the light in the hall. Grandma Bone was the only person in the house who forgot the routine. You'd think she would remember Paton's endowment, considering the number of times she'd been showered with broken glass.

"I like candlelight," said Billy, who had brought his rat down to enjoy a snack. "So does Rembrandt."

"So do I," said Charlie.

Indeed, it was a very cozy scene, with the warm

stove humming quietly in the background and the candle flames bathing the room in a comforting glow. And then Charlie had to go and close the curtains, and the safe, snug mood was banished in an instant for, staring up at the window, were two faces; their pale, yellowish eyes had an animal gleam, and their low brows were covered in tufts of hair.

Charlie screamed.

"What's that all about?" said Uncle Paton, hurrying into the kitchen.

"It's them," said Charlie in a shaky voice. "The things we saw outside Diamond Corner."

The two, hooded figures began to back away from the window.

Uncle Paton ran to the front door and flung it open. "What do you want?" he called.

Glowing eyes turned toward him, and then the two strangers began to slink away, up the street.

"Hold it!" shouted Uncle Paton. "Identify yourselves."

The hooded figures increased their pace.

"Oh, no, you don't!"

Charlie reached the door just in time to see his uncle leap down the steps and pursue the strangers. At this moment, they dropped on all fours and put on a tremendous burst of speed. But Uncle Paton's legs were the longest in the city. In three bounds he had caught up with them.

"Gotcha!" he cried, grabbing one of the strangers by the scruff of the neck.

Charlie wasn't quite sure what happened next, because the street light above Uncle Paton suddenly exploded and glass fell in a silvery shower over all three figures.

A howl of fury echoed down the street, followed by a cry of pain from Uncle Paton.

"Ye gods, it bit me!"

"We are not 'its', Mr. Yewbeam," hissed a voice. "We are human."

"Who . . . ," Uncle Paton began.

But the two creatures had vanished into the shadows.

HUNTING THE WILDERNESS WOLF

Up and down Filbert Street, doors and windows began to open, some boldly, some cautiously. Voices called into the night.

"What's going on?"

"Who's there?"

"It's Mr. Yewbeam from number nine."

"You all right, Mr. Yewbeam?"

Someone said, "Was it the wolf?"

Before Paton could reply, Agnes Prout, the Yewbeam's next-door neighbor, cried, "It must have been the wolf! It's come into the city."

At this, several doors were hastily slammed shut.

Clasping his wrist, Uncle Paton reeled back down the road. As Charlie ran to meet him, Benjamin and his mother rushed across the road, led by an excited Runner Bean.

"Are you OK, Charlie?" Benjamin cried.

"Yes, I'm OK, but my uncle's not."

Mrs. Brown stared in horror at the blood seeping through Paton's fingers. "Paton, what happened? Can I help?"

"It's nothing," Paton said gruffly. "Maisie will patch me up."

"But you're covered in glass!" Mrs. Brown picked helplessly at the glittering splinters on Paton's shoulders.

"Please, Patricia," Paton begged. "You'll cut yourself." He began to mount the steps of number nine with Charlie supporting his elbow.

Benjamin's mother refused to go home. She stood resolutely on the sidewalk, determined to get to the bottom of a mystery that was almost on her very doorstep. "It was the beast, wasn't it?" she said gravely. "Everyone's talking about it. They call it the Wilderness Wolf. You can hear it howling every night. It must live in the wilderness across the river."

"Patricia," Paton said firmly. "I was not attacked by a wolf."

"What, then?"

"It was HUMAN!" Without looking back, Paton strode into the house.

Charlie thought he should apologize. "Sorry," he said, turning to Benjamin and Mrs. Brown. "My uncle's hurt. 'Night, Ben. 'Night, Mrs. Brown."

"'Night, Charlie," Benjamin said anxiously. His mother was getting one of her I'm-going-to-get-to-the-bottom-of-this looks.

Mrs. Brown marched purposefully back to number twelve with Benjamin and his dog at her heels. "I'm going to get to the bottom of this," she said.

"Whatever's happened?" cried Maisie as Uncle Paton lurched into the kitchen.

"Uncle Paton's been bitten." Charlie helped his uncle into a chair.

Paton rolled up his sleeve. "Can you get me a bowl of clean water, Maisie, and some disinfectant?"

"You've never been bitten by a dog!" Maisie rushed to the sink and began to fill a bowl. "You could get rabies, Paton."

"It wasn't a dog," Paton said wearily. "No, it most certainly wasn't a dog."

"Thank goodness for that." Maisie came to Paton's side with her bowl. Taking his wrist she began to dab it with a clean cloth.

Charlie flinched when he saw the teeth marks. Maisie's constant dabbing was having an effect. As the blood was wiped away, the wound on Uncle Paton's wrist could clearly be seen.

"Looks like a wolf bite to me," Maisie observed as she examined Paton's wrist. "Those marks, like fangs they are — it's not the front teeth that went the deepest, it was those two on either side, the canines."

"I can't explain it." Paton allowed Maisie to bind his wrist with a length of white muslin. "The creature spoke to me. What's more — it knew my name."

"Well, I never." Maisie straightened up and took her bowl back to the sink.

All this time, Billy had been sitting perfectly still,

hugging Rembrandt to his chest. He looked frightened, but also puzzled.

"What is it, Billy?" asked Charlie. "Do you know something about those beings?"

"Not exactly." Billy's frown deepened. "I was just thinking."

"Thinking what?" Charlie sat beside him.

"Well, I was wondering, really."

"Wondering what?"

"It was the voice; when it howled it sounded like the voice we hear at night. It's difficult to explain, but it was using the same kind of language."

"But it's a wolf we hear at night, Billy love," said Maisie. "People call it the Wilderness Wolf."

"And the one that attacked me was most certainly human," added Uncle Paton.

Billy made a politely stubborn face. "They were the same," he insisted.

Uncle Paton gave a huge shrug. "In that case, we must conclude that they are related. In truth, I am too battle-weary to ponder these riddles any longer. I am going to bed. And you boys should be on your way too very soon. School tomorrow." He stood up, wincing slightly as his left hand grasped the back of his chair.

Maisie listened to Paton dragging his feet up the stairs. She shook her head. "Your uncle's not quite right, Charlie, if you know what I mean. I hope that bite wasn't poisonous."

Charlie didn't have a chance to find out if Uncle Paton had recovered from his bite. Monday mornings were always a scramble. Clothes were hastily flung into bags, breakfast was eaten at breakneck speed, and then Charlie and Billy were off, running up Filbert Street to catch the Academy bus.

Maisie waved them off, shouting, "I'll let you know if your uncle's any worse. Take care now, boys."

Academy students were not allowed access to telephones, radios, or televisions. Several homesick children had tried to smuggle in cell phones, but there were spies in the academy, ready to betray a friend just to gain favor with the Bloors. The cell phones were always discovered and confiscated, their owners put in detention.

Cook was Charlie's only link with the outside world, but he wondered if fear of Grimwald would deter her from giving him a message.

Cook didn't appear in the cafeteria all day. At tea time, Charlie leaned over the counter and very quietly asked one of the kitchen assistants if Cook was ill.

"She looks all right to me," said the woman, a friendly person called Valerie. "I expect she's too busy to come out to the counter."

Charlie was worried. "Could you, er, give her my regards?"

"Of course, love." Valerie grinned.

A voice said, "Is Cook a friend of yours, then?"

Charlie swung around. Dagbert had sneaked up behind him so softly, Charlie had no idea he was there.

"N-not especially," Charlie stammered. "It's just that the food is better when Cook's on."

Dagbert's blue-green eyes flashed. "I wasn't accusing you of anything, Charlie."

Charlie hurried away from the counter. He'd lost his appetite. Billy followed him out of the cafeteria.

"Is there any news about your uncle?" Billy asked.

"Of course not," Charlie said impatiently. "I haven't seen Cook, have I?"

Billy walked off, looking offended.

When Cook didn't appear at breakfast time on Tuesday, Charlie began to feel frantic.

Fidelio ran up to Charlie as he marched around the grounds during first break. "You look as if a black cloud has settled right there on your shoulders," Fidelio said, giving him a friendly punch.

"Don't!" Charlie pushed his friend's hand away.

"You're touchy."

Charlie apologized. "I'm just worried about my uncle. He was bitten by a, well — a thing, and I haven't seen Cook, so I'm worried about that, too, because of Dagbert . . ."

"Charlie, stop!" Fidelio protested. "Calm down and tell me what's going on."

Fidelio was a great listener. Charlie realized he should have confided in him before. He described his weekend, beginning with the visit to Mrs. Kettle and ending with the attack on his uncle. "People kept saying it was the Wilderness Wolf, the one we hear howling at night, but Uncle P. says it was quite definitely human. And — this is the weirdest bit — Billy says their voices are the same."

"Hmmm . . ." Fidelio stopped in his tracks. "The same?"

Charlie was suddenly distracted by a very interesting scene. Tancred was walking beside an extremely pretty girl; glossy blond hair rippled over her purple cape, falling almost to her waist. Her complexion was flawless, her lips full and pink, and her gray eyes fringed with long, curling lashes. "Hey, is that Tancred's . . ."

"Girlfriend," said Fidelio. "Tracy Morsell."

"Really? You know a lot."

"I do," Fidelio agreed. "I keep my ear to the ground. And over there is poor Emma Tolly, whose heart is breaking."

Following Fidelio's gaze, Charlie saw Emma sitting alone on a log in a far corner of the grounds. She had a pile of books on her knees, and even from a distance, Charlie could tell that she was upset.

"Does she . . . ?" Charlie turned to Fidelio.

"Does she like Tancred? I'll say. Haven't you noticed?"

"I'm an idiot." Charlie slapped his head. "It's obvious, now that you mention it. Poor Em."

The sound of the hunting horn echoed across the grounds, calling them back to class, and Charlie ran over to help Emma with the books that had tumbled off her knees. They lay scattered around her feet, their pages flapping like white wings in the icy breeze.

Emma took the books from Charlie with a grateful smile. "Silly of me to try and work out here," she said in a small voice. "I had this crazy idea that if I got all my homework done, I wouldn't have to go to the King's room tonight."

Charlie shook his head. "Wouldn't work, Em. They'd find something else for you to do."

"I know," she said.

Fidelio joined them as they walked back into school. They were the last to leave the grounds.

That night Charlie waited for the sound of distant howling. The grunts and heavy breathing of the sleeping boys around him seemed even louder tonight. And then he saw that Billy was awake, too. Charlie could just make out the white blur of his head as he sat up in the bed beyond Dagbert's.

"Billy?" Charlie whispered. "Can you hear anything?"

"I heard the howling once," Billy said softly. "But it was very faint."

"What did it say?"

"I'm not sure . . ." Billy hesitated. "It might have been 'father.'"

They heard, then, the distant but unmistakable sound of gunfire.

With a little moan, Billy dived under the covers.

Charlie lay back on his pillow. *I hope they haven't killed it,* he thought.

At number twelve Filbert Street, Benjamin Brown was still wide awake. He wished Charlie could have shared the past two days with him. So much had happened. It had all begun with a hastily arranged meeting in the town hall. Mr. and Mrs. Brown decided to take Benjamin along with them. "It will be good for you," said Mr. Brown. "You might learn something."

Benjamin doubted it until he heard that the subject for discussion would be the Wilderness Wolf. And he did, indeed, learn something. He learned that people lied when they were afraid. Fear was rife in the large hall that night. You could see it in people's eyes; you could hear it in their hushed and nervous chatter. Benjamin sat between his parents, right at the front. The Browns liked to observe the minutest details on occasions like this.

There were five people on the platform. They sat behind a long table; each had a clipboard and a glass of water set before them. Benjamin recognized the chairman, Mr. Marchwell, a prominent councilman who often visited his school; he also recognized Charlie's next-door neighbor Agnes Prout.

Mr. Marchwell opened the proceedings with a short speech. He told his audience that they were all there for the same reasons: one, to discuss ways and means of identifying the "unusual utterances" (a long-winded description of howling, Benjamin reckoned) coming from across the river, and two, to decide whether the creature responsible for the utterances was a threat to the citizens.

At this point, Agnes Prout rudely interrupted Mr. Marchwell with a shout of, "Threat? Of course, it's a threat. It's a wolf, for heaven's sake!"

A few people applauded this outburst. Benjamin

was glad that his parents kept their hands in their laps.

"We don't know that it's a wolf, Miss Prout," said Mr. Marchwell.

"You bet we do," Agnes retorted. "I saw it. It bit my neighbor Mr. Yewbeam. I saw the wound; a stream of blood poured from his wrist, a positive stream."

Mrs. Brown put up her hand.

Mr. Marchwell leaned forward slightly. "You have a question . . . Mrs., er . . . ?"

"Brown," said Benjamin's mother, standing up. "Trish Brown. I would just like to state that Mr. Yewbeam told me he was bitten by a human, a deluded person perhaps, but certainly not a wolf."

Benjamin felt proud of his mother. He felt even prouder when she stood her ground against a torrent of ridicule from Agnes Prout.

"Rubbish, Mrs. Brown. Absolute nonsense! Either the poor man wasn't himself, or you're deaf. That was no human, it was a wolf."

"If Mr. Yewbeam were here...," began Mrs. Brown.

"Well, he isn't," said Agnes, "so that's that."

Mrs. Brown went an angry shade of red and sat down. Mr. Brown patted her back.

"Well done, Mom," Benjamin whispered. She gave him a resigned sort of smile.

Benjamin looked up at the bright lights beaming down from the ceiling. It would have been impossible for Charlie's uncle to attend the meeting. They would all have been plunged into darkness and covered in glass the moment he walked through the door.

The audience had become very lively. Hands were showing up all over the place. People began to shout out of turn. In vain, Mr. Marchwell raised his hand, begging them to be civilized, to allow one another to be heard.

"I saw it down Cruckton Avenue!"

"Someone told me it was on Piminy Street!"

"I heard it was seen in Cathedral Square!"

"A great, gray beast, fangs like knives!"

"It's been eating cats!"

"And dogs!"

"Next it'll be our babies!"

"Our kids!"

"It's got to be killed!"

It took some time for the hubbub to die down, but Mr. Marchwell was a determined person and he managed to keep the rest of the proceedings under tight control. Only at the end did hysteria begin to creep into a few voices again.

A decision was made. The mayor would be apprised of the citizens' strong feelings about the "thing" in the wilderness, and a hunt would be organized. The so-called Wilderness Wolf would be flushed out and captured or killed. As the creature was silent during daylight hours, the hunt would begin at dusk the following day.

When the meeting broke up, small groups began to form on the sidewalk outside the town hall. Benjamin could hear excited voices. Violence was in the air. He began to think that the people in those angry, grumbling groups were more dangerous than any wilderness wolf.

Mr. and Mrs. Brown walked home in silence. Benjamin looked up at their disapproving faces and decided not to ask any questions. Just as they were climbing the steps of number twelve, they heard a melancholy howl stealing through the cold night air.

Benjamin shivered. "It doesn't sound dangerous," he said. "It just sounds sad."

"Sad indeed," agreed Mr. Brown. "There's something not right about this."

Five minutes later, sitting in his bright cozy kitchen, Mr. Brown put forward a theory. "It's like this," he said. "We hear a sound from the wilderness, right? An animal cry, if you like, but a call of some kind. A call for help. Now this 'thing' that attacked Mr. Yewbeam was human, he says."

"Paton Yewbeam's no fool," Mrs. Brown broke in. "He said it was human and I believe him, absolutely."

"So do I, Trish," her husband said hastily. "So do I. Thing is, it bites, which is an animal trait, so maybe there's a connection between the thing in the wilderness and Mr. Yewbeam's attacker."

Benjamin had been listening intently to his parents' conversation. Having inherited a double dose of their curiosity, and also their powers of analysis, deduction, and intuition, he was fast becoming an excellent detective himself.

"I've got a hunch," said Benjamin.

Mr. and Mrs. Brown regarded Benjamin's ideas very highly.

"A hunch, Benjamin!" Mrs. Brown said in a thrilled voice.

"What is it, boy? Tell us!" Mr. Brown eagerly studied his son's face.

"Well . . ." Benjamin decided to prolong the attention he was getting. "Well, it's just that Charlie told me that one of the boys, Asa Pike, hasn't been seen in school this term. He's endowed, like Charlie, only he's a kind of beast at night."

Mr. Brown nodded impatiently. "Asa? Yes, we know about him."

"Well . . ." Benjamin paused again. The look of anticipation on his parents' faces was very satisfying. "What you might not know is that Asa, who was once a good friend of Manfred Bloor's, well, Asa helped Charlie to find his father, and I reckon Manfred was pretty angry about that, so he might have trapped Asa somewhere as a punishment."

The Browns regarded their son with admiration and delight.

"Benjamin, you might be right," said Mr. Brown.

"Having possibly identified the howl, can you suggest how the howler might be rescued?" Mrs. Brown asked her son.

At this point Benjamin told a white lie. He said, "No," when all along an idea had been forming in his mind. Behind him lay Runner Bean, asleep in his basket. Runner Bean could find anything, Benjamin reckoned. And if he could sniff something belonging to Asa, the big dog could surely find him. Benjamin kept this idea to himself. He didn't want his parents' help. He wanted to find Asa on his own, or maybe with Charlie.

"We'd better do something soon," said Mr. Brown, "or the hunt will kill that poor boy before they realize who he is. I'll go and see the mayor."

"He won't believe you," Mrs. Brown said sadly. "He doesn't hold with all the stuff that goes on at Bloor's Academy. He knows about the endowed children, of course, but he doesn't like to admit it."

"I expect I'll think of something," said Benjamin.

Finding something belonging to Asa wasn't as easy as Benjamin had hoped. He discovered that Asa's parents had never been seen. No one knew where they lived. They appeared to have no friends and no relations. Any item that Asa might have worn or touched lay inside Bloor's Academy, an impossible place for someone like Benjamin to enter. The Bloors certainly wouldn't be happy to assist in Asa's rescue. He had changed sides. They would consider him a turncoat and a traitor.

By the time Benjamin got home from school the next day, the hunt was already underway. Half the city had turned out to watch. Forty able-bodied men were assembled on the bridge that led to the wilderness. In charge were the chief of police and Officer Wood. They were joined by a motley group of determined-looking men, dressed in an assortment of trenchcoats, suits, jackets, and raincoats. Their heads were covered by woolly hats, hoods, berets, and even a Stetson. A few pairs of rain boots and sneakers were to be seen, but most wore sturdy leather boots. Half the men carried rifles; the others took flashlights and clubs.

A cheer went up as the forty-two men marched across the bridge and turned right, down a path that ran beside the river. A few meters farther on, it disappeared into dense undergrowth — the beginning of the wilderness.

From a path on the city-side of the river, Benjamin's father had watched the whole proceedings. He returned home a worried man.

"It's not right," he told his wife and son, as they ate their scrambled eggs and spinach. "There's going to be a catastrophe, you mark my words. All those guns; someone's going to be killed in the wilderness, and it might not be the beast-boy."

Benjamin suddenly thought of Charlie's friend Naren. She lived with her father and mother in a little house deep in the wilderness. It was a beautiful, secret place, a sanctuary for lost and injured animals. Would it remain secret, when a group of angry men came tramping through the trees with guns and clubs and torches?

I wish I could talk to Charlie, thought Benjamin.

Charlie had fallen asleep. He woke up to find some-one shaking his shoulder.

"Charlie, there's something on the wall behind you. A word." It was Dagbert's voice.

Charlie sat up and rubbed his eyes.

"Look! Look behind you," Dagbert insisted.

Charlie looked around. On the wall above his bed

was the word "good-bye." It was written in a patch of moonlight, in shaky spiderlike letters that seemed as though they were a little uncertain of themselves.

"Naren!" Charlie whispered to the wall.

One by one, the letters began to fade.

"Naren!" said Charlie, forgetting to whisper. "Where are you going?"

There was no answering message. The wall remained blank. The slice of moonlight disappeared and the room returned to its usual inky darkness.

"What's going on?" asked Dagbert.

ASA'S DISGUISE

Charlie turned over and pretended to be asleep. He felt a sharp thump on his back. "Don't!" he whispered harshly.

"Tell me about those words on the wall," Dagbert hissed.

"No," said Charlie. "It's a private message."

"I won't tell anyone."

"Huh!" Charlie got up and went to the bathroom. If there was going to be an argument it would be safer to have it where no one could hear them. Just as he expected, Dagbert followed him.

Charlie closed the door. The moon slipped from behind the clouds again, and the light was bright enough for the boys to see each other's faces.

Charlie stood with his back to the bathtub. The cold tap dripped; a loud, insistent rhythmic drip. Dagbert stood by the sink, his face silvery green in the moonlight.

"I'm not a spy," Dagbert said. "You can trust me, you know."

"You're joking." Charlie sat on the edge of the bathtub. "You stalk me like a spy and you've turned nearly all my friends against me."

"Not all."

"Most. Why do you do it?"

Dagbert slid to the floor beside the sink and put his hands on his knees. He gazed at his long fingers, lifting them, one by one, and finally linking his hands together.

Drip, drip, drip went the tap, while Charlie waited for an answer.

Dagbert's crinkly hair began to unfold, as though invisible hands were tugging it straight. It became dark, flat, and shining. "The moon rules my life," he said at last. "Like the tides. I'm mean when the moon is hidden by clouds, worse when most of it is shadowed by the earth. I'm not going to ask you to forgive me, Charlie, because I can't help what I do. But if you tell me about those words on the wall, I promise I won't follow you anymore."

Charlie considered Dagbert's proposal. He wouldn't have to tell Dagbert where Naren lived. Besides, if Naren had said good-bye, it probably meant that she had left the cottage in the wilderness. "I know this girl," Charlie began. "She's called Naren, although her real name is much longer. It's Mongolian. Her parents were drowned in a flood . . ."

"Nothing to do with me," Dagbert said quickly. "Go on."

"She was adopted by Ezekiel's son, Bartholomew, and his Chinese wife. They live outside the city, at least they did once."

"But the words . . . the words on the wall," Dagbert repeated insistently.

"That's her endowment," said Charlie. "She can send messages through the air. As long as the curtains are open and the moon is shining."

"Do you mean like a text message on a cell phone?"

Charlie frowned. "Not at all like that. She doesn't need any . . . instruments. All she has is my glove as a kind of homing device."

"I see." Dagbert looked impressed.

"We'd better get back to bed," said Charlie.

"There's just . . ." Dagbert couldn't finish his sentence. Something was happening to him. He began to shake violently.

Charlie stood up, his eyes never leaving the trembling boy on the floor. Dagbert's fingers slowly uncurled and he held his hands out to Charlie.

Speechless with horror, Charlie couldn't touch the unnaturally long sticklike fingers, for they had begun to glow. A soft green light was pouring through Dagbert's skin; his face, his bare feet, and his hands had a phosphorescent glow. Even the skin covered by his pajamas gleamed faintly through the thick cotton.

Charlie fought a desperate urge to get as far away as possible from the glowing boy. "What's happened to you?" he whispered.

The boy on the floor was shaking so badly his voice came out in a halting splutter. "G-g-g-get . . . s-s-sea gold . . . cr-cr-creatures," he stuttered. "Un-under . . . m-my . . . p-pillow."

It took Charlie several seconds to make sense of Dagbert's speech. When he finally grasped what the afflicted boy wanted, he dashed into the dormitory and felt under Dagbert's pillow. His fingers touched one, two, three . . . seven small hard objects. Holding them cupped in his hands, he ran back to the bathroom and, with some difficulty, placed them on Dagbert's palms, closing his glowing fingers over them. Five tiny gold crabs and a golden fish in one hand, a sea urchin in the other.

Dagbert shut his eyes and bent his head. Slowly, the shaking stopped. Gradually, the green, phosphorescent glow faded. Dagbert opened his eyes and gave a twisted half-smile.

Charlie knelt in front of him. "What's going on, Dagbert?"

"It's my birthday," Dagbert replied. He glanced at his watch. "To the minute. One o'clock precisely."

"Your birthday? I don't understand."

"I'm twelve," said Dagbert. "I knew something would happen to me, but I never guessed what it would be."

"What does it mean?" In spite of the extraordinary moment, in spite of the shock and amazement, Charlie was unable to suppress a yawn. He got to his feet, leaning on the wall for support.

Dagbert stood up, still shivering a little. "It means that I am as strong as my father. And you mustn't tell a soul. NOT A SOUL. Because my father mustn't know. Not yet. Do you understand?"

"I understand. And I promise not to tell." Charlie yawned again. "Let's both keep our promises, shall we?"

"Agreed," Dagbert said solemnly.

They stumbled back to bed. The last thing Charlie heard before he fell asleep was the tinkle of sea-gold creatures.

It was a great relief to see Cook at breakfast the next morning. She looked almost like her old self. She had a message for Charlie. Leaning over the counter, she said quietly, "Your friend Benjamin has contacted me."

"Ben!" said Charlie.

"Shhh. Do you want the whole world to hear?"

"Sorry," Charlie mumbled.

Talking to Cook was always tricky, especially when you were in a breakfast line. Luckily, Billy was immediately behind Charlie, and Fidelio behind him.

Cook leaned farther over the counter. "He wants you to get some of Asa Pike's clothes. It's to do with the howling. Did you hear the gunshots last night?"

"Certainly did," said Billy.

"Do you want milk on your oatmeal, Charlie?" Cook asked as two girls strolled by.

"Yes, please."

"There was a hunt." Cook poured milk into Charlie's bowl. "Hit something, so I heard. Let's hope it was no one we know."

"Do you mean . . . ?" Everything suddenly fell into place. Charlie walked over to one of the tables. How slow he'd been, putting two and two together.

When Billy and Fidelio joined him at the table, Charlie whispered, "It must be Asa out there in the wilderness. At least Benjamin thinks so."

Billy nodded very slowly, as though he were still thinking about something. "Me too. That's why Ben wants the clothes, so Runner Bean can follow the scent."

"The only clothes belonging to Asa will be that old coat and hat from the drama department," muttered Fidelio. "Olivia's in drama. She'll be able to find them."

"That old coat," said Charlie affectionately. "Asa could never disguise himself properly, could he? I owe him everything. I've got to help him." He didn't add, *If Olivia will listen to me.*

Dagbert arrived at their table, holding his bowl of oatmeal. "Can I sit here?"

Fidelio grinned. "Can't smell fish today, so I guess it's OK."

Dagbert's face remained expressionless. "Thanks." He took a seat between Charlie and Billy.

Charlie sneaked a glance at him. There was no trace of the extraordinary phosphorescent glow that had radiated from Dagbert the night before. In fact he looked so downright normal, Charlie was finding it difficult to believe he hadn't dreamed the scene in the bathroom.

When Charlie stood up, Dagbert took no notice. And when Charlie left the cafeteria, Dagbert didn't follow him. He didn't creep after him at the end of assembly either, or into the blue coatroom. Did it mean that he was going to keep his word?

"Let's talk to Olivia at break," Fidelio suggested as he and Charlie went to their French class.

"OK." Charlie didn't relish a talk with Olivia, but he couldn't think of a better idea.

Emma was right about Olivia, however. Just as she had predicted, Olivia had already grown tired of her feud with Charlie. Besides, he was looking so preoccupied she longed to know what was going on. So it was Olivia who came up to Charlie and Fidelio during the first break rather than the other way around.

Charlie was very relieved. Words of apology had been chasing themselves around in his head. Now he was saved the trouble of choosing the right ones.

"What are you up to, Charlie Bone?" Olivia asked casually, as she pirouetted on the frost-hard ground.

Standing just behind Olivia, Emma grinned.

"Matter of fact, I was going to ask if you'd help us," Charlie said gravely.

Olivia pirouetted again. "What's it worth?"

"Your help?" Charlie floundered.

Fidelio came to his rescue. "There's something we're going to find very difficult to do without you, Liv. So you tell us what your help is worth."

A delighted grin spread across Olivia's face. "What have I got to do?"

"We need to find the clothes Asa used to wear as a disguise," said Charlie. "I'm sure they came from the drama department. You know, that old coat and hat, and the weird mustache that was always falling off."

"I know." Olivia clicked her glittery shoes together and hopped back and forth. "He used to stick on false eyebrows, too. And there were those funny old boots with holes in them."

"Yes, yes," Charlie said excitedly. "Thing is, do you know where they're kept?"

"Of course I do." Olivia came to a standstill at last. "Most of the stuff is kept in the basement, under the theater. I'll get the clothes for you during lunch break. There'll be more time then."

"Fantastic, Liv!" cried Charlie.

Fidelio nudged him. "The terms, Charlie, remember? What do you want for helping us, Liv?"

Olivia rolled her eyes at the sky. "Oh, I don't know. Yes, I do. One of Mrs. Onimous's chocolate fudge rolls . . . AND . . . you've got to tell me why you want Asa's clothes."

Charlie hesitated. He was always hesitating these days, never sure whom he could trust. Fidelio had no such qualms. He told Olivia about the distant howling and Benjamin's theory that it was Asa, and that

Runner Bean could find him if he got a scent of Asa's clothes.

"So if I get the clothes, I can come into the wilderness with you, right?" Olivia started hopping again.

"If we can come with you into the costume department," said Charlie, beginning to feel dizzy as he watched Olivia do a few twirls.

"You're on. When are you going into the wilderness?" Feeling dizzy herself, Olivia staggered to a halt.

"Saturday. Early. Seven o'clock."

"I'll be there." Olivia couldn't resist a last-minute twirl as the horn rang out across the grounds. "Hey, look at that," she said. "Dagbert Endless has made friends with Gabriel Silk."

Amazing but true. Charlie saw Dagbert and Gabriel heading for the door, side by side, deep in conversation.

"Must be the moon," Charlie murmured.

"The what?" asked Fidelio.

"Nothing."

Emma was smiling until Olivia had to go and say, "Look at those two lovebirds."

The smile left Emma's face. Tancred Torsson and Tracy Morsell were ambling over the frosty ground as though there were no such thing as a school bell. Tancred's arm was around Tracy's neck, his hand resting on her shoulder, and Tracy was gazing up at him as though he were the only boy in the whole world.

"Better buck up, you two!" Fidelio bellowed, undaunted by the fact that they were a year above him.

Tancred and Tracy took no notice, anyway.

"They didn't hear you," said Charlie. "Come on, race you to the door."

"I'll get there first," screamed Olivia, rushing away. "Bet you another chocolate fudge."

The boys raced after her, but Charlie was aware that Emma's run was very halfhearted. Olivia won her bet, though no one had taken her on.

Drama lessons took place in the school theater. It was here that Mrs. Marlowe, head of drama, put on the very popular productions that she herself wrote, produced, and directed. She was a small, vivacious woman, her face wrinkled from the many expressions that continually passed across it. Her hair, usually tied in a ponytail, was described as salt and pepper, in other words white and gray, and she wore exotic-colored shawls, long velvet skirts, and suede boots dyed to match her outfits.

Luckily, Olivia was Mrs. Marlowe's favorite, so when the teacher caught her and her friends about to creep down into the costume department at lunchtime, she wasn't as angry as she might have been.

The heavy velvet curtains had been pulled across the stage, and when Olivia opened the trapdoor at the back, she had no idea that Mrs. Marlowe was sitting alone in the dark auditorium, dreaming up her next production.

"Hello! Who's there?" Mrs. Marlowe sprang up the steps at the side of the stage and peeped through the curtains. "Olivia! What are you doing? And you two boys — you aren't in drama."

"So sorry, Mrs. Marlowe. We do apologize." Fidelio could really lay on the charm when he wanted to. "We had no idea you were there or we'd have asked. The thing is, I've written this musical. We're putting it on in the summer, in Olivia's backyard — she's starring, of course — but I wondered if we could borrow some costumes, and Olivia was going to ask, but she couldn't find you."

Charlie and Olivia stared at Fidelio in admiration. How had he managed to come up with such a good excuse so fast?

Mrs. Marlowe was certainly impressed. "A musical! How marvelous!" she purred. "I hope you'll invite me. Of course you may borrow some costumes, but let me know what they are, so that I can check them out." She withdrew her head and then, popping it briefly through the curtains again, added, "Be careful, kids. One of the bulbs has gone out. It's a bit dark down there."

"We'll be OK, Mrs. Marlowe," Olivia said cheerfully. She placed one foot on the wooden steps and descended backward into the room below. Charlie followed. Fidelio came last.

Olivia flicked a switch, and a light hanging almost above her head illuminated a part of the room nearest to the steps. Tall pine cupboards stood in rows against one wall, while a procession of leather trunks and large wicker baskets ran down the center of the room. On the other side, a line of ancient stone pillars created shadowy recesses where nothing at all could be seen.

"That's where the other light should be." Olivia pointed to the ceiling at the other end of the room.

"I hope Asa's stuff's not down there." Charlie gave a small shiver.

"No, it'll be at this end," Olivia said confidently. "And it won't take long. Mrs. Marlowe's very efficient. See, everything's labeled. All the clothes from 1900 to 2000 are at this end. They get progressively older until you reach bearskins and loincloths . . ."

"In the dark," said Charlie.

"There's so much," Fidelio exclaimed. "I think I really will write a musical."

Olivia picked out three large trunks and suggested they take one each. A label marked "1900–2000. Coats. Male." hung from the handles of all three trunks.

Charlie was the first to swing back a lid. He leaped away with a screech as a large beetle scuttled over the rim.

"You wait till the bats come out." Olivia laughed.

Charlie flung a look at the distant shadows, and then at the utter blackness behind the line of pillars. Was it his imagination, or did something glint in there? A bat's eye, or a beast's shiny fang? He turned his attention to the clothes in the trunk.

It was Fidelio who found Asa's coat. "This is it. I'd know it anywhere." He pulled out the long, tattered garment that Asa used to wear on weekends when he was spying for Manfred.

"Now the hat!" said Olivia, opening a cupboard

labeled "1900–2000. Headgear. Male." A wall of hats was revealed inside the cupboard.

Charlie came to help. But Asa's cap was not among the top hats, bowlers, fedoras, panamas, and various military headgear that hung before them.

Olivia tried a second cupboard. "Ah, this is more likely," she announced, scanning the rows of stained, moth-eaten hats.

Charlie pounced on an old tweed cap with several holes in it. "Asa's!" he declared. "I know it is."

They decided not to search for the boots. After all, one old black boot looked pretty much like another. Charlie lifted the lid of a box marked "Beards, et cetera." but there were too many to choose from. And then he saw the label on one of the cupboards. "Masks." He just had to take a look. Inside the cupboard hung masks of every description: painted, glittering, black, white, animal faces, skulls, clowns, ghosts, vampires, and monsters.

"Oh wow!" cried Fidelio, taking out a scarlet mask with black sequined eyebrows and a yellow mouth.

"This is all I need. A masked musical. I really will write one."

The others helped him to choose ten more masks: three animals; two monsters; a sad, white face; a warty man; two golden faces; and a black mask with gold-rimmed eyes. It reminded Charlie of the dark, hunched figure he'd seen in the hall. "Let's get out of here," he said.

The horn sounded just as they were climbing up to the stage. Charlie rolled the coat and hat into a tight bundle and tucked it under his arm. He took a last look at the shadowy steps, and then Olivia shut the trapdoor.

"Can you lock it?" asked Charlie.

"No. It's never locked. Someone could be trapped down there." She giggled.

In the room beneath them, someone limped from behind a pillar. A large, wicker basket creaked as it took the weight of the hunched, black-cloaked figure. Huddled in the gloom, it cursed Charlie Bone, over and over and over again.

THE PERILOUS BRIDGE

On Friday afternoon, Billy Raven changed his mind. He told Charlie that he wouldn't be spending the weekend with him after all.

"I thought you wanted to help us find Asa," said Charlie.

Billy slowly untied the laces on his sneakers. They were sitting in the blue coatroom. Charlie was pulling off his cleats.

"It's the wilderness," Billy said at last. "All those animals; not that I don't like animals, I do, but their voices — there are so many in a place like the wilderness, all speaking different languages, *boom, boom, chatter, chatter*, into my head. I'd rather stay here with Cook."

Children passed back and forth in front of them, skipping over boots, scrambling under benches, finding shorts, losing shirts. Charlie leaned closer to Billy.

"You've left Rembrandt at my place, Maisie'll be in a tizzy."

Billy pulled off his sneakers and sat staring at them. "Perhaps Maisie can bring him here and leave him with Cook."

Charlie shrugged. "I'll ask her. Well, I'm off to pack my bag now. See you on Monday."

"Good luck," said Billy.

Charlie had managed to hide Asa's clothes at the bottom of his bag. When he got home, he pulled out the old coat and hat and stuffed them in his wardrobe. Benjamin was already ringing the doorbell when Charlie went down for tea.

"What are you two up to?" asked Maisie when the boys walked into the kitchen. "You've got plots and adventures written all over your faces."

"Have we?" Benjamin anxiously felt his chin.

"You're telling me, and so's Runner Bean." Maisie began to search the fridge for a meaty bone she'd been saving.

Charlie wasn't sure how much he should tell Maisie. He didn't want to worry her. "We've got a few things planned for tomorrow," he said casually. "A sort of hide-and-seek with Runner Bean."

"So that's it." Maisie gave Runner his bone.

They sat down to their tea. Uncle Paton often didn't appear for meals, so Charlie wasn't too concerned. He would talk to his uncle later, he thought, in private. He wanted his advice on the project they were about to undertake.

"By the way, your uncle's gone," said Maisie, handing out her freshly baked scones.

"Gone!" uttered Charlie. "What do you mean, gone?"

"Don't look so stricken, Charlie. He's off on his usual visit to the sea."

"To see great-grandpa?" asked Charlie.

"That's the one," said Maisie. "Not a word to Grandma Bone. We don't want her going down there spoiling everything."

"No," Charlie murmured. He glanced at Benjamin, who was obviously having the same thought. They hadn't expected Uncle Paton to join them in the wilderness, but it would have been comforting to know that he was aware of the venture, and would be ready to help if things went wrong.

Benjamin was already having misgivings. He wondered if he should have told his parents where he was going. Charlie gave him a reassuring grin. "Fidelio will be with us," he said, "and Olivia."

"Oh?" Benjamin didn't know whether to be pleased or angry. Olivia was a bit too showy for his liking.

"Sounds to me like it's more than a game of hide-and-seek," Maisie said suspiciously. "I hope you're not going to do anything silly, boys."

"Not in the least bit silly, Mrs. Jones," Benjamin answered gravely.

A second later the phone rang. Even before Maisie answered it, Charlie had a nasty feeling that a second complication was about to arise.

"It's for you, Charlie," Maisie called.

Charlie's feet dragged a little as he went into the hall.

"Cheer up, it's your friend Fidelio." Maisie handed Charlie the receiver.

"Hi, Charlie, bad news," said Fidelio's cheerful voice.

Charlie sighed. "What now? Don't tell me you can't come tomorrow."

"Sorry, Charlie, I totally forgot. Promised Dad I'd go to this audition. It's for a summer tour. Really, really important. It could make a difference to my future career. . . ."

"Sure, sure," Charlie said glumly. "OK, genius, we'll have to go without you."

"How about next weekend?" Fidelio suggested.

"Too late," said Charlie. "Asa might be injured. We have to find him tomorrow."

"Could be dead."

"NO," said Charlie. "I won't believe that he's dead.

Good luck with the audition, Fido!" He put down the receiver.

Maisie gave Charlie a wary look as he returned to the table. "What's all this about death?" she said.

Charlie decided to tell her a small part of the truth. "We were talking about the Wilderness Wolf. Fidelio thought it might be dead. We heard shots in the night."

"That was the hunt," said Maisie, "but nothing was killed as far as I know. Though I haven't heard the howling for a couple of nights."

Charlie and Benjamin exchanged glances.

On Saturday morning Charlie woke up to hear a light pattering on his windowpane. It was still dark and at first he thought that snow was beating against the window. When he looked out, he saw Benjamin and Runner Bean standing beneath the street light.

Charlie pulled on his warmest clothes. Before he left the room, he pushed the black kettle farther under his bed. It was hot to the touch, not hot enough to burn him, but certainly hotter than the temperature in the room. *If this is a warning,* thought Charlie, *there's nothing I can do about it now.* He scanned the room for a glimpse of the white moth — his transformed wand — the guardian of his room. He saw it, at last, on the curtain rod, its silver-tipped wings upright like a single sail.

"Wish me luck," said Charlie.

The moth spread her wings and flew down to his shoulder.

"You're welcome to join us," said Charlie. "Very welcome."

By the time he opened the door, Benjamin had been joined by Olivia. She wore a navy coat, thick leather boots, and a striped scarf wound several times around her neck.

"Ready for anything!" sang Olivia as she bounced into the hall.

"SHHHH," hissed Charlie and Benjamin.

Charlie cast an anxious glance at the stairs. He

expected both his grandmothers to come rushing out of their rooms, but luckily they must have been fast asleep.

Olivia held up a red canvas backpack. "Got food for a week in here," she whispered. "Raided the fridge before I left home. Told Mom I was spending the day with Emma. Mom's working anyway. She won't be back till Sunday night."

Charlie decided to take some food of his own. Olivia often ate exotic and unpronounceable food. Tiptoeing into the kitchen, he returned with a bag of cookies and some cold cooked sausages. He tucked them into his own backpack, on top of Asa's coat and hat. "Let's go," he said.

When they left the house, a thin line of pale green light was beginning to show above the distant hills, but as they walked down toward the river, the light faded and they were plunged into a dark, grayish gloom.

There were two bridges over the river, one an ancient narrow iron bridge that the council had declared unsafe for use; the other, built over large stone arches, was wide and strong and completely safe. Charlie had used the iron bridge to visit Naren, but today he chose the stone bridge. Nothing must jeopardize their rescue mission.

Runner Bean seemed to know that something was expected of him. He ran ahead in total silence, not a bark to be had from him. Only his furiously wagging tail betrayed his excitement.

When they had crossed the bridge, the three children walked down the path where, only a few days ago, the hunters had marched into the wilderness. Olivia pulled a large flashlight from her backpack. Its strong beam helped them to navigate the dense undergrowth that bordered the forest. Once they were through and into the trees, the brambles and coarse grass receded. They even found a narrow path.

It was time to put Runner Bean to work. Charlie took the bundled coat and hat from his backpack and held them out to the dog. Runner Bean sniffed them. He growled and backed away. Animals had always been afraid of Asa; a creature that was human by day and a beast at dusk worried and confused them. Instinct told them to avoid such things.

"Come on, Runner," coaxed Benjamin. "Please. We need you to do this." He took the clothes from Charlie, laid them on the ground, and patted them. "Runner, come on."

Runner Bean approached the bundle cautiously. He sniffed the clothes, first the coat, then the hat. He growled again, and then, suddenly, he was away, running along the narrow path, leaping off it now and then to sniff the grass, and running on again.

"He's got the scent!" cried Benjamin, chasing after his dog.

"He's got something, that's for sure," Olivia agreed, following Benjamin.

Charlie picked up the clothes and ran after them. He was surprised how fast Olivia could move, and Benjamin too, for that matter. The beam from Olivia's flashlight was shooting all over the place, anywhere but on the ground, and Charlie found himself straying off the path, bumping into trees, and stumbling over creepers.

There was a cry up ahead, and then another. Too late, Charlie flew into Olivia, who had bumped into Benjamin.

"I've lost him," said Benjamin.

A series of distant barks sent them running forward again. Now at last, a pale light was beginning to filter through the trees. The barking changed direction. They all stopped and listened. Now here, now there, Runner Bean was everywhere at once. They left the path and ran into the trees, only to be drawn back again by another bark.

"He's teasing us," Olivia complained. "He can't smell anything. He's just playing a game."

"Maybe he is," said Benjamin.

Several minutes went by. The barking stopped. They waited and waited. Nothing. Benjamin called to his dog, but there was no answering bark.

"Time for a snack," said Olivia, passing a chocolate bar to Charlie.

"I can't eat," said Benjamin. "Runner's in trouble or he'd have come back. He always comes when I call."

As winter light began to fill the wilderness, an icy breeze picked up, and the whistling and rattling of the bare branches all but drowned a very distant howl.

Charlie's scalp prickled. "Was that the — thing, or Runner Bean?"

"Not sure," said Benjamin.

"Whatever it is, we'd better find it," said Olivia. "That's what we're here for, isn't it?" Taking the lead, she galloped along the path, while the boys raced after her.

Charlie wasn't sure when, or where, the path ended, but he gradually became aware that it was gone and they were now following Olivia on a course that was all her own.

"I suppose she knows where she's going?" Charlie called to Benjamin.

"Yes, I do," cried Olivia. "My hearing is a hundred percent, and I know the howl came from this direction."

They were now in an extremely dense part of the wilderness. The trees grew so close together that the low sun could only throw tiny splashes of light on the soft, mossy ground.

Olivia stopped and the boys ran up to her. "I'm waiting for another howl," she said.

Another howl came. A long, low, melancholy howl that drew closer and closer until Runner Bean burst through a thicket and came bounding up to them. His hair was matted with grass seed, his ears were back, and his eyes were wide and fearful.

"What is it, Runner?" Benjamin clasped his dog around the neck. "What have you found?"

Runner Bean growled. It was a grumbling, angry sound. He definitely didn't want to go back the way he'd come.

"He saw something, didn't he?" said Olivia.

"Found something, I bet," said Charlie.

"Show us, Runner, come on." Benjamin attempted to push his way through the thicket before him.

Runner Bean lowered his head and growled again.

He began to leap around the children, almost as though he were trying to stop them from seeing what he had found.

"OK, OK, Runner, we've got to find it!" Charlie pushed the big dog's head away and waded through the low tangle of branches, until he and the others were standing in a small sunlit glade. A mound of dead leaves lay in the center, a mound shaped like a grave. A bunch of snowdrops had been placed at one end.

On the other side of the glade, a figure huddled between the great, gnarled roots of a tree. Briefly, it turned its face to them. There was no mistaking the wide nose and low hairy brow. It was one of the creatures who had bitten Uncle Paton.

The children were at a loss. They had expected to find Asa, or, at least, the beast that he could become.

"Who . . . who are you?" Charlie took a step closer to the creature.

It snarled at him and then began to whimper.

Olivia grabbed Charlie's arm. "Don't go near it."

"It's OK, Liv." Charlie brushed her hand away. "Look, it's, I mean, she's" — he knew instinctively that it was a woman — "she's not going to hurt us. She's sad. Maybe she's just buried someone."

"Asa?" Benjamin whispered.

Charlie walked over to the woman and crouched in front of her. "Do you know Asa Pike?" he asked gently.

Slowly, she turned her head toward him. Close up, she didn't look so bad. There was kindness in her yellow eyes, and a dimple in her sallow cheek.

"I am Asa's mother." Her voice was faint and husky.

"Is that . . . ?" Charlie looked back at the grave.

"Asa's father." The woman's yellow eyes brimmed with tears.

"Did they kill him?" Charlie asked.

The woman looked up fearfully as Benjamin and Olivia crept closer. Rather than stand over her, they knelt on the ground behind Charlie.

"You're Charlie Bone." The woman gave a dismal

little sigh. "Because of you . . ." She glanced at the grave, and her eyes brimmed again.

"I'm sorry if something I've done has caused you trouble," said Charlie.

She sighed again. "Yes, yes. But you couldn't help it, could you, poor boy?"

Olivia crawled a little closer. "Asa's not dead, is he?"

The woman shook her head. "I do not know. They've taken him, hidden him. He was in a cave, imprisoned there, couldn't change his shape from beast to boy, because of the darkness, you see. We brought him food and I told him not to howl, but he couldn't stop himself."

"And then the hunters came," said Benjamin.

"Yes, and then the hunters came." Her voice was so faint they could barely hear it.

Charlie hesitated before saying, "So it was the hunters who killed your husband?"

The woman began to shake. She twittered like a bird, whimpered, covered her face with long-fingered, hairy hands. "They killed him. They killed him. He was trying to lead them away from our boy. There was a shot and he fell. I dragged him into the shadows, covered him with branches and leaves so they wouldn't see him. But the man who shot him saw him fall, saw the ground all bloody where my poor husband dropped. He thought he'd crawled away to die. So they left."

"And they didn't find Asa," said Olivia.

"Not the hunters, no. But when I went to tell our boy his father was . . . dead" — she closed her eyes and screwed up her face — "Asa was gone. His cave was empty, the barred gate unlocked. They've moved him deeper underground, I know it, so his howling can't be heard."

"Who's 'they,' Mrs. Pike?" asked Olivia. "It is Mrs. Pike, isn't it?"

The woman looked up. "Yes, that is my name."

"The Bloors took Asa, didn't they?" said Charlie.

"Them. Yes," she said sullenly.

The children looked at one another. They had

come to rescue Asa but found instead his mother, who seemed to need their help as much as Asa.

"I think we should take you somewhere, Mrs. Pike," said Charlie, "somewhere safe, in case the hunters come back. Where's your home?"

"Far, far." Mrs. Pike began to sway back and forth. "Can't go back, not with my boy here, somewhere."

Olivia stood up. "Mrs. Pike, you can't stay in the wilderness. You'll freeze to death. And, like Charlie said, the hunters might come back." Now that the woman had a name, Olivia spoke just as she might to a friend.

Mrs. Pike responded with a rueful smile. "I can't walk. I fell when I was moving my husband. My ankle was badly twisted."

"Worse and worse," muttered Benjamin.

Runner Bean whined in sympathy. He had remained on the other side of the glade, not sure what to make of things.

Charlie had been thinking. There was only one place where they could take Mrs. Pike — the Pets' Café. "I know someone who will take care of you," he said. "His name is Mr. Onimous. I'm going to pull you up now. Olivia, go around the other side of Mrs. Pike and help."

Mrs. Pike didn't object when they heaved her onto her one good leg, but she groaned horribly when they dragged her away from the grave.

They decided not to return by the stone bridge. By now it would be too busy. They would have to use the slightly dangerous iron bridge. None of them was very heavy, and if they were careful, they should be able to get safely across. The Pets' Café wasn't far from the bridge, and with luck they should reach it before anyone noticed the odd-looking person hobbling between them.

They found the narrow path again, and soon, as the trees began to thin, they saw two rough wooden fence posts ahead of them. Charlie knew they had reached Bartholomew Bloor's cottage. The sanctuary.

Supporting Mrs. Pike, they shuffled into a yard that had once been full of animals. It was utterly deserted.

"What is this place?" Olivia asked.

"My friend Naren lived here," said Charlie. "Her father is Dr. Bloor's father, but he isn't like the other Bloors. He hates them. He felt safer away from the city, but still near to the Red King's castle. He wanted it to be a secret place. He must have left with his family as soon as he heard hunters in the wilderness."

"I knew them," rasped Mrs. Pike. "They were good to us. Go and see, boy. See if they've really gone." She pulled away from Charlie and leaned against the top bar of the fence.

Charlie ran to the cottage and looked in the window. The table was there and two chairs, but everything else had gone: the photographs on the wall, the lamps, the kettle, the pots and pans, the china ornaments, and the mementos that Bartholomew had collected on his many travels. All gone.

"No one there," said Charlie, walking back to the little group.

Mrs. Pike began to moan. "Not gone, not gone. What will become of them? It was a good place and they were kind."

All at once Charlie understood why Mrs. Pike was so concerned for Bartholomew and his family. "You lived here, didn't you?" he said.

Mrs. Pike nodded. "In a barn, for a while." She made a funny little noise at the back of her throat, her head fell forward, and she began to slide to the ground.

Olivia caught her, just in time. "She's fainted. Take her arm, someone. This isn't going to be easy."

Easy it certainly wasn't. How they managed to haul, lift, and drag Mrs. Pike as far as the bridge, Charlie would never know. The poor woman would regain consciousness, hop a little way, then slump into their arms like a dead thing. When they finally reached the bridge, Charlie ached all over, and he could see that the others were in the same state. Their troubles had hardly begun.

"That's not safe," Olivia declared, staring at the thin band of wrought iron disappearing into the mist.

"It's OK, Liv. I've crossed it several times," said Charlie. "So's Benjamin — and Runner Bean."

"You're crazy," said Olivia.

"It's the only way," Benjamin pointed out.

"What about her?" Olivia looked at Mrs. Pike, slumped against Charlie's shoulder.

As if in answer, a wave of fog came swirling toward them over the river. Now they could hardly see more than a few inches in front of them. Olivia shined her flashlight into the advancing fog. It hardly penetrated at all. "Useless," she said.

"We'll feel our way," Charlie said heartily. Someone had to be positive, after all. "Come on. Benjamin, you go first with one hand on the railing, and one hand holding the back of my jacket, to guide me. I'll walk backward and I'll haul Mrs. Pike along, while Olivia follows, making sure that Mrs. Pike's feet don't fall over the side . . ."

"And take us all with her," Olivia said grimly.

No one could think of a better plan, and so they began the perilous trek across the river. They had only gone a few meters when Benjamin cried out, "The railing's gone . . . I can't see . . . I can't see anything. The fog's too thick — and — and something's happening."

Charlie grabbed the last bit of railing before the link was broken. A roaring, rushing sound filled his ears and, to his horror, he felt water washing over his feet. *This can't be happening,* he thought. *The river was at least thirty feet below the bridge. How can it rise this far?* He thought of Dagbert's endowment.

Olivia's feeble croak came drifting toward Charlie. "My feet are soaked. Is the river tidal? I mean, do you think there's a special time of year when it rises?"

Charlie wondered if now was the time to tell a lie. He knew the river wasn't tidal, but he had to keep up their spirits. "Could be," he said. "We'll have to crawl. Safer that way."

"But we'll get wetter. We'll drown," wailed Benjamin.

"I don't know where the next bit of railing is, or even if there is one, I . . . oh!"

A radiant light suddenly illuminated the area all around them.

"It's your moth!" cried Benjamin. "Look, Charlie! Over your head —"

Charlie looked up. There, fluttering in the air above him, was the white moth, her silvery wings throwing out brilliant shafts of light.

"Thank you!" breathed Charlie. "What would I do without you, Claerwen the moth!"

"I can see the railing," Benjamin shouted. "Yes. I've got it. Come on, Charlie."

By now, all three children were on their knees. It was just as well. Driven by the swirling river, the bridge began to heave from side to side. Charlie felt himself sliding toward the water. With one hand, he clung tight to Mrs. Pike; with the other, he clutched the edge of the bridge.

Frozen with terror, Benjamin couldn't move another inch. "We're going to drown!" he cried.

"We will if you don't keep going," yelled Olivia.

Behind her, Charlie could just make out the dark shape of a very wet Runner Bean; he was crawling slowly toward them on his belly. The bridge suddenly tilted violently. Everyone screamed as they slid across the bridge, clinging to whatever they could find. There was a howl of fear, and when Charlie looked over Mrs. Pike's sprawled body he could see Olivia, one arm thrown around a railing, the other wrapped tightly around Mrs. Pike's feet. Beyond Olivia, the bridge was empty.

"Was that Runner howling?" shouted Benjamin. "Is he OK?"

"Keep going, Ben," Charlie grunted.

"I can't, I can't. I'll fall in."

We'll all fall in, thought Charlie, *and that will be the end of us.* He imagined Runner Bean struggling against the vicious current. He wouldn't be able to struggle for long.

Slowly, the bridge swung back until it was straight again. They waited for the next heave. It never came.

All at once the iron beneath them felt firm and steady. When Charlie stood up, his feet held to the bridge as though it had an almost magnetic force. And yet he could move quite safely.

"Can you feel that?" he called to Benjamin.

"Yes. Yes. I feel safe now," said Benjamin. "And I can see the other side, where your moth is flying."

"Wow!" Olivia stood with legs wide apart. "It's amazing. And look, Mrs. Pike's feet aren't sliding about anymore."

"Let's get going!" Charlie glanced unhappily at the empty bridge behind Olivia. He felt sick with apprehension. There was now a very good chance that they would survive, but what would Benjamin do when he discovered that Runner Bean had fallen into the river?

The wilderness was still shrouded in thick fog, but the mist was rolling back from the water, and Charlie could just make out the far end of the bridge. He half closed his eyes, squinting into the distance. Could he believe what he was seeing?

"What are you staring at, Charlie?" asked Olivia.

"There's someone at the end of the bridge," Charlie said softly.

"Where?" Olivia swung around. "Oh, wow!"

"I'm not seeing things, then?"

"No, Charlie," Olivia said in awe. "I can see him, too."

The figure itself was indistinct. It appeared to be dressed in dull gray, but there was nothing obscure about the red cloak, or the shining silver helmet with its brilliant scarlet crest.

"A knight," Charlie murmured.

Benjamin looked back. He was too late to see the knight, for he had vanished into the mist. All Benjamin could see was an empty bridge.

"Where's Runner? HE'S GONE!" cried Benjamin. He pounded over the bridge, leaped onto dry land, and rushed along the bank beside the swirling river.

MERROMALS

All the excitement had roused Mrs. Pike. Heaving herself upright, she asked, "What's going on?"

"Benjamin's dog fell into the river, Mrs. Pike," Olivia told her. "And now Ben's rushed off to find him."

"In that?" Mrs. Pike stared at the foam spilling across the water. "He'll drown, poor boy."

"He's very sensible," Olivia assured her. "And at least we're safe. Look, just a little way now, and we're there."

Charlie thought, *Benjamin's not safe.* But Asa's mother seemed to need his help more than anyone else just then.

Mrs. Pike managed to hop the rest of the way over the bridge, but needed Charlie's arm to steady herself on the steps up to the road.

"Charlie Bone, there's a light on your head," Mrs. Pike observed when they got to the top.

"Oh, yes. She's my wand," said Charlie, "or rather

she WAS my wand. Her light helped us to get across the bridge."

"A wand . . ." Mrs. Pike spoke in a faraway sort of voice. "How very useful."

A narrow lane bordered by tall hedges led into the town. Once on High Street there would be only a short way to go before they reached the Pets' Café.

The town was not busy that morning. It was misty and cold, and no one paid much attention to two children and a hopping person whose face was hidden by a large hood. Mrs. Pike couldn't move as fast as Charlie would have liked, but at last they turned into the cobblestoned alley called Frog Street.

Standing at the very end of Frog Street, the Pets' Café had an ancient look about it. Who could tell how long it had been there, for it was built into the thick city wall, and that was nine hundred years old. Above the window there was a sign decorated with whiskers, paws, tails, and wings. No one was allowed to enter without a pet. Luckily, Charlie knew the owners well.

It was now ten o'clock. The café opened at half past

ten. Charlie rang the bell. There was, of course, no answer. The owners, Mr. and Mrs. Onimous, didn't like people arriving early. They wouldn't open the door on principle.

Charlie banged on the window and shouted, "Help! Mr. Onimous, come quickly. PLEASE!"

Mrs. Pike gave a small moan and sank to the ground.

"Mr. Onimous, come quickly!" cried Charlie again. "There's been an accident."

The door opened very suddenly and a large man wearing a yellow sweater stood glaring down at them. "You know we don't open until half past ten," he bellowed.

Norton Cross was the doorman, or bouncer, as Charlie liked to call him. It was Norton's duty to prevent anyone without a pet from entering the premises.

"This is an emergency, Mr. Cross!" wailed Olivia.

Norton folded his arms across his chest. "Where are your pets?"

Charlie had no answer.

"I suppose you call a moth a pet," said Norton.

"Ummm . . . ," Charlie began.

"There's one on your head," said Norton.

"Ah, yes. My pet," Charlie agreed.

"And yours?" Norton asked Olivia.

"You're wasting time," Olivia said angrily. "I haven't actually got . . ."

At this point there was a moan from the ground. Mrs. Pike raised herself on all fours and crawled forward. She looked up at Norton. He stared back, lost for words.

"You'd better come in," he said at last.

Olivia and Charlie helped Mrs. Pike to her feet and heaved her into the café. Breathing heavily, she allowed herself to be steered through the café, around the counter, and into the kitchen.

"Visitors," Norton announced as he held back the curtain behind the counter.

The Onimouses' cozy kitchen never failed to lift Charlie's spirits. It was here that the three famous cats resided, when they were not out on an important errand of their own. Not for nothing were they called the Flames. Today, all three were asleep on top of a cupboard, their thick bright tails hanging over the side like upside-down question marks. One was yellow, one orange, and the third a coppery red.

Mr. Onimous could almost have been an animal himself. Very small, round, and hairy, with sharp bright teeth and long pointed nails, he reminded Charlie of a cuddly kind of rodent. As for his wife, Onoria, she was in every way the exact opposite of her husband. She was six feet tall with thin, wispy hair and the longest nose you're ever likely to see on a human being.

When a not-quite-human-looking person hobbled into their kitchen, the Onimouses didn't blink an eye. To them, she was just another poor creature, obviously in need of their help.

"Sit down, my dear." Mrs. Onimous pulled out a chair for their visitor.

Mrs. Pike sank into it with a sigh and laid her head on the table.

"What troubles have we here?" asked Mr. Onimous.

Olivia said, "This is Mrs. Pike. She's twisted her ankle. But we need to use your phone, Mr. Onimous. It's urgent. Runner Bean may have drowned and Benjamin's gone looking for him."

"The river has risen," Charlie added. "It's as high as the bridge. Benjamin could drown, too! And I think maybe I should go back and look for him."

"You just wait here, Charlie Bone. Heaven, help us!" Mrs. Onimous ran to the telephone in the café.

Charlie and Olivia could hear her gabbing away in a rather high voice, while they stood waiting uneasily on either side of Mrs. Pike.

In less than a minute, Mrs. Onimous was back. She looked annoyed. "The police say they've had no reports of a high river. In fact, Officer Singh says he noticed it was particularly low when he came across the bridge this morning. And if a boy is looking for his dog, that's his business. His parents must report him missing if anything is to be done about it."

"The river WAS up," Olivia said angrily. "It washed right over my feet. My boots are still wet. I saw it . . . unless . . ."

"Dagbert-the-drowner," Charlie said quietly.

Olivia stared at him. *Dagbert*, she mouthed.

"Kids, take off your shoes and put them by the stove," said Mr. Onimous, "and then sit down and tell me about this poor lady." He nodded at Mrs. Pike.

Charlie and Olivia pulled off their wet shoes and socks and placed them by the stove. But when Charlie sat down he found he was incapable of giving the Onimouses a clear explanation about what had happened. He was too concerned about Benjamin. So it was Olivia who launched into a lengthy account of Asa's imprisonment, the hunting party, and the shooting of Mr. Pike.

"Murder!" cried Mrs. Onimous. "Just because people are" — she glanced at Mrs. Pike's coarse, reddish-colored hair — "outsiders, it's no excuse. Whatever we are, whoever we are, murder is murder."

"I agree," said Olivia. "But I don't think Mrs. Pike

211

wants to bring an action, or whatever you call it. I don't think she wants to be seen, if you get me."

Mr. Onimous gently touched Mrs. Pike's shoulder. "You're with friends now, dear. We'll do what we can for you. There's a nice cozy room above the café. You can stay as long as you like. We'll find that son of yours, if he's still . . ."

Mrs. Onimous looked hard at her husband and vigorously shook her head.

"I expect they've hidden him somewhere dark and . . ." Mr. Onimous frowned and put his hand over his mouth, as though struck by a sudden thought. "By golly . . . I wonder?"

"Do you think you know where he is?" asked Charlie.

"Tell us," cried Olivia.

"Can't, kids. Got to ponder it a bit." Mr. Onimous sat down and stroked his furry chin.

His words had had an effect on Mrs. Pike. She lifted her head and gazed around at them, her yellow eyes full of hope. "He can be saved, my Asa?"

"He can, my dear," Mr. Onimous said confidently. "Now, can you tell us a little about yourself, and how you came to this city? Forgive me, but it seems that you are very much a stranger here."

"I am." Mrs. Pike clasped her hands together and said, "I would like some water, please."

"What am I thinking of?" Mrs. Onimous leaped to put the kettle on. "You shall have herbal tea, my dear, a good restorative drink. And seedcake perhaps, with juicy raisins and revitalizing spices."

"I thoroughly recommend it," said Mr. Onimous, fetching a glass from the cupboard. "But first some water."

"And frozen peas for the ankle?" Olivia suggested.

"Frozen peas it is. I see you know a thing or two, Olivia." Mr. Onimous set a glass of water before Mrs. Pike and then delved into the freezer for a bag of peas.

While Mrs. Pike was being attended to, Charlie stood up. Benjamin was still very much on his mind. Someone should be looking for him. But when Charlie made for the door, Mrs. Pike began to speak, and her soft, husky voice drew him back. Before he knew it, he was sitting down again and listening to an incredible story.

Words poured out of Mrs. Pike as though she'd been holding them back for years, waiting for the time when she could talk about her family, and the extraordinary place that she'd come from. "We live in what you might call enchanted places, forests moving with the secret currents in the air. They say that Cafall the Changer began it all. He was one of the Red King's sons. A wicked one. But Cafall was changeable, you see. All of a sudden goodness would come over him. It was in one of these righteous moods that he took flight from the castle. Evil was growing there, and he could take no more. So he sailed away and found, by chance, the land of the Merromals. Merromals are people like me." Mrs. Pike's heavy brow lifted slightly and she gave a wry smile. "Not all Merromals look like me and Mr. Pike. A mutual attraction drew us together.

"Well, Cafall took a Merromal wife, and they had a son, and that's when the changing began. Their child was a boy by day and a beast at dusk. And so it went on, through the generations."

Mrs. Pike took several noisy sips of herbal tea. It was obvious that she had more to say and her rapt audience remained silent, waiting for her to continue. Charlie politely dropped his gaze when her huge teeth bit into the seedcake, but Olivia couldn't stop her nose from wrinkling.

"It's very gratifying to be so carefully listened to." Mrs. Pike brushed a few crumbs from her chin and continued. "I will tell you about my family."

"Please." Mr. Onimous nodded eagerly.

"We brought our son to this kingdom fifteen years ago. Merromals don't travel well, but we, Mr. Pike and I, decided that we must see more of the great world that we all live in. I expect you're wondering how we came by our education. . . ." She looked around the table, but no one would admit that such an idea had crossed their minds. Mrs. Pike smiled. "Well, I'll tell you. It was books. Cafall took his father's great book of legends when he left the castle. Since then we have collected more legends, more words. We have printers, yes, really. We have libraries, many of them. When Merromals travel, they always come home with more books, more subjects, more words, more ideas. We are a very educated people, although sometimes our children find schoolwork hard. It was like this for Asa."

Charlie remembered that Asa had failed his last exams. He waited for Mrs. Pike to continue, but she was intent on eating at that moment. She had stuffed the rest of the cake into her mouth and was chewing heartily.

"More cake, Mrs. Pike?" Mrs. Onimous hastily cut extra slices and pushed the plate across the table. "Come on, Charlie, Olivia, eat up. There's plenty more."

Charlie was glad that Mrs. Onimous had been the first to speak, and by doing so broke the spell. He took a slice of cake, waited for Mrs. Pike to swallow, and then asked, "Why did you send Asa to Bloor's Academy, Mrs. Pike?"

She looked at him in surprise. "Where else would he go? It's where the Red King lived, where other endowed children go. Not that you'd call Asa's affliction an endowment, exactly. But we felt he would fit in, and he did, for a while. Manfred Bloor took him under his wing, and life was quite good for Asa . . . and then . . ." Her voice trailed away.

"And then he changed sides," Olivia put in. "He helped Charlie to get his father back."

"The Bloors will never forgive Asa, will they?" Charlie said sadly.

Mrs. Pike patted Charlie's hand. "He did the right thing. It's not your fault, Charlie Bone. We were proud of our Asa for helping you against the Bloors. But we didn't expect their wrath to be so terrible. If Manfred hadn't been injured like that . . ." She glanced up at the three cats.

"I know," said Mr. Onimous, following her gaze. "It's hard to believe they could do that to a person."

"They were leopards once," Charlie said defensively. "What do you expect?"

Everyone looked up at the three bright tails, and Leo, the orange cat, woke up, almost as though he felt their eyes on him. He stretched and yawned, and then regarded the scene below with haughty golden eyes.

"I can't feel sorry for Manfred," said Charlie. "He put my father in a trance so deep, he would never have woken up if it hadn't been for the cats."

"We know, dear," said Mrs. Onimous.

There was a question that Charlie had been wanting to ask Mrs. Pike. Now seemed the right time. "Were you in our empty house, Mrs. Pike, a week ago? I thought I saw you in the street outside, when my uncle, er, when the streetlight kind of exploded."

Mrs. Pike turned to look at Charlie. She seemed a little fearful. Her mouth twitched and her hands began to tremble. "In your house?" she whispered.

"The place that used to be our house," Charlie amended. "I don't live there at the moment, but when my parents come back from their vacation, and the builders have repaired it . . . oh, please. I'm sorry."

Charlie couldn't continue because Mrs. Pike appeared to be very distressed. She had covered her face with her hands and was shaking quite violently.

Mrs. Onimous put an arm around the troubled woman. "There, there, dear. Charlie meant no harm, I'm sure."

"I'm really sorry," Charlie said in an undertone. "I didn't mean to upset anyone."

Mr. Onimous took a handful of tissues from a box on the dresser and offered them to Mrs. Pike. She grabbed the tissues, dabbed her eyes, rubbed her cheeks, and loudly blew her nose. When all this was done, she stopped shaking, squared her shoulders, and said in a firm voice, "I can't deny it. You deserve the truth, Charlie Bone."

Charlie was taken aback by Mrs. Pike's sudden, forthright manner. "Thank you," he murmured.

There was an expectant hush while Mrs. Pike dabbed her nose again and cleared her throat. Unfortunately, the silence was broken by Olivia.

Unable to bear the strain any longer, she begged, "What is the truth, Mrs. Pike?"

Mrs. Pike flashed a reproving glance at her. "I'm coming to it," she barked.

Olivia smiled self-consciously and sank back into her chair.

Raising her voice several notches, Mrs. Pike announced, "We were blackmailed."

Everyone looked startled, but before a word could be said, Mrs. Pike continued. "It was that man Weedon who caught poor Asa. He took him away and locked him up in the dark. When our boy didn't come home we went to the academy, very late so no one would see us. The Bloors told us we'd get our boy back if we found something they wanted: a box, inlaid with mother-of-pearl. They reckoned it was in your old house, Charlie. We were to search every inch of it, and not return until we'd found the box. No box, no boy, they said." Mrs. Pike swallowed hard and blew her nose again.

Charlie waited for her to resume her story, but

when this didn't happen, he asked, "Did you find the box?"

"Not a sign of it." Mrs. Pike sighed. "It isn't in that house, I'd swear to it. The old man, Ezekiel, said he knew that Lyell Bone, your father, had hidden it, Charlie. But when Lyell was under that terrible spell he forgot all about it. They could never make him tell them where it was. But now he's better, they're afraid he's suddenly going to remember where he put it."

"He never mentioned a mother-of-pearl box to me," said Charlie. "I wonder what's in it?"

"It must be very valuable," said Olivia excitedly.

"Something of the utmost importance," declared Mrs. Onimous.

Her husband added thoughtfully, "A matter of life and death. Oh, dear. Oh, my word."

"What is it, Orvil?" his wife demanded. "You look so grim."

Mr. Onimous grinned unconvincingly. "I just had a silly thought, but it's nothing."

Charlie realized he must have had the same thought

221

as Mr. Onimous. "It isn't silly," he said. "You think they'll want to stop my father from coming back, don't you? In case he finds the box before they do."

"It did cross my mind," Mr. Onimous admitted.

Charlie got to his feet, angry and defiant. "If they think they can get at my father again, they're wrong. He's thousands of miles away."

"Of course he is, Charlie," Mrs. Onimous said calmly. "He's quite safe."

"I'll tell him about the box as soon as he comes back," Charlie went on, "and we'll find it together."

"What can be in it?" said Olivia. "I can hardly wait to find out. Couldn't you look for it now, Charlie? I'll help."

"Lyell might have given the box to someone else," Mr. Onimous suggested.

The room went quiet as they all thought about this. Olivia had just begun to say, "But who . . ." when they heard Norton Cross open the café door and say, "Blow me down!"

"Goodness, it's time to open the café!" Mrs. Onimous ran around the table and through the beaded curtain. She gave a cry of surprise and appeared a second later with Benjamin Brown. At his side walked a very wet-looking dog.

"Ben!" cried Olivia and Charlie.

"I thought he'd drowned." Olivia jumped up and hugged the bedraggled dog.

Benjamin smiled at everyone. "Someone saved him. Look." He pulled from his pocket a long scarlet feather. "I found this under Runner's collar. It's a kind of message, isn't it?"

"The knight," said Charlie slowly.

"What knight is this?" asked Mr. Onimous.

While Mrs. Onimous rubbed Runner Bean with a towel, Olivia described the knight they had seen standing in the mist at the end of the bridge. "At first I couldn't believe my eyes," she said, "but Charlie saw him, too. He wore a red cloak and a silver helmet with red feathers floating from the top."

"The Red Knight," Mr. Onimous scratched his chin.

"Are you going to tell us who he was?" asked Mrs. Onimous.

"No one knows for sure." Mr. Onimous's bright eyes blinked several times before he said, "It was believed that the knight and the Red King were one and the same."

LYSANDER AND LAUREN

"The Red King!" Charlie felt an overwhelming surge of hope. "Of course. Who else could stop the river from drowning us? And who else could have saved Runner Bean?"

Olivia looked dubious. "The king is just a tree, Charlie. We saw him. He'll be a tree forever now."

"We don't know that for certain." Charlie looked at Mr. Onimous. "Do we, Mr. Onimous?"

The small man spread his hands. "Who knows, Charlie? In this city anything is possible. Now I must attend to my café. Mrs. Pike, you stay here, and we'll get you settled later." He rushed out of the kitchen, carrying a tray of dog biscuits and bowls of bird seed.

Mrs. Pike had been listening to them all with a frown that grew deeper every moment. Mention of the Red King brought her no relief. "I am beyond saving," she said sadly. "The Bloors want me dead for sure. I failed to find the box, and knowing about it has sealed my fate. I wasn't to tell a soul. They'll guess that I've told you. They wanted to drown ME, Charlie, not you or your friends."

"It was just the river, Mrs. Pike," Olivia said emphatically. "No one was trying to drown you. I mean, who would have seen us so early in the morning, in all that fog?"

Mrs. Pike couldn't be consoled. "If Asa's alive, they'll try and turn him again. He's a changer, after all." She made a soft, grunting noise and Runner Bean backed into a corner with a growl. "Dear me, the dog's afraid of me, and I've never harmed an animal in my life."

"He's not afraid, he's just confused," said Benjamin, trying to sound polite.

The sound of barking came from the café; this was followed by several catcalls, a low whinny, and a voice that kept repeating, "Dog ahoy! Dog ahoy!"

There was no mistaking the familiar call. It had to be Lysander's parrot, Homer. Charlie, Benjamin, and Olivia said good-bye to Mrs. Pike, Charlie promising that whatever happened, Asa would be rescued.

"And you'll be quite safe here, Mrs. Pike." Olivia gave the forlorn woman's arm a squeeze. "They're brilliant, the Onimouses."

The three children trooped out of the kitchen, emerging behind the counter in the café. Standing on the other side of the counter were Lysander and a very pretty girl with a parrot on her shoulder. Lysander's parrot was sitting on his head.

"Hi, everyone," said Lysander. "This is Lauren, oh, and Cassandra."

"I'm Lauren; she's Cassandra," said the girl, tapping the parrot's foot. "Are you going to sit with us?"

It seemed a very good idea. The other three walked around the counter and joined the line.

"You owe me a chocolate fudge," Olivia reminded Charlie.

"You deserve two," said Charlie, checking his pocket for the right money.

The Pets' Café was remarkably busy. Perhaps on gloomy days, pets needed to socialize as much as their owners. Before they could reach the only empty table, the five children had to jump over cats and rabbits, squeeze past a giant dog and a miniature pony, and duck under a low-flying owl.

"Phew!" Lysander dropped into a chair and wiped a hand across his brow. "What a crowd. This place is becoming almost too popular. Homer's favorite foods have already sold out." He passed a chunk of cake up to his parrot. "Try that, Homer."

Homer took the cake in his beak, placed it under one foot, and pecked at it very daintily.

"What a great place," Lauren declared, gazing around the café. "I wish you'd brought me here before, Lysander."

Charlie had been trying to place the girl. She was so pretty, with her dark, wavy hair and dimpled cheeks, he was sure he would have noticed her at Bloor's. "You don't go to our school, do you?" he said.

Lysander laughed. "No fear of that. She goes to a nice, normal school, don't you, Lauren?"

"Actually, you go to my school," Benjamin said

shyly. "But I don't suppose you would have noticed me."

"Hang on." Lauren studied Benjamin closely. "Yes, of course. You're Benjamin Brown. Your parents are famous detectives, aren't they?"

"Well, not really famous." Benjamin blushed and leaned down to give Runner Bean a second beef treat.

Lysander wanted to know what Charlie and his friends were doing in the Onimouses' kitchen.

"It's a long story," Charlie said uncertainly. He knew Lysander could be trusted but wasn't so sure about Lauren.

There was no stopping Olivia, however. Hardly pausing to draw breath, she recounted almost every moment of their near-disastrous morning, from the time they reached the wilderness until Benjamin appeared with Runner Bean and the red feather.

While Lysander remained silently pensive, Lauren praised Olivia for her excellent storytelling.

"Not that I think it's a story," Lauren told Olivia.

"But it's so incredible. I mean, I know you guys at Bloor's are very, well . . . interesting to say the least but, hey" — she lowered her voice — "a not-quite-human person right here, in the kitchen?"

"As a matter of fact, she is human," Charlie said gravely. "Look, you mustn't tell anyone about all this, Lauren. It's very secret, very private."

"He's right," said Lysander as though waking from a dream. "Lauren, you must promise never to repeat a word of what you've heard here today, even to your best friend."

Lauren stared at him reproachfully. "Lysander Sage, YOU are my best friend. And I promise never, ever to tell a soul."

Lauren looked so earnest, it was impossible to doubt her. Charlie breathed a sigh of relief. "Have you got any ideas, Lysander?" he asked.

Lysander passed another piece of cake up to Homer. "You said Mr. Onimous might know where Asa has been taken. We'll have to wait until he tells us. And then we'll bring Tancred in."

"Tancred?" Olivia scowled. "What can he do?"

"Tancred will be essential, and so will your moth, Charlie." Lysander glanced at the white moth resting just above Charlie's left ear. "She saved your lives today, and I'm sure she will again."

"And the Red Knight," Benjamin said quietly. "He saved us, too."

"Indeed, the Red Knight," Lysander agreed.

It was decided that they should all meet up again the following afternoon. Lysander would try and persuade Tancred to come to the café, but he wasn't hopeful. Tracy Morsell didn't like animals, and Tancred was reluctant to be out of her company for more than a minute.

Olivia remarked that she found this really silly. Lysander shrugged and grinned at his girlfriend.

When Lysander and Lauren left the café, their parrots' heads bobbed up and down in time with each other, as though they too were dating.

"I used to think Lysander was so cool," Olivia said sadly.

Benjamin and Charlie set off for Filbert Street, while Olivia made her way up to Ingledew's bookstore. She had almost reached Cathedral Close when she saw a familiar figure dart up Piminy Street. Anyone else might have registered the appearance and passed on. Not Olivia.

"Hey!" she shouted. "Where are you going, Dagbert Endless?"

Several pedestrians looked at Dagbert, who froze in his tracks and slowly turned to face Olivia.

"Hi!" yelled Olivia. "Do you live up there?"

Dagbert stared at her. The expression in his blue-green eyes was so chilly it made Olivia's skin prickle.

"OK," she said, annoyed with her voice for sounding so shaky. "Who cares where you live?" She continued into the square and entered Ingledew's bookstore.

THE STREET OF MAGICIANS

Miss Ingledew had two customers, both interested in the same rare book. She smiled at Olivia and pointed to the curtain that screened off her living room.

Olivia found Emma at her aunt's desk, writing a list of titles in a large black book. She brightened visibly when she saw Olivia. "I was worried about you, Liv, going into that wilderness when it was still practically dark."

"You'd have been more worried if you'd been there," Olivia said cheerfully.

Miss Ingledew popped her head around the curtain to tell them that she had just made the best sale in years. Her two customers had bid against each other until the price of the rare book became so high, one of them had to pull out. "Let's celebrate," she said. "I'll close the shop for a while."

When the front door had been locked, Emma's aunt poured three glasses of sparkling cider and passed them around. Miss Ingledew was one of the few people Emma and her friends could trust, and as soon as Olivia had gulped down her cider, she hiccupped three times and then launched into an account of her adventure in the wilderness.

Olivia had a tendency to embellish the facts a little more every time she repeated them, but, to be fair, her story was more or less accurate.

When Olivia had finished, Miss Ingledew knocked back her cider and exclaimed, "Good grief, Olivia. The trouble you children get yourselves into. I seriously hope you won't return to that wilderness. Anything could happen."

"We definitely won't cross the iron bridge again," Olivia said evasively. "By the way, I saw one of the new boys running up Piminy Street. Dagbert-the-drowner. I know this sounds weird, but Charlie thinks he might have had something to do with the water rising so fast."

"It doesn't sound weird, Olivia. We all know what can happen in this place." Miss Ingledew poured herself another glass of cider. "I don't like Piminy Street. Too much happened there, in the past."

"Tell us, Auntie," said Emma.

Miss Ingledew looked at her watch. "I ought to open the store again soon. I don't want to miss another sale."

"But what happened on Piminy Street? Tell us, please," begged Olivia.

Miss Ingledew regarded her empty glass. She picked up the bottle of sparkling cider and put it down again. "It's the oldest street in the city," she said with a tiny shiver. "The great fire of the eighteenth century never touched it. Some said it was because so many magicians lived there. People like Feromel, the blacksmith, and Melmott, the stonemason. There was also a cobbler who made heart-stopping shoes, and several others whose talents I can't remember. They were usually at each other's throats, but the fire brought them together, just for a day, and their combined efforts were enough to ward off the flames. They've all gone now, of course."

"There's a kettle shop," Emma said thoughtfully. "Charlie got a very unusual kettle from there."

"Did he now?" Miss Ingledew looked interested, but someone was rapping on the front door and she reluctantly left the girls while she went to attend to her next customer.

Olivia often stayed over at the bookstore on a Saturday night. Her mother, a famous actress, couldn't always get home when she was working. Olivia hardly minded at all. She enjoyed sharing Emma's tiny bedroom, with its sloping ceiling and low oak beams.

That night, the girls fell asleep early, but the stirring events of the day kept breaking into Olivia's dreams until she found herself waking, with a bump, on the bare floorboards beside her bed.

"What was that?" cried Emma, sitting up.

"Only me," groaned Olivia. "I can't sleep, Em. I keep thinking about all the stuff that happened this morning. It does my head in, knowing that Piminy Street is so close, with all its bewitchery maybe still going on."

"I know what you mean." Emma drew the covers up to her chin. "Especially if Dagbert-the-drowner lives there."

"Shall we take a look, just to satisfy our curiosity?"

Not wanting to sound like a wimp, Emma reluctantly whispered, "OK."

A small window was set between the beams behind Emma's bed. To anyone less than six feet tall, it only afforded a view of the sky, but when Emma stood on her pillow she could see the backs of the houses on Piminy Street.

Olivia climbed onto Emma's bed and they stood, on tiptoe, on the pillow.

A narrow alley ran between the backyards of the houses on Piminy Street and Cathedral Close. A single streetlight cast a dim glow over brick walls, trash cans, bags of garbage, and untidy patches of weeds. As the girls scanned the dismal scene for anything of interest, one of the yards caught their attention. The small cobblestoned space was filled with gray forms that cast eerie shadows across the walls.

"They're bits of people," said Olivia, "made of stone."

"All broken," Emma observed.

"Or unfinished," said Olivia. "A man without a head, a woman without arms . . ."

"And animals," Emma added with excitement. "A lion's head, a horse that looks perfect, except . . ."

"It hasn't got a tail," said Olivia. "I like the giant dog with only two legs."

"He's sitting down. Look, you can see one of his back feet."

"Oh, yes." Olivia clutched her friend's arm. "Em, do you think they were made by that old stone-mason, Melmott, or whatever he was called?"

"Well, if they were, he can't be around to bring them to life." Emma's laugh was slightly hollow, for she wasn't absolutely sure that this was true.

A bright orange flare suddenly lit a wall a few houses down from the stonemason's yard.

"What was that?" Olivia climbed up on the head-board to get a better view. "I think someone's started a fire. I wish I could see more. Look, there's another flash." Olivia jumped down onto the pillow. "Shall we go and have a look?"

Emma shook her head. "It's too late. We can't go snooping around in the dark. Anyway, it's probably someone's log fire. It's not against the law to burn logs in a fireplace."

"At this time of night? What if there *is* a fire? These old houses would burn like firewood. We ought to find out what's going on."

"I could find out," said Emma.

Olivia could only just make out her friend's face. Emma looked deadly serious.

"You mean . . . fly?" whispered Olivia.

"Yes. You must hold the window open as wide as you can." Emma took Olivia's place on the headboard. Her head and shoulders were now above the windowsill. She took a deep breath and imagined herself soaring up toward the stars. She imagined black wings beating in the blue velvet sky — and now she could feel them, strong and pliant, lifting her up, up, up!

Standing with her arms extended against the wide-open window, Olivia heard the soft crackle of newly formed feathers. She felt a rush of air sweep past her face, and then saw two black wings beating in the midnight sky. "Good luck, Em," she called.

Emma flew above the alley, until she came to a yard illuminated by intermittent bursts of brilliant light. She perched on a wall, gazing at a small window, bright with sparks and flashes. If she were to find the source of these pyrotechnics, Emma would have to fly closer.

Taking another breath, this time for courage as much as anything, Emma swooped across the yard and alighted on a narrow sill outside the fiery window. The glass pane glistened with drops of condensation. Beyond the shining droplets, an extraordinary scene appeared to Emma. In the center of the room stood a tall figure, its head covered by a metal helmet with a glass visor. It wore dusty blue coveralls and long leather gauntlets, but it was quite definitely female.

A blazing furnace belched smoke and flames as

the woman thrust a pair of giant tongs into its heart. She withdrew a long, flat object, every inch glowing a brilliant red. Clamped in the tongs, the object was held by the woman on an iron block with concave sides — an anvil, Emma presumed.

Reaching up to a shelf, the woman found a large hammer and began to beat the glowing metal. *Clang, clang, clang!* The sound reverberated around the walls, while shadows grew and vanished with the leaping and dying of the flames.

Metal on metal wasn't the only sound that Emma heard. Beneath the clanging, a voice had begun to chant, not tunefully, but somehow in rhythm with the beats, a low, humming, indecipherable chant, like a spell.

And now Emma could see clearly what lay on the anvil. Taking shape beneath the hammer was a gleaming sword; its sides were razor thin, its tip so sharp it seemed to melt into the shadows.

"A sword," breathed Emma.

Who, in this day and age, would want a sword?

Who would need a sword? This blacksmith clearly wasn't Feromel, so who was she?

Emma lifted off the windowsill and flew onto a wall. Happily, there was no imminent danger to the surrounding houses. The fire was contained in the furnace. They could all sleep peacefully in their beds. But there was much to ponder.

Emma could see Olivia waiting patiently by the window, and flew up to tell her about the blacksmith and the sword.

"A sword?" In her excitement, Olivia slipped off the headboard. "Ouch." She climbed up again. "Are you coming in now, Em?"

"I want to see what's on the other side of those houses," said Emma. "I don't often get the opportunity to be a bird. I might as well take advantage of it."

Olivia wasn't sure if this was a good idea. If enchanters still lived on Piminy Street, there might be one who could recognize a girl in bird feathers. But tonight Emma was in an adventurous mood. Before Olivia could say another word, Emma had swept up and over the blacksmith's crooked slate roof and down onto Piminy Street.

The front of the blacksmith's was quite a surprise. Displayed in the window were a variety of homely looking kettles; the largest, made of copper, gleamed so brightly it cast a pinkish glow on the cobblestones. There was nothing to suggest that a blacksmith worked at a fiery furnace on the other side of the building.

Emma perched on a streetlight and surveyed the row of ancient houses. Piminy Street held a curious energy. The air crackled with unheard sounds and strong emotions. Emma was tempted to fly back to the safety of the bookstore, but found herself drawn farther down the street. She fluttered between trees, glancing at windows and tiny mice scuttling for cover. Somewhere a cat pounced, somewhere else a dog barked. Didn't Olivia say that she saw Dagbert Endless running down here? And wasn't that a fish shop, with a badly painted sign hanging on the wall? Perching on the dilapidated sign, Emma looked through the window above it. A slight gap between the curtains gave her a narrow view of the room beyond. Emma caught her breath. Eerie, underwater colors swirled across the wall, and on the bed lay someone whose face was shining.

Holding back a cry, Emma flew to a tree and sat there, ruffling her feathers and listening to the wild beat of her heart. "Dagbert. Dagbert-the-drowner," she twittered to herself.

An owl sitting in a tree on the other side of the road hooted, as if to say, "You should be asleep. Nights are exclusively for owls."

Emma fell silent. Gradually, she calmed down. She had seen more than enough for one night. If there were other houses that held sinister enchant-ments, she didn't want to know about them. She rose out of the tree — and plummeted back in astonish-ment. She would have fallen to the earth if she hadn't managed to cling to a branch at the last minute.

Directly beneath Emma stood a boy she recog-nized. Eric Shellhorn. He was not alone. As Emma peered down through the naked branches, a figure moved out of the tree's shadow. Its face was covered by a mask with glittering, silvery eyes.

"Now!" commanded the masked figure.

"Now!" Eric repeated in a small voice.

The little boy walked toward one of the shops. Emma couldn't see what lay beyond its darkened window. Eric had stopped now. He was staring at the door. His concentration was so fierce, tiny shock waves rippled through the night air.

Suddenly, the door opened and a stone man walked out. His gait was slow and awkward, his legs lifting too high and his knees bending with a groan. When his stone feet hit the ground, a dull thud rumbled through the earth, like distant cannon fire.

AN UNBEATABLE SWORD

"Are you sure it was Eric?"

"Yes." Emma answered Olivia's question in a husky whisper. She was lying in bed with her eyes closed, wanting to sleep but knowing she wouldn't be able to. Images of the moving stone man, the shining boy, and the fiery sword kept running through her mind. Closing her eyes against them was useless.

"What on earth's going on in Piminy Street?" said Olivia, rather too loudly in Emma's opinion.

"You heard what my aunt said. Even the great fire couldn't destroy those old houses. So many magicians lived there." Emma yawned. She felt exhausted.

"Yes, but why have all these things started happening NOW?"

Emma wished Olivia would give her a bit of peace. She didn't want to think about what she had seen. "Maybe they're always happening, but no one's noticed."

A loud *Hmmm!* came from the other side of the room. "I don't think so, Em. Something's happened. Something to do with Charlie, probably."

"Why Charlie?"

"Because his father's turned up after ten years. That's bound to upset things for some people, isn't it?"

"Why?" Emma asked sleepily.

"I don't actually know," Olivia admitted. "It's just a feeling."

Both girls gave themselves over to a bit of silent thinking for a while and then, miraculously, fell asleep.

On Sunday morning, when Emma and Olivia went down to breakfast, they found Miss Ingledew, in a blue velvet bathrobe, entertaining Paton Yewbeam. He must have arrived while it was still dark. They were both drinking black coffee, and were obviously in the middle of a rather serious conversation.

Miss Ingledew seemed flustered. She jumped up and began to get breakfast ready. Paton said, "Morning, girls," in a distant kind of voice, while he watched Miss Ingledew waft around the room.

Olivia nudged Emma. "Are you going to tell them about last night?"

"Last night?" Miss Ingledew put four cereal bowls on the table with a heavy clatter. "What happened last night?"

Emma sat down and told them about the stone man, the shining boy, and the fiery sword.

It took the two adults some time to digest this news. They drained their coffee cups, and then Paton said, "Can you go through that again, Emma?"

Emma went through it again.

"What does it all mean, Mr. Yewbeam?" asked Olivia, who thought that Paton Yewbeam knew almost everything there was to know.

"What does it mean?" Paton rubbed his chin. "I don't know, Olivia."

Olivia was not disheartened. "I bet you do. I mean, I bet you've got a bit of an idea about what's going on."

Paton smiled. "All right. I admit I've got a bit of an idea. It goes like this. Charlie's father . . ."

"I knew it had something to do with Charlie!" cried Olivia. "I knew —"

"Please! Let Mr. Yewbeam speak," said Emma.

Olivia subsided.

"Thank you." Paton winked at Emma. "As I almost said, Charlie's father comes out of a trance, a spell or whatever you like to call it, after ten years. That's going to put a lot of people out, especially the people who put him 'under,' shall we say. There was a reason for the terrible thing they did. We've always assumed that it was Ezekiel Bloor's revenge for the accident that put him in a wheelchair for life. But now that Charlie has told me about the Pikes searching his old house for a certain box, I'm absolutely convinced that Lyell Bone was punished for something he knew about, something he steadfastly refused to give up: the contents of that box."

"But why would that cause all those weird things to happen on Piminy Street?" asked Olivia.

"Things have rather come to a head, Olivia, my dear," said Paton, "now that Lyell has, so to speak, woken up. Piminy Street was once full of magicians. If you ask me, someone has stirred them up."

"Y-e-e-s." Olivia poured cornflakes into her bowl in a slow and thoughtful stream.

"They've got that little boy Eric working for them," said Miss Ingledew, jamming sliced bread into the toaster. "Charlie's aunt, Venetia, married Mr. Shellhorn just to get her hands on the poor child."

"I'm going to investigate," Emma announced. "I want to know why that blacksmith was making a sword."

"For the knight," Paton told her. "The Red Knight on the bridge."

"Do you think it could be the Red Knight, Mr. Yewbeam?" asked Emma.

"I really couldn't say."

"I still want to see the blacksmith." Emma looked very determined. "I mean, she seems to be the only one in the street who is kind of good."

"You're not going without me," said Olivia.

Miss Ingledew wanted Paton to go with the girls.

"I don't like to think of them alone on Piminy Street," she said.

Paton cast a gloomy look out the window. "It's too late for me. The sun's up. Besides, I suspect that whoever was making that sword will be more likely to talk to the girls if they're on their own, rather than with a peculiar chap like me."

Miss Ingledew shook her head at Paton and said she would go around to the Kettle Shop herself if the girls weren't back within half an hour.

Emma and Olivia bolted down their breakfasts, dressed hurriedly, and left the bookstore. They were so eager to find the mysterious sword maker, they didn't even bother to brush their hair. Almost unheard of for Olivia.

Piminy Street was silent and deserted. The girls headed toward the Kettle Shop. They hadn't gone far when they heard footsteps behind them. A voice said, "Are you two spying?"

The girls swung around. Dagbert Endless walked up to them. "What are you doing here?" he asked.

"I don't see that it's any of your business," Olivia said hotly.

"Maybe not, but I'd still like to know." Dagbert's aquamarine eyes flicked from Olivia to Emma. "Well?"

"As a matter of fact, we've come to buy a kettle," said Emma, trying to sound casual.

Dagbert gave her a pitying look. "On a Sunday? The shops are all closed. You'll have to do better than that."

"We don't have to do anything," Olivia snapped.

Dagbert stared at her. "Want to change your mind before something nasty happens?"

Olivia's mouth became a grim, defiant line.

"OK." Dagbert looked past them at a sewer grate in the road. His mocking expression changed to one of cold intensity. Suddenly, water began to gurgle beneath the grate. It flipped open with a clang and the water gushed out in a muddy fountain. The girls were covered in it. Screaming, they ran past the grate, up toward the Kettle Shop. But the water pursued them; twisting away from its natural course, it swept around their ankles in a thin, snakelike tide. The pressure was so great they felt themselves slipping to the ground, unable to withstand the force.

Emma was the first to fall; Olivia, grabbing Emma's arm, came crashing after her. As they dragged themselves toward the Kettle Shop they heard, for the first time, Dagbert's terrible laughter. It bubbled out of him in horrible gloops and burbles.

Olivia, pulling herself upright against the door of the shop, began to bang the knocker, noticing, in spite of her predicament, that the knocker was, in fact, a small, bronze kettle.

"Help!" cried Olivia. "Someone, please help!"

Emma, scrambling to her feet beside her, added, "We're drowning!"

The door was opened so abruptly, both girls tumbled headlong into the shop, one on either side of the large woman standing on the threshold.

Mrs. Kettle glared across the muddy stream at Dagbert. "STOP THIS NONSENSE!"

Dagbert made a deep, gulping sound, almost as if he were swallowing a bucket of water.

"I suspected something like this," said Mrs. Kettle, with a scathing look at the wriggling water. "Well, you can keep your water to yourself, fish boy!"

Dagbert gazed angrily at the water which appeared to be drying up very fast. Lifting his chin, he marched past the Kettle Shop without even glancing at the owner.

Mrs. Kettle slammed the door. "Well, now, you are in a pickle, aren't you?" she said to the girls.

"We were in a pickle," said Olivia. "Thanks for saving the day. I'm Olivia Vertigo and this is my friend Emma Tolly."

"Pleased to meet you. I'm Katya Kettle." She peered closely at Emma. "Have I seen you before?"

"Um, you might have," said Emma.

"Hmmm. Come in then, both of you. I'll get you some dry clothes. You're soaked to the skin." Mrs. Kettle led the way through an arch and into a warm room at the back of the shop. "Get those things off," she commanded, giving the girls a friendly push toward the stove. "I'll be right back." She disappeared through a thick metal door, studded with screws.

Emma and Olivia removed their socks, shoes, jeans, and jackets. Luckily the brief shower hadn't permeated Olivia's pink and silver top, or Emma's blue sweater.

When Mrs. Kettle reappeared, she was carrying two large pairs of coveralls and two pairs of thick, woolen socks. "These won't be a perfect fit," she warned. "Just roll up the parts that are too long."

Grinning shyly, Emma pulled on her coveralls and socks. Olivia took her time, sizing up the huge garment and wondering how she could jazz it up a bit. "Have you got a brooch or something?" she asked Mrs. Kettle.

The big woman hooted with laughter. "I don't go in for such things. Pretend you're a princess in disguise." She hung their wet clothes on a wooden rack above the stove.

Olivia grimaced and stepped into the coveralls,

rolling up the sleeves until her pink and silver cuffs were revealed.

"I can see you're a bit of a fashion queen," said Mrs. Kettle, with a chuckle. "Cup of tea, girls?"

Before they could reply there was a loud and urgent knock on the shop door.

"I hope it's not that blasted fish boy again," said Mrs. Kettle, striding back into the shop.

"Well, well, it's you," they heard her say. "What's up, young man?"

There was a mumbled reply and the next minute Charlie Bone walked into the room.

"Good grief!" Charlie blinked at the girls in disbelief. "What an outfit, Liv. Is that the latest fashion?"

"I think it suits me," Olivia said haughtily.

Emma burst out laughing. Charlie joined in, and then Olivia began to giggle. Mrs. Kettle laughed loudest of all. Still spluttering with mirth, she went through her metal door to make some tea.

It was only then that Emma noticed Charlie was

carrying his old black kettle. "You've brought it back," she said.

"Yes." Charlie put the kettle on the floor. "I wanted Mrs. Kettle's advice."

"What's it for?" asked Olivia.

"Mrs. Kettle gave it to me." Charlie explained how the liquid in the kettle warmed up when trouble was brewing. "It got so hot last night it was almost boiling."

"Last night?" said Emma thoughtfully.

"And how come you're both dressed like plumbers?" Charlie asked them. "Are there any burst pipes around here?"

"You could say so." Olivia told Charlie about Dagbert and the water.

Charlie frowned. "I hoped he wouldn't use his power like that," he said quietly. "I just can't figure him out."

Mrs. Kettle walked in with a tray of tea, and as they pulled their chairs up to the table, she asked, "So, what brings you here, girls? I know you weren't just escaping from the fish boy when you burst in. You were coming to see me, weren't you?"

Olivia looked at Emma, and Emma said, "Yes."

"So what's the story?" Mrs. Kettle filled four mugs with tea and handed them around, while Emma hesitated, wiped her nose, and cleared her throat.

"Er, are these your coveralls, Mrs. Kettle?" Emma asked.

"Of course. There's no one else living here."

"Oh." Emma stared into her mug. "No one at all?"

"Not a soul," said Mrs. Kettle.

"Oh." Emma looked around the room, searching for words. It seemed a bit rude to ask a homely person like Mrs. Kettle if she were a blacksmith.

Olivia had no such qualms. Losing patience, she asked, "Are you a blacksmith, Mrs. Kettle?"

"Indeed I am," said Mrs. Kettle evenly. "And are you a bird, Emma?"

Emma reddened. "Yes. I can be. Sometimes."

"So you were sitting on my windowsill, watching me at work last night?"

"I wasn't spying," Emma said quickly. "I was just — exploring."

"Of course you were, my dear. Don't worry. There's no harm in watching a blacksmith at work."

"We came around," Olivia blurted out, "to find out about the sword you were making."

"Sword!" Charlie stared at Mrs. Kettle.

"Ah, the sword." She suddenly looked very grave. "You're not to breathe a word of this to anyone you can't trust with your lives." She studied each of them with an expression that was both fierce and solemn.

"We won't," said Charlie earnestly.

Mrs. Kettle's features softened. "I have inherited certain skills from my ancestor Feromel. I seldom use them, if ever. By that, I mean that I do not use the magic side of my talent, although I still make tools, harnesses, and even iron furniture. I have never been asked to make a sword before — a very, special, unbeatable sword — so, naturally, I was overjoyed by the request."

Charlie leaned eagerly toward Mrs. Kettle and said, "Who asked you?"

Mrs. Kettle smiled. "A knight with a red crest on his silvery helmet."

"It sounds like the one we saw on the bridge," said Charlie.

Both speaking at once, the girls asked Mrs. Kettle, "What did he say? Who was he? When did he come?"

Mrs. Kettle put up her hand. "Hush, my dears. I can't answer three questions at once. He came a few nights ago, very late. He wore a tunic of chain mail and a shining helmet with scarlet feathers, all streaming in the moonlit breeze. His face was covered by a visor, and he spoke not a word."

"How did you know he wanted a sword?" Charlie leaned so far forward he knocked over the sugar bowl.

Mrs. Kettle set the bowl upright and spooned the sugar back into it.

"Sorry," said Charlie, "but, please; how did you know what he wanted?"

Mrs. Kettle put her hand into the deep pocket of her cardigan. She withdrew a folded piece of paper, opened it, and put it on the table. "That's how I knew."

The children stared at the single word on the paper.

Caledfwlch

"I can't even say it," said Charlie. "It doesn't make sense."

"It does to me," said Mrs. Kettle. "That word told me that the knight was no ordinary knight, and certainly not a trickster or a hoaxer."

"But what does it mean?" Charlie persisted.

"Are you sure you don't know, Charlie Bone? Doesn't it sing out at you?" Mrs. Kettle looked earnestly into his face.

Charlie stared at the word. "No. I'm sorry. It doesn't mean anything — unless . . . is it Welsh?"

"There you are," said Mrs. Kettle. "You knew it all

along. It is indeed a Welsh word. It is the name of King Arthur's sword, but it's mentioned only in the old Welsh legends. Their words have remained a secret code, used by those who can be trusted."

"Wow!" Olivia sighed. "I feel honored."

"Not a word of this to a soul." Mrs. Kettle put a finger to her lips.

The three children vigorously shook their heads, and Charlie murmured, "Only to someone I could trust with my life."

"When's the knight coming back for his sword?" asked Emma, thinking she might do a little more night-flying.

"No idea. I'll just have to wait. The hilt needs working on. I think I shall use some gold, and maybe silver." Mrs. Kettle gazed over their heads. "I might even use a pearl or two."

Charlie suddenly remembered why he'd come to the shop. "I almost forgot." He lifted Feromel's kettle onto the table. "This got boiling hot last night."

"Did it, indeed?" Mrs. Kettle put her hand on the

blackened iron. "It's cool now. But last night was a dangerous time. A few doors away the stone men began to move."

Emma's mouth dropped open. "You know about that?"

"I've been watching that boy," said the blacksmith. "Him and his dreadful companion. I suppose you saw them, too, while you were out flying."

"I couldn't believe it," said Emma. "Eric stared at the door and this huge stone man came walking out. It was horrible."

"I THOUGHT it was Eric," Charlie murmured.

Mrs. Kettle stood up and put their empty mugs on the tray. "Time for work," she said. "Your clothes are dry, girls."

Charlie decided to leave before the coveralls came off. He arranged to meet the girls at the Pets' Café in the afternoon. Picking up his kettle, he left the shop, thanking Mrs. Kettle as he went.

Charlie had just turned onto Filbert Street when he saw Benjamin running up the road toward him.

"Charlie! Charlie! Have you seen Runner?" cried Benjamin.

"No."

"He's run off. He tugged his leash out of my hand and then he was gone." Benjamin's face was creased with worry. When he reached Charlie he bent over, panting heavily. "I've got a cramp now."

"It's not like Runner to go off like that," said Charlie.

"He's never, ever done it before. Where could he have gone, Charlie?"

Charlie tried to think of all the places Runner Bean might want to go without Benjamin. Only one place came to mind. "Chattypatra," he said.

Benjamin straightened up. "Chattypatra? Do you mean he might have gone to Darkly Wynd?"

"That's where Runner's girlfriend lives. He was really goofy about that little dog, wasn't he?"

"Yes, he was," Benjamin agreed.

"Let's go, then," said Charlie.

"Oh, no, not Darkly Wynd," groaned Benjamin. "I hate that place."

"So do I," said Charlie. "But if you want to find Runner, I bet that's where he'll be."

As they jogged up to Darkly Wynd, Charlie realized he was still holding his black kettle. It was beginning to make his arm ache and he wished he'd left it at home. He told Benjamin about his meeting with the girls and Dagbert's efforts to drown them. He didn't mention the sword, however. Even though he trusted his friend, Benjamin was not endowed.

Benjamin's anxious frown had grown deeper. "Dagbert tried to drown us too, didn't he?"

"I think so."

When they reached the alley leading to the three number thirteens, the boys slowed down. Charlie wasn't surprised to feel the kettle heating up. The temperature in Darkly Wynd was always several degrees lower than anywhere else and the warmth from the kettle was rather comforting.

Ahead of them stood the tall block of houses with their black balconies, their pointed roofs, and the stone beasts that framed the long windows.

"I don't think Runner's here," said Benjamin in a low voice, "unless they've taken him inside." He gave an involuntary shudder.

Charlie caught a slight movement out of the corner of his eye. Was it a curtain, or was the house shifting very slightly? Benjamin gasped for air, and croaked, "Charlie, something moved. One of those stone creatures above the window."

They stood where they were, fearfully watching Great-aunt Venetia's house. Suddenly, the door was flung open and Miranda ran down the steps with a dog on either side of her, both barking like mad.

"Runner!" cried Benjamin, rushing toward the big dog.

"I saw you coming," said Miranda. "My m . . . m . . . she wanted to lock your dog in the cellar. But I kept him safe for you. She doesn't like dogs, my m . . . m . . ."

Benjamin flung his arms around the big dog, who licked his master with such enthusiasm, Benjamin's happy face began to glisten.

Charlie noticed that Miranda's eyes were swollen and two red streaks ran down her cheeks. "Are you OK, Miranda?" he asked.

Miranda gave Charlie a desperate look. "No. I don't think I am," she whispered. "My m . . . m . . ." She obviously found it impossible to say the word "mother."

"What's my great-aunt been doing to you?" said Charlie.

"She doesn't like me." Miranda cast a fearful look behind her. "She only likes Eric, and Eric, he . . . he isn't my brother anymore."

"What? What has he . . . ?"

Runner Bean gave a sudden yelp of warning. As he leaped up the steps, the troll beside the door gave a hideous grin and sprang into the air.

"Look out, Miranda!" cried Charlie. He tried to pull her out of the path of the flying troll, but unbelievably, the troll twisted in midair and came straight for Miranda, thumping her on the back.

The little girl slumped to Charlie's feet, and then fell onto the sidewalk, her face as white as a sheet.

THE STOLEN CLOAK

Charlie and Benjamin were both too shocked to speak, or even to move. Chattypatra licked Miranda's hair, whining pitifully, and then Runner Bean began to howl. The dog's mournful voice brought the boys to their senses. Charlie knelt down and gingerly touched Miranda's shoulder. Very softly, he spoke her name.

Miranda's eyelids fluttered. She moaned.

A man appeared in the doorway. He had receding brown hair and wore glasses. When he saw Miranda he gasped and ran down the steps.

"What happened?" the man shouted at Charlie.

"I . . . ," Charlie began.

"Miranda! Miranda!" The man bent over her. "Thank goodness. She's alive." He picked her up in his arms. "Tell me what happened?" he demanded.

Charlie could only tell him the truth, ridiculous as it

might sound. "That troll . . ." He whirled around. The troll was back in its place by the door, mute and unblinking. Just a lump of stone. Charlie took a deep breath and said, "I know you're not going to believe this, sir, but that troll flew down and hit Miranda on the back."

The man stared gravely at Charlie. "I believe you," he said. "I'm Mr. Shellhorn, Miranda's father. I think you must be Charlie." He turned to Benjamin. "And you're Benjamin, because of the dog. Miranda told me about you."

"I suppose you're my great-uncle," said Charlie.

Mr. Shellhorn looked rather surprised. "I suppose I am. Look, Charlie, can you take Chattypatra away from here?"

Charlie was taken aback. "I can't, sir. What will Miranda do without her?"

"She'll miss Chatty, of course. But I'm afraid something might happen to the dog if she stays here. I can bring Miranda around to see her, from time to time, if I . . . if my wife . . ." He glanced nervously at the open door. "I must get Miranda indoors. Please, boys. Please, take the dog."

Miranda's eyes blinked open and she said, "Something thumped me in the back. It hurts."

"Yes, darling. Let's get you inside." Mr. Shellhorn carried Miranda up the steps and into the house. Chattypatra rushed after them, but the door closed before she could reach it.

"Now what?" Benjamin sighed.

"We take Chattypatra," said Charlie. "What else can we do?"

Chattypatra set up a steady brokenhearted whine. The troll watched her. Charlie watched the troll. It turned its stony, malignant gaze in his direction.

"All right, troll. Do your worst!" Handing Benjamin the kettle, Charlie bounded up the steps, seized Chattypatra, and jumped to the sidewalk in one leap. "Run!" he shouted.

Benjamin ran. Charlie raced after him, with Chattypatra wriggling and squealing under his arm. Runner Bean bounded beside them, urging them on with encouraging barks. If they had been anywhere else in the city, windows would have been flung open and angry voices would have demanded to know what was going on. Not in Darkly Wynd. Most of the houses were deserted. The few people who did live there kept their heads down and minded their own business. They didn't want to know what was going on in the three number thirteens.

"I wish Billy was here," Charlie panted. "He could have had a word with this silly dog."

"Don't . . . call . . . her . . . silly," Benjamin puffed. He came to a halt, breathing heavily. "Look!"

Coming toward them were three cats. They walked side by side, copper, orange, and yellow. Their big tails were held aloft and their golden eyes were fixed on Charlie. Runner Bean sat back and gazed at them. Chattypatra fell silent. She stopped wriggling and watched the bright creatures until they stood beside Charlie, purring rhythmically.

"Hi, Flames!" said Charlie. "Would you mind having a word with this dog?"

The Flames needed no encouragement. Leo, the orange cat, lifted his head and directed a loud *meow* straight at the little dog's nose. Aries, the copper cat, took up the call, and then the yellow cat, Sagittarius, trilled a finale.

Chattypatra was entranced. She sniffed the Flame cats and vigorously wagged her tail.

"I think they've done it," said Benjamin. "Put her down, Charlie, and let's see if she runs back."

Charlie put Chattypatra on the sidewalk. She sat down, happily sweeping her feathery tail back and forth across the ground.

"Whatever they said, it's done the trick," said Charlie.

The Flame cats' work had only just begun. Their voices fell silent and they walked on, toward the three thirteens. There was deadly purpose in their strong swift pacing. They had come to keep a child safe, to protect her against a stone troll, a wicked stepmother, and a spell-making brother.

"I don't feel so bad now." Charlie breathed a sigh of relief. "If anything can keep that troll in its place, it's the Flames."

The three cats had reached Great-aunt Venetia's house. They climbed up to the troll and gazed steadily at him. Satisfied that he had not moved, they took up their positions: Aries on the top step, Leo by the door, and Sagittarius on the porch wall.

"Let's go home," said Charlie.

When the boys walked out of the dark alley, Chattypatra obediently followed them.

"WHAT'S THAT CREATURE DOING HERE?" shouted Grandma Bone.

The last person Charlie hoped to meet when he got home was his bad-tempered, dog-hating grandmother.

"That dog belongs to my sister. You've stolen it!" Grandma Bone gave Chattypatra a poke with her shiny black shoe.

"Don't!" cried Charlie. "She's not your sister's dog. She belongs to Miranda. I'm looking after her because Great-aunt Venetia doesn't like dogs."

"Nor do I," said Grandma Bone. "Put it out. Get rid of it." She lunged at the little dog, who rushed under a chair in the hall.

"I won't have it, do you hear?" screeched Grandma Bone. "Get the filthy thing out of here."

Charlie shouted, "Uncle Paton. Help!"

"He's not here," said Grandma Bone, with satisfaction. "Nor's your other grandma. You're all on your own with me, Charlie Bone. So get that dog out, or I'll kill it."

"Ahhhh!" screamed Charlie. He knelt on the floor, reached under the chair, and pulled out the trembling Chattypatra. Tucking her under one arm, he ran for the door, while Grandma Bone went for her secret weapon: a sword-stick disguised as a black umbrella.

"Aieeee!" Charlie pulled open the front door and leaped down the steps.

Benjamin was standing outside his house. Hearing

the screams, he was about to rush over to number nine, when Charlie burst out of the door and came running across the road.

"Grandma Bone!" yelled Charlie. "She's on the warpath. Says she's going to kill Chattypatra."

Grandma Bone. Runner Bean knew that name. He gave a hearty growl and would have leaped over to number nine if Benjamin hadn't grabbed his collar.

Charlie practically fell up Benjamin's steps and together they jumped into number twelve.

"Keep the noise down, boys," shouted Mr. Brown from his study. "We're very busy."

"Isn't Maisie going to give you lunch today?" called Mrs. Brown in a disappointed voice.

"I'm not going home for a bit," Charlie replied. "It isn't safe."

"Oh?" Mrs. Brown didn't sound very worried. As a detective she was used to unsafe places. Grandma Bone had a bad reputation, of course, but she had never actually killed anyone — as far as Mrs. Brown knew.

Benjamin had an idea. He looked into the study.

His father was sitting at the desk and his mother was writing at a small table, littered with papers. When she finally became aware of Benjamin, Mrs. Brown looked up. "We've been given another case," she told her son. "It's so intriguing we couldn't turn it down."

"Any news of the wolf boy?" asked Mr. Brown. "I called the mayor, you know, but he said Wilderness Wolves were out of his jurisdiction. A bad business, Ben, very bad."

"Well, there's no news, exactly," said Benjamin, adding, "I don't suppose you'll be having lunch today?"

Mrs. Brown looked slightly guilty. "I think there's some bread . . ."

"It's OK, Mom," said Benjamin cheerfully. "We'll go to the Pets' Café."

"What a good idea." Mrs. Brown smiled with relief. "There's lots of money in the sugar bowl."

The sugar bowl hadn't seen sugar since Mr. and Mrs. Brown decided to give it up. It was now used for spare cash, which could mount up considerably when the Browns were on a job that required many quick-change disguises.

At that moment, Chattypatra chose to introduce herself. She came bouncing up to Mrs. Brown, trustfully wagging her fluffy tail.

"Not another dog!" moaned Mrs. Brown, melting slightly as she stroked Chattypatra's silky head. "She's very cute, but we really can't . . ."

Charlie popped his head around the door. "It's OK, Mrs. Brown. We're taking her to the Pets' Café."

"Is she a stray?" asked Mr. Brown.

"No, but her story is tragic," said Charlie. "Ben will explain later. And please, can you tell Grandma Maisie where we've gone?"

The Pets' Café was not as crowded as it had been on Saturday. There were plenty of dishes full of delicious-looking food set out on the counter. Charlie and Benjamin were the only two in the line and they were able to have a quick chat with the Onimouses. When they heard Chattypatra's woeful history, they agreed to keep her at the café until her fate was decided.

"But what about the little girl?" asked Mrs. Onimous. "I'm sorry to say this, Charlie, but those aunts of yours should be locked up — and your grandma."

"I agree," said Charlie grimly.

Mr. Onimous leaned over the counter and, cupping his hand around his mouth, said softly, "And you say the brother is a . . . a stone animator?"

"Looks like it," said Charlie.

"Nasty business. Something must be done. Mrs. Pike's perked up a bit. But she'd be a lot better if she could find her son." Mr. Onimous moved farther along the counter as a small white-haired woman and her miniature pony joined the line. "Miss Blankhoff, good to see you," said Mr. Onimous. "And how's Brunhilda today?"

Charlie carried two plates of cheese straws, gooseberry tarts, and cinnamon cookies to a table by the window. Benjamin followed with a large bowl of beef treats, chicken drops, and kidney chips. He put the bowl on the floor and was surprised to see Runner Bean sit politely beside the bowl while Chattypatra bolted down every one of his favorite treats.

Chattypatra withdrew her head, happily licking her lips, but Runner Bean didn't attempt to move in on the bowl until he was quite certain that Chattypatra had had her fill.

"Will you look at that?" said Benjamin. "I mean that has to be love."

Charlie agreed but his attention was held by something else. From his position in the window he had a very good view of Frog Street and, although he couldn't be certain, he thought he saw a familiar figure dart along the side of the wall and disappear into a group of fast-approaching goats.

"Five goats," Benjamin observed. "Will there be room for them all?"

"They're tiny," Charlie murmured. "Benjamin, I think I saw Joshua Tilpin out there."

"It's not so surprising. He's always spying on you, Charlie."

"Let him." Charlie bit into a cheese straw.

They had to prolong their meal for another hour. The girls weren't expected until the afternoon, and by the time they turned up, Charlie had eaten twenty-five cheese straws, according to Benjamin. Charlie hadn't been counting. He felt a bit queasy.

"Chrysanthemum tea," Mrs. Onimous suggested, when Charlie staggered up to the counter, hiccupping constantly.

Charlie took the mug of tea and sniffed it suspiciously. Flowers floated on the top. They did smell rather nice. He'd just sat down again when Lysander arrived with Gabriel Silk. Lysander hadn't been able to persuade Tancred to part from his girlfriend. His own relationship with Lauren was far more easygoing, he informed them. Lauren had asked Lysander to say hi to everyone for her, because she always went to see her grandmother on Sundays.

"Lauren's cool," said Benjamin appreciatively.

Charlie hadn't spoken to Gabriel since the nasty incident with Dagbert. He felt slightly uncomfortable when Gabriel came and sat beside him.

"How are you doing, Gabe?" Charlie cast a sideways look at Gabriel's long, permanently sad face.

Gabriel couldn't help his expression. He might look sad but today he was feeling quite upbeat. "I'm doing all right," he said, putting Rita, his favorite gerbil, on the table.

"Look, you didn't believe all that stuff Dagbert said, did you?" asked Charlie.

"Of course not." Gabriel gave a melancholy smile. "I'm not stupid, you know, Charlie. I know what that fish boy's trying to do: drive us all apart so we don't help each other anymore. Well, it didn't work with me."

"Well done, Gabriel Silk!" Olivia gave him a congratulatory thump on the back.

Gabriel went pink. "Are you going to tell me what's been going on, then?"

So much had happened. First they had to bring

Gabriel up to date with the search for Asa and the death of Mr. Pike. And then Gabriel and Lysander listened incredulously to Charlie's description of the moving troll and the rescue of Chattypatra. When Olivia repeated Mrs. Kettle's account of the knight and the sword, Lysander could contain himself no longer.

"Who is he? And what's he going to do with that sword?" Desperate curiosity caused Lysander's deep voice to squeak like a parrot's.

"Even Mrs. Kettle doesn't know that," said Emma.

Gabriel seemed puzzled. "Hold on," he said, putting Rita back in his top pocket.

"What do you mean, 'hold on'?" said Olivia.

"Hold on! Hold on! Hold on!" screeched Homer from Lysander's shoulder.

"Shhh!" Lysander tapped the parrot's foot.

"Shhh!" said the parrot.

Gabriel waited until the parrot was silent and then said, "The knight was definitely wearing a red cloak when you saw him?"

"Definitely," said Olivia. "And he had red feathers in his helmet."

"That's interesting," said Gabriel.

"Why?" asked everyone else.

"Because the Red King's cloak has vanished." Gabriel looked around the circle of bemused faces. "You know the one I mean, don't you?"

Could there be any doubt? Charlie's immediate worry was that the cloak had fallen into the wrong hands. He had always wondered how such a precious garment had survived for nine centuries. He knew that Guanhamara, the Red King's daughter, had taken the cloak to Italy when the king disappeared. It had been passed down through her descendants, ending up in a battered trunk in Gabriel Silk's dilapidated house in the hills. And just once, Charlie had witnessed the cloak's extraordinary magic. For Gabriel had worn it in a battle with Harken the Enchanter. Mild, weedy, passive Gabriel had withstood the enchanter's murderous attack and come away completely unscathed.

"How could the cloak just disappear, Gabe?" asked Lysander. "I mean, a priceless thing like that? A thing of inestimable value? The Red King's very own cloak?" As Lysander spoke he began to throw his arms about in a kind of frenzy. "I mean, don't you keep it LOCKED UP?"

"Of course we do." Deeply offended, Gabriel's face was now bright red. "We are the guardians of that cloak. I suppose you don't think we deserve the honor? We treasure it; we guard it with our lives."

"Where did you keep it, Gabriel?" Emma asked softly.

"In a chest under my parents' bed. Sometimes, when I'm feeling a bit down, my father lets me put it on. He knows it comforts me. You understand my endowment, don't you?" Gabriel looked at Charlie and Charlie nodded. "Well, that cloak is the only thing I have ever been able to wear that once belonged to someone else. Last weekend I was depressed. I asked Dad if I could put the cloak on, just for a few minutes. He refused. When I begged him, he said, 'It's gone, Gabriel. Disappeared. We don't have the cloak anymore.'"

The others stared at Gabriel in dismay.

"So it was stolen," Lysander said grimly.

For the first time Charlie wondered if the knight on the bridge had been trying to save them, after all. And what of the sword? Could Mrs. Kettle have been mistaken? Perhaps the knight who came to her door was not one of the trusted. Perhaps he had learned of their secret language and used it to obtain a magical sword, a sword that might be used against the very people who were most in need of his help.

Charlie got to his feet. "We've got to warn Mrs. Kettle. I'm going there right now, before she hands over that sword to a . . . an impostor."

"Charlie, wait," said Lysander. "Just because the cloak was taken, it doesn't necessarily follow that the knight is an impostor."

"Doesn't mean he ISN'T, either." Charlie pushed back his chair.

The next moment, Charlie was grabbed by a strong,

285

hairy hand. "Charlie, my boy," said Mr. Onimous. "Don't go yet. I meant to tell you before. I've REMEMBERED."

"Brace yourself!" croaked Homer.

Lysander put a hand over Homer's beak. "What have you remembered, Mr. Onimous?"

"Where it was — the passage under the castle. Where the wolf boy might be kept." Mr. Onimous beamed at them all, so pleased with himself for having remembered such vital information. "My great-grandma worked at Bloor's you know, just a cleaner, but a very inquisitive one. She found a trapdoor at the back of the stage. She opened it and climbed down, into a dark room with old clothes hanging in cupboards. She wanted to go farther, but her lantern went out and she was a tiny bit scared, so she came up. Later, she asked the other staff about it. There was an old man, a footman or some such, who'd been born in 1799 — imagine — and he said, 'Ah, yes, there's a passage leading off that room, and it goes down and down and down, into the deep, dark earth. And there's an old, old story that says once, long, long,

long ago, that passage carried on and on and on, all the way to the river."

"We've been in that room!" said Olivia, her voice cracking with excitement. "But it was so dark at the back we didn't go too far in."

Mr. Onimous lost his smile. "There's a good chance they're keeping that poor lad down there." He looked at Charlie. "But I'm not saying you should go there, kids, no, not at all. I wouldn't like to think my words had set you on a dangerous, maybe deadly path."

It was too late for Mr. Onimous to take back his words. Once spoken, they had an immediate effect on Charlie. He was already bound on that dangerous and deadly path.

CHARLIE MAKES A DANGEROUS JOURNEY

Charlie's intention was to get to the Kettle Shop as soon as possible, but there were those in the city who were determined to stop him. Maimed and scarred as he was, Manfred Bloor still exerted a terrible power over some of the endowed children. Joshua Tilpin was one of his most fervent admirers, and he was more than willing to help Manfred take his revenge on Charlie.

Manfred knew that the Flame cats were responsible for his dreadful injuries, but they had been acting in Charlie's defense, so it was Charlie who must be punished. Besides, there was the matter of Asa. Manfred hadn't given up on the Wilderness Wolf, as everyone was calling him. A few more weeks in the dark, Manfred figured, and Asa would be his again: a savage creature of destruction who would do Manfred's bidding without question — unless Charlie Bone found the beast boy and released him.

Charlie was aware that certain dangers lurked in the city, but he had no idea where they were, and it took him several minutes to realize he was running in the opposite direction from the one he intended. By then it was too late for him to do anything about it.

Charlie had stopped running. He was descending a flight of narrow wooden steps that led down into an alley of impenetrable darkness. "What am I doing here?" he asked himself. "I was going to the Kettle Shop. How did this happen?" He tried to turn and climb back into the light, but he seemed to be stuck fast on the steps. The only way he could move was downward.

"Well, I won't go!" Charlie shouted into the darkness. "I'll stay here all night if I have to."

The steps shuddered. Charlie put his hand against the wall and, to his horror, found it sliding away beneath his fingers. The steps were moving farther and farther away from the light. As they speeded up, Charlie was thrown forward. He landed with a thump on cold hard stone. His legs felt like lead; it was useless to move them. He felt as though all the breath in his body had been knocked out of him, and he didn't have the strength even to cry out.

Fear had caused Charlie to close his eyes. Slowly, he opened them. There was a light a few meters ahead. It came from a large, ancient-looking lantern standing on the ground. Above the light three faces were illuminated, unsmiling faces lined with hard shadows. Joshua Tilpin and the Branko twins.

Dazed as he was, it didn't take Charlie more than a second to realize that the combined energy of Joshua's magnetism and the twins' telekinesis had drawn him down into this sinister alley. Their power was stronger now than it had been before, and pitted together, they created an almost irresistible force.

Somehow, Charlie managed to drag a voice out of his aching body. "What do you want?"

"We certainly don't want you," one of the twins answered with a brittle laugh.

"You've got to make a promise," said the other twin whose voice was deeper and more aggressive.

"A promise?" groaned Charlie.

It was Joshua's turn to speak; in a hard, expressionless voice he said, "You're to give up this foolish quest to find Asa Pike."

"And if I don't?" Charlie muttered through chattering teeth.

"No ifs," said the twins in unison. "You WILL give it up."

There was a scraping noise high above Charlie. He turned his head just in time to see a large lump of stone dislodge itself from the high wall beside him. Charlie shrank back; covering his head with his hands, he waited for the inevitable blow to his skull.

The stone never reached him. A violent gust of wind swept down the alley; caught in midair, the stone was flung off-course and came crashing down beside Joshua Tilpin. There was a high-pitched scream as Joshua was lifted off his feet and carried away. The twins, clinging to each other, suffered the same fate. Charlie could hear their feet hitting the walls of the alley as they tumbled through the air, wailing like banshees.

There was a deafening crack of thunder and a cloud of black dust whirled overhead. The screams of the airborne children blended into a pitiful, endless wail that was gradually drowned by the crackle of thunder and the steady patter of raindrops on the ground.

Charlie drew himself into a miserable huddle and waited for the storm to pass.

It takes considerable energy to rouse such savage weather and the perpetrator was left feeling a little tired. He would rather let the storm die slowly than bring it to a sudden conclusion.

When Charlie finally summoned up the courage to lift his head, he noticed that the lantern, though covered in dust, still burned. Someone had brought it closer to him. He saw two long legs encased in a pair of damp blue jeans. Dreading an even worse attack than the one he had already suffered, Charlie's eyes traveled nervously upward. He saw a thick navy jacket, a gray scarf, and above the scarf, a smiling face topped by a shock of blond, spiky hair.

"Charlie!" said Tancred.

"Tancred," breathed Charlie, "is it really you?"

"Of course it is. Are you OK, Charlie?"

"Well, I'm not dead." Charlie attempted to get to his feet but needed Tancred's arm to steady him.

"How did you know I was here?" asked Charlie.

"Followed your moth," said Tancred. "I knew it was her immediately. She was in quite a state, fluttering around my head, butting my cheek; she actually bit my chin when she thought I wasn't going fast enough. As soon as I saw the great drop where the steps should have been, I knew something pretty nasty was going on."

Charlie looked back. The steps lay in a broken heap, well below the level of the road.

"Had to jump down." Tancred examined a splinter in his thumb. "We'll never get out that way."

"The twins," Charlie murmured, "they're so . . . so strong now, and so coldhearted. And Joshua . . ."

"They'll be out of it for a bit." Tancred grinned. "Come on, Charlie. Let's get you home."

The candle in the lantern finally burnt out, and the two boys inched their way forward while the white moth flew ahead, lighting their way. Charlie was half expecting to stumble over a body, but there was no sign of Joshua or the twins.

"They'll be lying in a field somewhere," said Tancred. "I made sure the wind was strong enough to carry them out of the city."

Charlie marveled at Tancred's incredible endowment. "I wish I could do something useful," he muttered.

Tancred patted him on the back. "You're always doing something useful, Charlie. I feel ashamed to tell you the truth. Tracy Morsell kind of blew me off course for a while." He watched the bright moth hover, as she waited for them to catch up with her, and he laughed. "Do you know, that moth made me see the light?"

"How?"

"Tracy gave me an ultimatum. 'Follow that stupid moth and you're dumped, Tancred Torsson,' she said. I saw her for what she was, Charlie. A manipulative airhead."

"She's very pretty," said Charlie, trying to excuse Tancred's temporary defection. "So I can understand your . . . your . . ."

"Obsession? Oh yes, she's very pretty," Tancred said sourly.

They emerged, at last, into a road of shops and lights, and Charlie began to feel he was part of the real world again. "How do we get to Piminy Street from here?" he said.

Tancred looked surprised. "What do you want to go there for?"

It was time Tancred knew what had been going on, so as they made their way across the city, Charlie filled him in. It was the sword that really grabbed Tancred's attention, just as it had with Lysander.

"A sword?" Tancred's blue eyes lit up. "Wow! And you think this Red Knight is an impostor because he stole the king's cloak?"

"I don't know for sure, Tanc. I just feel I've got to warn Mrs. Kettle."

"I can't wait to see this kettle shop and meet the woman who's a blacksmith." Tancred dashed off and Charlie had to run to keep up with him.

The thunderstorm had sent almost all the citizens indoors. The children in the Pets' Café, having decided that Charlie would, inevitably, have run back to Filbert Street, gathered up their pets and made their way home. Benjamin had a hard time separating Runner Bean and Chattypatra, but Mr. Onimous managed to persuade the dogs with a doggy bag of beef treats for Runner Bean to carry home, and a bowl of ice cream for Chattypatra behind the counter.

The remains of the storm lingered above Charlie and Tancred as they hurried along Piminy Street. Tancred explained that he couldn't help it. "But the weather is a protection, Charlie," he said. "Can't you feel it?"

Charlie could certainly feel something. He sensed a deepening conflict on Piminy Street, almost as though battle lines had been drawn up. How many magicians had lived here? Who, among them, had been true to the name of the Red King, and who had used magic against their neighbors?

When they reached the Stone Shop, Tancred peered into the window. He shrugged himself deeper into his winter coat. "Think of it, Charlie. An army of moving stone. Who could defeat that?"

Charlie had no answer.

Outside the fish shop, Tancred hesitated again. He looked up at the window above the badly painted sign. Charlie had told him what Emma had seen, but Tancred would have stopped anyway. Here, he sensed, was an enemy he was born to oppose. He had no way of knowing that he and Dagbert shared the same stormy ancestor: Petrello, bringer of storms, fogs, and drowning tides.

Charlie watched the sign swaying and creaking in the wind. He tugged Tancred's arm. "Let's go, Tanc. I want to get to Mrs. Kettle."

"It's not even a shop," Tancred remarked. "They've got nothing to sell, whoever they are. But I can smell fish, all right." He stepped back from the window, holding his nose.

Charlie couldn't delay his visit any longer; he ran up to the Kettle Shop and began to rap on the door. Tancred joined him and they waited a few seconds before Charlie rapped again, using the kettle-shaped knocker with some force.

"Goodness me, Charlie Bone, what brings you here again? I'm very busy." Mrs. Kettle stood in the doorway with her arms folded across her chest. She was wearing oil-stained coveralls and her face was streaked with soot. She didn't look inclined to let anyone in.

"I'm sorry, Mrs. Kettle," Charlie said in a rush, "but something has happened, something that you should know about."

Mrs. Kettle leaned forward and looked furtively up and down the street. "You'd better come in. We don't want the whole street to know our business. And who's this you've brought along?"

"My name's Tancred Torsson," said Tancred, stepping into the shop. "I'm responsible for a little storm that might have breezed past your door just now."

"Little storm? It was a ruddy hurricane. You've certainly got your uses, my dear. I'm Katya Kettle. Pleased to meet you." She shook Tancred's arm so enthusiastically, he had to clutch his shoulder, fearing his arm might come out of its socket.

As they followed Mrs. Kettle into her back room, they were aware of soft plopping and tapping noises coming from every side of them. Looking around, they saw the lid of a blue kettle lift into the air and drop back again. The same thing happened with a copper kettle, and then a small iron one.

"What's going on, Mrs. Kettle?" asked Charlie.

"What do you think, Charlie, my dear? The amount

of energy in this street is enough to blow my roof off." Mrs. Kettle dropped into a chair and dabbed her shining forehead with an oil-stained rag.

"My storms don't usually have that effect," said Tancred, sitting beside the large blacksmith.

"Your storm!" She gave Tancred a wry half-smile. "That was only part of it. Wickedness is growing in this city, my boys. It's blossoming like a deadly giant flower, and it all stems from that wretched youth, Manfred Bloor. His hatred is so potent it will overwhelm us unless something is done about it."

"Does anyone know about the sword you're making?" asked Tancred, glancing at the large trembling kettle that Charlie had gone to examine.

Mrs. Kettle gave a shrug. "Who knows? They're aware of what I do. No one could fail to notice the sparks and hammering coming from the back of my little shop, but soon the knight will have his sword and then we'll see . . ."

Charlie swung around. "Mrs. Kettle! I don't think you should give that sword to the Red Knight."

"Whatever makes you say that?" Mrs. Kettle asked, looking genuinely astonished.

Charlie struggled to put his doubts into words. "The knight on the bridge was wearing a red cloak and . . . and Gabriel Silk, whose family keeps the Red King's cloak, well, he says that someone has stolen it — the king's cloak, I mean."

"Charlie Bone!" The blacksmith glared at him so indignantly he shrank against the kettle-laden table. "Stolen indeed! Borrowed, or reclaimed maybe, but never stolen. What made you say such a thing?"

"I don't know." Charlie looked away from her stern, copper-colored eyes. "But a sword like that, Mrs. Kettle, it's going to be unbeatable, isn't it? And in the wrong hands, it could be very dangerous."

"It will have to be dangerous, you silly boy. Feromel's words were in my head when I forged that sword. It was his magic that shaped the steel beneath my hammer. He was with me every step of the way."

"But suppose the knight is an impostor?"

The big woman stared at him in disbelief. "Do you think I wouldn't know?"

"No," said Charlie weakly. "I suppose not."

Mrs. Kettle stood up and wiped her face again. "Well, if that's all you came to tell me, you're wasting my time. I've work to do, as you very well know."

Behind Charlie, the big iron kettle gave a loud steamy whistle. The heavy lid shot into the air and then fell to the floor with a loud clang. Charlie was about to pick it up when he noticed the moon shining in the dark liquid that filled the kettle. He looked closer and the moon swam out of vision, only to be replaced by a circle of leaping flames.

"Don't look!" a voice commanded, but Charlie's gaze was held by the changing images inside the kettle. Now he could see a man beside a fire, feeding the flames with twigs. *I'm traveling,* thought Charlie, *but it's not the time. I mustn't travel . . . not into that!*

He could hear voices urgently warning him. There were distant footsteps, a hand reaching out, but the fingers that gripped his shoulder were as light as dust.

Now began the whirling, gliding, tumbling through space that Charlie had come to relish and to dread. The first few seconds of travel were always the worst, when he lost his foothold on the world he knew and fell into the unknown.

He landed on straw piled at the back of a room. A small window, high on a wall, perfectly framed the full moon. Charlie's gaze traveled from the moon to the man feeding the fire. He had never seen a man so tall and whose shoulders were so vast. He gave the impression of immense strength, and Charlie hoped he was not hostile, because he could obviously squash someone of Charlie's size like an unwelcome flea.

The only light in the room came from the fire, but when Charlie's eyes had become accustomed to the dark, he could see that the floor was bare, dusty earth, and the walls gray brick stained with soot. Beside the fire stood a large iron kettle, perhaps the very one that Charlie had fallen into.

As the man poked at the flames a cloud of ash floated out into the room, and Charlie sneezed.

"Faith!" cried the man, turning from the fire. He stared at Charlie almost fearfully. "What art thou? Some fiend they've sent to spy on me?"

Charlie stood up rather shakily and, clearing his throat, said, "Um, no, sir. I've come from . . . that is, I'm a traveler."

"A traveler?" The man dropped his poker and came toward Charlie, squinting down at him incredulously. "A traveler?" he said again. "Like Amoret?"

"Amoret?" Charlie's nervous mind whirled. "The Red King's youngest daughter? Yes, I think I am her descendant."

"Fate's gift to me." The huge man clutched Charlie's shoulder. "Know that I am Feromel, and this may be my last day on earth."

"Your last day, why?" asked Charlie in alarm. "How?"

"They want something and they shall not have it.

See!" From a table in the corner, Feromel picked up a bundle of red cloth. Opening the cloth, he revealed a shining sword hilt. The golden grip was decorated with ruby-eyed birds inside a diamond-shaped patterning. The cross was in the form of two winged leopards with sapphire spots.

The gleam of ancient gold and the beauty of the object lying on the scarlet cloth made Charlie gasp. "Did this belong to the Red King?" he whispered.

Feromel smiled. "I believe thou art one of the trusted."

"I hope I am," said Charlie fervently.

"Then know that the king's own hand hath fashioned this magic hilt. The sword itself has vanished; I hoped to make another, but it is too late for that."

There was a sudden, thunderous bang on the door and Feromel cried, "Quick, we must hide it." He leaped across the room, picked up the poker, and handed it to Charlie. "Keep the flame aside, lad, while I do the rest."

Trying his best not to tremble, Charlie took the

poker and pushed the blazing twigs to one side of the fire. Feromel had pulled on a pair of long leather gloves and, picking up the wrapped sword hilt in one hand, with the other he reached to the back of the fire and removed one of the chimney bricks.

Another assault of deafening thuds caused the blacksmith's thick oak door to groan. Charlie dared not look around. The heat from the fire was now so intense his eyes were filled with tears, but he clearly saw the dark gap in the bricks, and he watched Feromel's gloved hand, singed by flames, push the red bundle into the cavity and close it with a brick.

"It's done, lad. I thank thee!" Feromel removed the scorched gloves and thumped Charlie on the back.

The door could bear the force outside no longer. It crashed back into the room, and three figures strode over the splintered wood: a stone man, a stone woman, bearing a cudgel, and the troll that stood outside Great-aunt Venetia's house.

For all his immense strength Feromel didn't stand a chance. His great fist rebounded off the brutal stone figures, and his long legs buckled under the stone troll's battering head.

"Go, boy! Go! Save yourself!" called Feromel.

With a sickening sense of dread, Charlie realized that he couldn't go anywhere. He'd left behind the only thing that could take him back — his white moth.

THE HIDDEN SWORD HILT

Charlie rubbed his eyes with sooty fists. He blinked up at the firelit rafters, hoping desperately that he would see the tiny light of his moth. Perhaps she had followed him after all.

The stone people didn't appear to see him. They were intent on their destruction of heroic Feromel. Outnumbered and overwhelmed, the blacksmith wasn't going to give up until every spark of his life had been extinguished. Seeing the terrible punishment Feromel was enduring, Charlie threw himself at the stone man, who, with one swing of his great arm, knocked Charlie clean across the room. He pulled himself to his feet and lunged at the stone woman's legs, but it was useless; he might as well have tried to topple a tree.

The troll turned its vicious stony gaze on Charlie. It spun and kicked, knocking Charlie's legs out from under him. He fell to the ground again, and as he closed his eyes in pain, a bright light swam across his vision. The next moment he was floating.

"Charlie! Charlie!" The distant words drifted closer.

"Has he been traveling? He shouldn't have looked into that kettle." This voice was loud and fretful.

"I think he's coming out of it."

Charlie found himself looking down into a circle of inky water. Slowly, he lifted his aching head. All around him polished kettles winked and glinted. Their light was so bright, Charlie had to squint his eyes against the glare.

"Sit down, boy."

Charlie was led to a chair, where he gratefully rested his aching body. A large face, glistening with sweat, came close to his.

"What did you do that for, my dear?" asked Mrs. Kettle. "Scared the living daylights out of us."

"Sorry," mumbled Charlie. "It just happened. He needed me, but it was no use. I couldn't help."

Tancred handed Charlie a glass of water. "You were out for ages, Charlie, frozen to the spot. No sign of life at all. We couldn't move you."

Charlie took great gulps of the pleasantly icy water. "It was so hot in there," he spluttered.

"Where, my dear? Where did you go?" Mrs. Kettle's large face receded as she took a chair beside Charlie's.

Taking a deep breath, Charlie said, "Actually, I think I was right here, and so was Feromel."

"Feromel?" Mrs. Kettle clasped her hands expectantly. "You saw him?"

Charlie glanced at her eager face. "I'm sorry, Mrs. Kettle. I tried, but it was no use. I couldn't help him. The stone people were too strong."

Mrs. Kettle pressed her fingers to her lips. "You poor boy. You saw him die. The stone man killed him. We have always known that."

"Yikes!" said Tancred quietly.

There was a long silence while Charlie struggled with his conscience, unsure whether to tell Mrs. Kettle about the golden sword hilt. She was Feromel's descendant, and by rights, she should know of its existence, but Charlie was still troubled by the thought that the Red Knight might not be entirely friendly.

"Don't look so downcast, my dear." Mrs. Kettle took Charlie's hand and patted it. "You couldn't have done a thing. The die was cast. The dreadful deed had been done when your mind went plunging into that kettle. I've always wondered about it." Charlie followed her gaze to the big iron kettle, sitting on its table. "Sometimes, I've heard things, and then there've been times when I could swear I saw firelight blinking in its black water. I believe that old kettle reflected my ancestor's dreadful end. By why? I've asked myself. What was his purpose in recording his last day on earth?"

Charlie couldn't hold back the truth any longer. "Because he hid something, Mrs. Kettle, and maybe he hoped that one day someone like me, a traveler, would go back in time and see where he put it."

"Put what, Charlie?" asked Tancred.

Charlie looked from Tancred to Mrs. Kettle. "A

sword hilt. He said it had been fashioned by the Red King himself."

"What!" Mrs. Kettle leaped out of her chair. "Where is it, Charlie? Where did Feromel hide it?"

"In a chimney."

"A chimney?" cried the blacksmith, running to her metal door. "In the furnace, then. I must put out the fire."

"No, no," said Charlie. "No, it wasn't in the furnace. It was just a little fire that he had in his room."

"There's a chimney." Tancred pointed to the chimney behind a large iron stove.

Charlie shook his head. "It was quite near the ground, so it would be well below the top of that stove."

Tancred stared doubtfully at the heavy-looking stove. "It must weigh a ton."

Mrs. Kettle had no doubts at all. "Come on, boys, give me a hand." She strode over to the stove and began to tug it away from the wall.

The boys had no choice but to help her. Luckily

the stove had not been lit, so while Charlie pulled from floor level, Tancred got a grip just above him, and Mrs. Kettle heaved from the top. Gradually, one side of the big stove began to move away from the wall. When there was a gap of half a meter, Mrs. Kettle cried, "Stop, my dears. I can see into the chimney."

Charlie peered over the stove. "It's a very small hole," he observed.

"Then we'll make it bigger." Mrs. Kettle marched through the metal door into her work space and returned, almost immediately, with a very large hammer. Squeezing herself between the wall and the stove, she gave a mighty push with her large bottom. The stove moved back another foot at least, giving the blacksmith enough room to swing her hammer against the chimney.

Crack! One blow was enough to shatter the bricks above the hole. Enveloped in a cloud of black dust, Mrs. Kettle took another swing, and then another. At the third blow, a pile of bricks tumbled out of the chimney, burying Mrs. Kettle up to her knees.

"Aha!" the blacksmith cried triumphantly. "Charlie, it's your turn. You saw where Feromel put the precious object."

Kicking the fallen bricks out of her way, she moved from behind the stove and pointed to the large hole she had made. "What do you think, my dear?"

Charlie didn't know what to think. He tried to imagine the dark room where he had helped Feromel to hide the sword hilt. Could this really be the very same chimney?

"Go on, Charlie!" Tancred's enthusiasm blew little clouds of dust into the air, and Charlie began to cough.

"Cool it, Tancred!" Mrs. Kettle said reprovingly. "Here, Charlie, put these on." She handed him a pair of oversized gloves.

Charlie cautiously pulled them on. His movements were slow and almost reluctant, for he was filled with misgiving. Perhaps such a precious object should never be found, and certainly not by someone like himself, a boy who had never proved himself worthy to touch such a great king's possession.

"What's holding you back, Charlie?" Mrs. Kettle asked gently.

"The gloves are too big," he muttered.

"Take them off, then. There's no fire in the chimney today." Mrs. Kettle laughed and Tancred joined in. Their laughter seemed out of place on such a solemn occasion.

Charlie removed the right glove and laid it on the stove. He pushed several bricks aside with his feet and then knelt before the wide hole in the chimney. He could see the bricks at the back, patched with tar and soot. He leaned forward and ran his gloved hand over the surface of the wall. One of the bricks wobbled slightly beneath his fingers. Charlie told himself he hadn't noticed it. He was thinking of the stolen cloak. If the Red Knight was a thief, should he be given a magic sword?

"I'm not sure if this is the right place," he said.

"It must be. Feromel lived here. The house was hardly altered." Mrs. Kettle gave Charlie a long hard look. "Are you sure, my dear? Try again."

Once more Charlie ran his hand over the wall. The loose brick made a light, grating noise, but he took no notice.

"What was that?" Tancred exclaimed. "I heard something." He knelt beside Charlie. "Sounded like something kind of wobbling."

"It was just loose mortar," Charlie insisted.

Tancred wasn't convinced. Putting his head and shoulders right into the chimney, he felt the wall with both hands. "Here it is!" He pulled the loose brick away and brought it into the light.

"Well!" Mrs. Kettle clapped her big hands against her cheeks. "I can hardly believe it. What's in there, Charlie? What's behind the brick? Go on, FEEL, my dear."

Charlie put his right hand into the cavity. His fingers closed on a hard object wrapped in cloth. For a moment he hesitated and then slowly he pulled the bundle out of the wall. Beneath a film of dust, a dull red cloth could be seen. Charlie found he could hardly breathe. The only sound in the room seemed to come from his racing heart. He handed the bundle to Mrs. Kettle.

"Oh, Charlie!" She gasped. "Shall I?"

"Of course," said Tancred impatiently. "Open the cloth. Let's see it."

For a moment, Mrs. Kettle was too overcome to move. She gazed reverently at the dusty bundle and then very slowly unwrapped it.

In the bright light of the kettle room, the sword hilt looked even more magnificent than Charlie remembered it. Speechless with awe, they all gazed at the golden patterns, the shining birds, and sapphire-studded leopards.

"That is the most beautiful thing I've ever seen in my entire life," said Tancred.

"Not only beautiful, but invincible," said Mrs. Kettle. Lowering her voice so they could hardly hear her, she added, "And magical."

"Supposing it doesn't fit your sword?" asked Tancred, who could be surprisingly practical at times.

Mrs. Kettle threw back her shoulders. "Follow me!" she commanded.

The boys followed her through the metal door into the room she called her smith. Lying on a rough worktable was a long metal box. Mrs. Kettle raised the lid and they beheld the gleaming sword. Even though it was unfinished, a shiver of dread ran down Charlie's spine; it looked so very dangerous.

The sword tapered to a treacherous point, but the top ended in a narrow strip of metal about six inches long.

"No handle," Tancred observed. "I mean, no hilt."

Once again, Mrs. Kettle unwrapped the dusty bundle. She gazed solemnly at the magnificent sword hilt and then very carefully lifted it closer to her face. Peering beneath the two winged leopards, she happily exclaimed, "There!" and turned the end of the sword hilt toward the boys.

They saw a dark space in the center, a narrow cavity made to fit something very like the top of the sword.

"Charlie," said Mrs. Kettle, "lift the sword."

Charlie rubbed his sooty hands on his trousers and then gently lifted the narrow strip of metal at the top of the sword.

"Good. Hold it steady," commanded Mrs. Kettle.

She smiled at them, but Charlie could tell that she was nervous and only half-believed the hilt would fit the sword. "Higher, Charlie," she said, her voice trembling slightly.

Charlie lifted the sword another few inches, and Mrs. Kettle slowly eased the hilt over the top. It slid into place so smoothly it seemed as if an irresistible force were drawing the winged leopards down onto the shining blade.

"Made for each other." Tancred sighed.

Almost as he spoke, a great wind rushed across the floor of the smith, and a long sigh came from somewhere deep within the ancient walls.

Charlie looked at Tancred.

"Wasn't me," said Tancred, anxiously looking around the room.

"It was Feromel," said Mrs. Kettle, and a tear shone in her eye. "Thank you, Charlie. He is at peace." She laid the now complete sword back in its box and closed the lid.

"I didn't do anything, really," said Charlie, a little embarrassed. "It just happened."

"You did a great deal, and now you must run along." She glanced at the window. "It's getting dark and they may be lurking about already."

"Who?" asked Tancred, raising his shoulders nervously.

"Manfred and his cronies, whatever or whoever they are." Mrs. Kettle's face was grim as she led the boys back through the ocean of kettles. And when Tancred and Charlie stepped into the dusky street, a low whisper followed them through the closing door. "Don't do anything foolish until the Red Knight has his sword."

"And how will we know that?" asked Tancred as the two boys hurried down the badly lit street.

"Perhaps she'll get a message to us."

Both boys speeded up. They felt that eyes were watching through cracks in the darkened windows. But when they passed the fish shop, Tancred stopped again and stared up at the window above the sign. "Dagbert's not there," he said. "I can't smell fish."

Charlie walked on to the Stone Shop. He squinted into the shadows beyond the window. The stone man was there: the very same figure that had stormed into Feromel's house and crushed the life out of him. Charlie stepped back from the blank stare of the protruding stone eyes. "Let's get away from here," he murmured huskily.

"You're on," said Tancred, running up to Charlie and then overtaking him.

When they got to the end of Piminy Street, Charlie decided to take a chance and visit Ingledew's bookstore. It was closer than Filbert Street and, with any luck, Uncle Paton would be there.

Tancred scooted off through the dark, calling, "See you tomorrow, Charlie."

Charlie grinned to himself. He sprinted happily around the corner and into Cathedral Close. There was a light on in the bookstore. Charlie knocked and two seconds later Emma opened the door.

"Where've you been?" she said. "Your uncle's here."

Charlie bounced down into the shop. It felt so good to be surrounded by soft lights and thousands of books, to be enveloped in warmth, and to see Uncle Paton gazing pensively over the top of his half-moon glasses.

"I've got so much to tell you," Charlie said.

THE SHRIVELING SHROUD

Billy had regretted his decision to spend the weekend at school almost as soon as the other children had left. He watched Mr. Weedon lock and bolt the heavy doors and he was overcome with loneliness. Now he didn't even have Rembrandt to keep him company. Perhaps Cook could find a way to get the rat into school. This thought cheered Billy and he went in search of Cook.

Billy looked in every cafeteria and kitchen, even the green kitchen, where Mrs. Weedon was banging saucepans onto the counter.

"Have you seen Cook?" Billy asked timidly.

"I have not!" snapped the beefy woman.

On some days this reply might have sent Billy scuttling away. Mrs. Weedon always made him uneasy, but today he stood his ground. "Do you know where she might be?"

"Not at all. I'm in charge today."

Billy gave a nervous cough. "Um, will I get supper?"

"An egg," she said grudgingly. "In here. Six o'clock sharp. I wasn't expecting you. No one told me."

"Sorry," said Billy. He backed out.

More than an hour to go before supper. And then what? Bed, he supposed. Billy went to his dormitory and began to read *The Children of the New Forest* for the fifth time. He had just got to the part where the children's family home is burnt down, when he heard something scratching the door.

"Blessed!" Billy jumped up and ran to open the door. He was so pleased to see the old dog he went down on his knees and hugged him.

"Where's Cook?" Billy asked in slow grunts.

"Frightened!" barked Blessed.

"I know. She's frightened of the fish boy. But where is she?"

Blessed's head dropped.

"Is she in her room in the east wing?"

The old dog wheezed, or was it a sigh? Billy wasn't sure. "Come on, let's go and look."

Billy was never sure which door, out of the many on the fourth floor, belonged to Cook, but he knew that Blessed would lead him to the right one. After climbing two staircases and wandering down several dark and echoing hallways, they came at last to an unpainted door with a pair of small walking shoes beside it.

Billy knocked. There was no reply. He opened the door just a crack and peeked in. A clean apron lay on a very tidy bed. There was a chair, a chest of drawers, and a cupboard. A threadbare carpet beside the bed was the only comfort for bare feet on the splintery floorboards. A pair of slippers had been placed at the end of the bed. They looked unworn.

Billy looked at Blessed. "I don't believe Cook lives in this room," he said in a series of light barks that he knew Blessed would understand.

Blessed's only reply was to hang his head.

"What is it? You look worried, Blessed. There's something you're not telling me. Aren't we friends anymore?"

"Friends! Friends, yes," barked Blessed. "Hide-and-seek!"

"OK. We'll play for a bit."

Hide-and-seek was Blessed's favorite game, probably because he was very good at it. His nose always led him straight to Billy's hiding place, although, sometimes, just to make things more exciting, he pretended that his sense of smell had temporarily deserted him.

Billy and Blessed played in the empty hallways and dormitories until just before six o'clock, when Billy hurried down to the green cafeteria.

The egg was waiting for him, a hard-boiled egg, sitting on a plate with a thin piece of bread beside it. A note on the table said, *Wash the plate when finished.*

Billy peeled the cold egg and thought of the hot runny eggs that Maisie gave him when he stayed with Charlie. Blessed watched with a sad expression as Billy ate the cold egg and thin bread.

"Nice?" the old dog asked.

"Horrible," said Billy. He went into the kitchen, washed his plate, and put it on the counter.

"What next?" Billy asked Blessed.

"Hide-and-seek," said Blessed.

It was better than sitting alone in the dormitory.

Blessed chose to hide first. They began in the hall. Billy closed his eyes while he counted to a hundred. He could hear Blessed's claws pattering up the main staircase. On the landing Billy was certain the claws turned left, and then they faded into the huge silence that filled the building.

"One hundred," said Billy under his breath, and he set off up the stairs.

Blessed couldn't open doors, and he seldom bothered to close them; this led Billy to ignore all the doors on the second and third floors. Only the bathrooms were accessible to Blessed and he was not in any of them.

As Billy trudged up one of the many staircases, he became aware that he was approaching the attics, and his heart sank. Mr. Ezekiel used to give him cocoa in a gaslit room up in the attics. He would bribe Billy with chocolate and promise that soon nice, kind parents would come and adopt him. They never came. And the cocoa and promises had stopped when Billy made friends with Charlie Bone.

Billy reached the top of the staircase and sniffed the air. It was muggy and stale. Gaslights in iron brackets sent weak flickering beams down a narrow hall.

"I'm not going down there," Billy said to himself. But then he saw a shadow move across a half-open door. *I'll give you one more chance, Blessed,* he thought, and he tiptoed as softly as he could into the dark room behind the door.

To Billy's astonishment, he found that the floor of the room was lit by thin lines of light. Cracks in the ancient floorboards were letting in light from the room below. Curious to see what lay beneath, Billy carefully lowered himself to the floor and put one eye to a large crack. What he saw made him gasp with horror.

Directly below him Manfred Bloor lay on a red velvet sofa. His head was propped on a silk cushion, and his face was covered in orange bugs. Stifling another gasp, Billy stared at the tiny moving creatures. Behind their writhing, Manfred's pale face was changing. If Billy could believe his eyes, Manfred's scars were fading.

"Magic bugs," Billy whispered to himself.

Slowly and shakily Billy lifted his head, but before he could get to his feet, a voice from the doorway said, "What have we got here?"

"A spy," came the icy reply.

Suddenly, a ghostly gray shroud came flying toward Billy, smothering him in smoky folds, choking him until he felt he would never breathe again, blinding him with impenetrable darkness, deafening him with a thousand silences, and pinning him to the floor in a net of steel.

Sometime later, when Billy was not certain that he could really be alive, he smelled, through his smoky cage, a distinct and doggy scent.

"Blessed," rasped Billy. "Is that you?"

The reply was a desperate howl that made no sense at all to Billy. There followed a series of grunts, barks, and whines. Billy could understand none of it.

"Help me, Blessed," he croaked. "Pull this awful thing off me."

He waited. There were no more barks. No howls. Not even a whimper, and Billy knew that the old dog had abandoned him.

He can't understand me, thought Billy, *and I can't understand him. They've stolen my endowment, the only thing I had, the only thing that made my life worth living.*

In her secret apartment beneath the kitchens, Cook awoke from an uneasy sleep. She could hear a dog whining in the distance. Cook got out of bed, put on her slippers, and opened her bedroom door. The whine continued, low and urgent.

Cook pressed a switch and soft light illuminated a cozy sitting room. Snug armchairs with plump cushions were gathered around a small stove. The walls were hung with bright pictures, and gold-patterned china twinkled reassuringly from the shelves of an old oak dresser.

Cook crossed the room and opened a small door

in the corner. A dark cupboard was revealed. She opened another door at the back of the cupboard and saw Blessed sitting at the bottom of a flight of steps. Cook's room was very secret indeed.

"Well, what is it?" Cook yawned. "You've woken me up all for nothing, I suppose."

Blessed barked. Cook couldn't speak his language, but she recognized the urgency in his voice.

"Come in, then, you blessed dog."

Blessed didn't want to come in. He turned his back and began to waddle up the steps.

"I'm not following you at this time of night," Cook whispered harshly.

The old dog looked back at her and gave such a mournful howl, Cook realized that something was very wrong indeed.

"Wait a minute, then." She rushed back to get her bathrobe. Slipping it on, she put a flashlight in her pocket and followed Blessed through the two doors, carefully closing each one behind her. As she climbed the steps she told herself she was being very foolish.

Something nasty was going on at Bloor's Academy; she'd already seen the fish boy and Dorcas Loom crossing the landing, long after the other children had left.

There were two ways of entering Cook's secret apartment. One began in a broom closet in the kitchen, but Blessed found the other route easier to navigate. At the top of the stairs Cook followed him along a hallway that led, in endless curves, to a very small door. Beside the door a dog-size panel in the wainscot opened to let Blessed through. Cook raised an eyebrow. She'd put on weight since Christmas and wasn't about to get stuck in a dog flap. She unlocked the very small door, opened it, and gently pushed at a cupboard standing in front of it. Squeezing herself between the cupboard and the door, Cook emerged into a carpeted corridor. Blessed was waiting for her.

"Now what?" Cook asked the old dog.

Blessed set off at a trot, which, at his age and size, wasn't that fast. Cook hurried after him. When Blessed approached the eerie region of the attics, Cook slowed down. She was beginning to feel very nervous. *Any minute now,* she thought, *and Lord Grimwald will come lurching out at me, in his dreadful sea-boot stride.* "Blessed," she called in a whisper. "No farther."

But the old dog increased his pace, and now Cook was sure that a child was in trouble, and she remembered the promise that she had made to herself: to keep the balance between light and darkness, between the children bent on evil and those who only wished each other well. Cook's endowment was tranquillity.

They came at last to the gaslit hallway. With a soft growl Blessed padded into a dark room. Cook took a few steps into the room; she stumbled against a bundle lying on the ground. Shining her flashlight on the floor, Cook saw Billy Raven's white head beneath a gray weblike shawl.

"Billy!" Cook dropped to her knees and began to tear at the soft, clinging fabric.

A voice from the hall said, "I wouldn't do that if I were you!"

Cook got to her feet and swung around. The beam

from her flashlight lit two familiar faces: Dagbert Endless and Dorcas Loom.

"What are you doing here?" Cook demanded. "And what have you done to this poor boy?"

"Nothing that he didn't deserve," said Dorcas.

"Deserve? Deserve? You wicked girl!" cried Cook. She could feel Dagbert's eyes on her, and her legs felt like jelly. She hoped the light from the gas jet was too weak for him to see her face clearly, but unfortunately, it only made her look younger, and he began to recognize her features.

"I know you, don't I?" Dagbert said slowly.

"Of course you do; I'm Cook," she snapped.

"No, I mean from long ago. I've seen your photo somewhere." He grinned. "My father has it."

"Don't be silly," cried Cook, adding, "Is your father — around?"

"He's gone back to the North," said Dagbert. "He doesn't much like it here."

Cook wasn't sure she believed him. "Go to bed," she told him, "while I attend to this poor boy."

"You mustn't do that," said Dorcas in a low, chilly voice.

"No, Cook. Leave him be." Dagbert took a menacing step toward her.

"Go to bed," she ordered, "right this minute."

"Go to bed," they jeered. "NO. WE WON'T!"

Cook saw a large shadow loom behind the children. She almost dropped her flashlight in terror, she was so certain that Lord Grimwald would come striding in. But he didn't.

"YOU'LL DO AS YOU'RE TOLD!" roared a voice.

The two children were grabbed by the scruffs of their necks and hauled backward.

Cook raised her flashlight a little. She smiled with surprise and relief. "Dr. Saltweather!"

"Good evening, Cook!" Dr. Saltweather held the two squirming children in a firm grasp. "Are these kids bothering you?"

"They certainly are," said Cook. "And they've done something awful to poor Billy Raven."

"He's a little creep," yelled Dagbert, "and you don't

know what you're getting into, you old fool." He swung his foot at Dr. Saltweather, kicking him viciously in the shin.

"Stop that!" barked the music teacher.

"I'll do what I like," screeched Dagbert. "We've had permission."

"Not mine," said Dr. Saltweather. "Now, get back to your miserable beds." Releasing Dagbert and Dorcas, he gave them both a shove toward the stairs.

Dagbert stood very still. He glared at Dr. Saltweather with shining aquamarine eyes. A foggy cloud spread around the teacher and began to fill the hallway. Even Dorcas staggered backward, coughing violently.

Cook found she could hardly breathe. The fog was filling her lungs, and if she could believe her eyes, there were fish swimming through the walls and seaweed floating in the blue-green water all around her. Was it possible to drown in an attic? she wondered.

"STOP IT!" thundered a voice.

Dr. Saltweather seemed impervious to the choking fog and the watery images.

Dagbert gave a horrible, burbling laugh. "You're drowning."

"I CANNOT DROWN!"

Cook could not be sure what she heard. The words were spoken in a deep whisper that swam around her head. *Cannot drown. Cannot drown. Cannot drown.* She became aware that the fish were fading, the seaweed withering, and the fog retreating.

Dagbert stood in the hallway looking puzzled. A frightened Dorcas clung to his arm.

"Go to bed," Dr. Saltweather ordered, this time in a calm, clear voice.

The two children turned meekly away and ran down the stairs.

"How did you do that?" asked Cook incredulously.

"I'm not called Saltweather for nothing," the doctor replied with a smile.

"Well!" She took a deep breath and stared at the music teacher's weathered face and crown of foamy white hair. "Are you . . . are you one of us, then?"

Dr. Saltweather closed his mouth and laid a finger

across his lips. "I prefer that no one knows," he said. "I am not endowed, exactly, but I do have authority in certain areas." He rubbed his hands together. "Now, let's get this little lad out of his predicament."

The gray shroud was not easy to remove. It clung to Cook's fingers and wrapped itself around Dr. Salt-weather's sleeves. Time and again they peeled the threads away from Billy's head, only to see another part of the shroud creep up and bury him again. But eventually the doctor gathered up the last strands and held the dreadful gray thing in his hands.

"This, I believe, is what they call a shriveling shroud," he said gravely. "It shrivels the thoughts, rather than solid matter."

"It's been knitted," Cook observed. "On very large needles."

"A talent Dorcas has inherited from one of her nastier ancestors, no doubt." Dr. Saltweather rolled the shroud into a ball and put it in his pocket. "I'll deal with it later."

Cook knelt beside Billy. "He's coming around, the poor child."

"What happened?" groaned Billy. "I was looking for Blessed. And then . . . and then . . ."

"Best not to think about it, Billy," Cook said gently.

Without a word, Dr. Saltweather bent down and lifted Billy into his arms. "Where shall we take him, Cook? This boy should not be left alone tonight."

"Follow me," said Cook, "but never tell a soul about the place I shall take you to."

"On my life," said the doctor, "never!"

THE RESCUE BEGINS

Monday dawned, cold and gray. It was so dark Maisie put all the lights on in the house.

Grandma Bone was up unusually early for her. "You know what'll happen when my brother appears," she warned from her rocker by the stove. "All the lights will explode."

"I'll deal with that when it happens," said Maisie, "but I can't cook breakfast in the dark."

Charlie could hear them arguing as he brushed his teeth in the bathroom. When he went back to his room, Uncle Paton called softly through his door, "Come in here, Charlie. We must talk."

Charlie looked into his uncle's room. Paton was sitting at his desk. A candle placed beside him had almost burnt out. Charlie got the impression that his uncle hadn't even been to bed — it was strewn with papers.

"I've got to hurry," said Charlie anxiously, "or I'll miss the school bus."

"This won't take long. Come in and lock the door behind you."

Charlie did as he was told and came to stand beside his uncle. "Have you been to bed, Uncle P.?" he asked.

"Too busy." Paton flapped a hand. "But it's all worked out, Charlie. I'm quite pleased with myself. I've managed to contact Bartholomew Bloor and . . ."

"And Naren?" cried Charlie. "Where are they?"

"Shhh!" Uncle Paton commanded. "Keep your voice down. Never mind where they are; I know a few of Bartholomew's old haunts and I asked the Browns to help me find him. They really are the most tenacious detectives; they tracked him down in no time. Bart's an awkward fellow, but he's agreed to help. His van will be waiting near the bridge — the stone bridge, not that deadly iron contraption. He'll wait until dawn if he can."

"Near the bridge," Charlie repeated, stifling a yawn.

"North side. Under the trees." Uncle Paton peered into Charlie's face. "Are you listening? You are intending to spring the wolf-boy tonight, are you not?"

"Yes. Yes, I am."

"Julia and I have been doing some research, and it's true what Mr. Onimous told you. There is a passage from the academy that ends beside the river. It comes out in a small grove of trees above the path. I'm sure the Bloors are aware of it, so you'd better look out, Charlie. Will you be alone?"

"Not exactly. Tancred and Lysander will be involved, and Billy, because he can speak to the beast."

Uncle Paton looked down at the papers on his desk. His face was very solemn. "I feel that I should not be allowing you to do this, Charlie. It's extremely dangerous. And if any harm should come to you — I can't imagine how I would explain it to your parents. But . . ."

"But I'd do it anyway," said Charlie.

"You would do it anyway." Paton sighed. "So all I can

do is to make it easier for you. I wish I could be there, but I am too conspicuous, and my endowment . . ." He gave a wry smile.

"Streetlight explosions would really give the game away," Charlie said cheerfully.

Paton nodded sadly. "Remember, Bartholomew will be waiting at the north side of the bridge. Asa's mother will be there — and someone else."

"Someone else?"

"Mmmm. A slight complication, but it can't be helped. Venetia's husband, Mr. Shellhorn, contacted me last night. He got my name from Mr. Onimous." Paton scratched his chin while Charlie listened with growing interest.

"Mr. Shellhorn has decided to escape — that was his word for it — from your great-aunt. It's for his daughter's sake. She isn't safe in that awful house. So, together, they will make their way to the Pets' Café, and Bartholomew will pick them up."

"What about Eric?" asked Charlie.

Paton shook his head. "Mr. Shellhorn has reluctantly

decided to leave the boy. He's changed completely. He adores Venetia, it seems, and it would be too risky to let him in on the secret."

"The troll!" Charlie exclaimed. "They'll never get past it."

"The troll, dear boy, has gone."

Charlie gaped. "How? It must weigh a ton."

"Your friend the blacksmith is a mighty strong lady," said Uncle Paton. "The troll is under lock and key, and if Eric doesn't know where it is, he can't get it moving."

"Phew. Where will Bartholomew take them all?"

"To a far, far place where they'll all be safe. And, as you know, Bartholomew Bloor's the best man in the world for that sort of mission."

There was a sudden loud rap on the door. "Are you in there, Charlie?" shouted Grandma Bone, rattling the door handle. "You'll miss your bus."

Uncle Paton rolled his eyes and gave Charlie a little push toward the door. "By the way," he whispered, "you'll need Olivia."

"Why?" mouthed Charlie.

"Distractions." Uncle Paton's voice was so soft Charlie could hardly hear him. "Illusions. White vans."

Grandma Bone yelled, "Why should I care if you miss the bus, you stupid boy?"

Charlie grinned, unlocked his uncle's door, and leaped onto the landing. "Almost ready," he called.

Charlie didn't notice the change in Billy until first break. Billy was sitting in the coatroom, reading a book, when Charlie found him.

"I want to talk to you about tonight," said Charlie.

"Why?" asked Billy.

"We're rescuing Asa, and it's important to get the timing right."

"Is it?"

"Billy, are you OK?" Charlie bent over his small friend.

"I don't know," said Billy. "I had a funny kind of weekend. I was playing hide-and-seek with Blessed and then . . . and then . . ."

"And then what?"

"I don't know. When I woke up in the dormitory this morning, I couldn't remember anything that had happened."

Charlie sat beside his friend. "But you feel OK?"

"I suppose," said Billy. "Except I can't understand Blessed anymore, and he can't understand me." Billy closed his book. "Charlie, do you think it's going to be like that with all the animals? Have I lost my endowment?"

"You can't have, Billy. I need you to talk to Asa."

"Oh." Billy looked doubtful. "I'll try. Will you wake me up when it's time?"

"Of course."

The blue coatroom began to fill up with children, and Charlie had to end the conversation. He headed out to the grounds, where he found Tancred and Lysander pacing around the field together. They stopped when they saw Charlie, and in a low voice, Lysander asked, "Have you decided on tonight, Charlie?"

"It has to be tonight," Charlie told them, "because someone's going to be waiting for Asa."

"Good," said Tancred. "The sooner, the better. But I think we should wait until well after midnight. I've seen the Bloors' lights burning at one o'clock in the morning."

"Two o'clock, then," said Charlie.

"Do you think you'll be able to wake up?" asked Lysander.

"Dad gave me a new watch before he went away. It's got an alarm." Charlie proudly displayed the watch with its black face and sparkling circle of numbers.

"Wow!" Tancred said obligingly. "That's impressive. I hope it doesn't wake the whole dorm."

"Are you still sure you want to do this, Charlie?" Lysander suddenly looked very serious. "I wouldn't blame you if you called the whole thing off. It won't be easy, down there in the dark."

"And Asa might bite you to death," Tancred said lightly.

Charlie grinned, though at that moment, it was the last thing he felt like doing. "Where will you two be?"

"I'll be watching Manfred, and he'll be dealing with Dagbert," Tancred said, and Charlie nodded at his blond friend.

"So I've got nothing to worry about, then. See you tonight." As Charlie walked back to the school he saw a knot of children surrounding Joshua and the twins. Joshua had a black eye, one twin had a blue nose, and the other's forehead was wrapped in a wide bandage. Joshua pointed at Charlie, and the group of children turned and stared at him.

Charlie gave a cheery wave.

At lunch Charlie had butterflies in his stomach; he could hardly eat a thing. Throughout the rest of the day his heart beat extra fast, his hands felt cold and clammy, and during the last class, French, he found, much to his annoyance, that his knees were knocking. "I am NOT nervous," he said to himself.

Fidelio leaned toward him. "What was that, Charlie?"

"Silence!" commanded Madame Tessier.

"Tell you later," Charlie whispered.

"SILENCE!" screamed Madame Tessier.

Charlie managed to get Fidelio alone in the dormitory before supper. He told his friend everything.

Fidelio frowned in concern. "Shall I come with you, Charlie? I mean, just you and Billy, alone in that awful place, with a wild beast?"

"Asa's not really wild," said Charlie.

"How do you know? He's been a beast for at least two weeks now. He could be utterly savage. Why don't you give it up, Charlie?"

"Asa risked everything for me," said Charlie gravely. "I can't just let him . . . rot."

Fidelio shrugged. "OK. I'll keep an eye on Dagbert if he wakes up."

"Oh, he'll wake up all right," said Charlie.

There was still one person Charlie had to contact. Olivia. Fidelio insisted on going up to the girls' dormitory with Charlie. "You could run into Matron up there," he said.

They did. She was standing right outside Olivia's door with a pile of sheets in her arms. "You're out of bounds," she snarled.

"I've just come to borrow a book," said Charlie.

"You can go without it." Lucretia Yewbeam's small black eyes locked onto Charlie's. "I've been hearing some very unpleasant things about you, Charlie Bone. We're all disgusted with the way you've turned out. Still, with a father like yours, who could expect . . . ?"

"What do you mean?" cried Charlie, clenching his fists. "My father's worth a hundred Yewbeams."

"He is a Yewbeam, stupid boy. At least a poor excuse for one." She smiled spitefully as Charlie raised his fist.

"Charlie!" Fidelio grabbed his arm. "Let's get out of here."

They were about to turn away when the door behind the matron opened and Olivia looked out. "Hi, Charlie. I've got that book you wanted," she said, waving a small book of French verbs.

Lucretia Yewbeam stepped away from the door.

"Eavesdropping is an appalling habit." She spat. "Get downstairs, all of you."

They were only too happy to obey.

In the deserted art room, Charlie outlined his plan to Olivia.

"I'd rather come with you." Her eyes had a dangerous sparkle. "I want to know what it's like down there. There could be treasure . . . anything. Are you going to wear pajamas, Charlie? You might need rubber boots, I mean, if the passage leads to the river . . ."

"Liv, shut up and listen," said Fidelio. "You've got a job to do."

"Well, what?" said Olivia angrily. She folded her arms and waited.

"Illusions, Liv. That's all I want from you. I don't need you underground."

"Oh." Olivia looked disappointed. "Where do you want these illusions?"

"All over the city. I know Manfred's just waiting for something to happen. He knows I'm going to try and rescue Asa, but he doesn't know when. He doesn't even know if I know where Asa is." Charlie glanced at Olivia's impatient face. An unwelcome thought had popped into his head. "I suppose I don't know for sure. I'm just guessing because of what Mr. Onimous said."

"And your gut," Fidelio said encouragingly. "Your gut tells you, doesn't it?"

"Yes, my gut." But Charlie's gut also told him that he didn't actually know if Asa was somewhere deep beneath the academy, somewhere in the dreadful, inky darkness beyond the costume department. It was all rather hit or miss.

"So what sort of illusions do you want?"

Olivia's sharp voice brought Charlie back to earth. "Vans, Liv. Smallish white vans, a bit battered." He described Bartholomew's dented old van as best he could. "Your illusions will be a distraction from the real one, in case someone tries to follow. There should be five or six parked around the city, and I'll need them between two o'clock and dawn."

"You're joking," Olivia declared.

"No, I'm not," said Charlie solemnly.

"OK, you're not joking." Olivia grinned. "Emma will help me to stay awake. Actually, I think I'm going to enjoy this."

As they left the art room, a tall, slightly hunched figure appeared at the far end of the hall. It began to limp toward them and Charlie froze. Manfred was out and about again. He waited for the masked figure to come closer.

Fidelio and Olivia stood on either side of Charlie, watching the tall figure move into the beams of the only light in the hall.

Charlie's mouth fell open. There was no mask. There were no scars. Manfred's face was as smooth and pale as it had ever been.

"Surprised, are you, Charlie Bone? Shocked, are you?" Manfred limped up to Charlie and stood in front of him. "It's a good thing I'm blessed with clever friends, isn't it?" He stroked his flat cheek. "I bet you never expected to see me like this again, did you?"

Unable to think of a reply, Charlie coughed.

"We always hoped for the best," Olivia gushed. "It's just great to see you looking so — so handsome, Manfred."

Fidelio spluttered behind his hand.

"SIR," barked Manfred. "You will call me sir."

"Yes, sir," Olivia replied meekly.

"Get ready for supper. You shouldn't be here!"

"Yes, sir," they replied.

They hurried past Manfred, not daring to look at one another, but when they reached the end of the hall, Manfred called, "I'm watching you, Charlie Bone, so don't get any silly ideas."

"No, sir," Charlie mumbled.

There was a tense, stifling atmosphere in the King's room that night. Joshua Tilpin looked very much the worse for wear. His hair was plastered with bits of paper, dust, cobwebs, and pencil shavings. Torn plastic wrappers stuck to his sleeves, and his hands were covered in crumbs.

The twins, aware that Tancred was responsible for their bruises, kept aiming books and pencil cases in his direction, but their strength seemed to have been depleted and Tancred easily repulsed them with a few stiff breezes.

Dagbert watched everything with a calm, calculating expression. Occasionally, he caught Charlie's eye, and his face told Charlie everything. Dagbert would do anything that Manfred asked.

During two hours of homework, Emma was the only one to smile. Tancred had invited her to sit beside him and, blushing furiously, Emma accepted. The smile came later. It was only the ghost of a smile, but it lasted a long time and it lifted Charlie's spirits considerably.

After homework the children dispersed in silence. Charlie didn't even glance at Tancred and Lysander. He knew he must give no hint of tonight's secret arrangement.

In the dormitory Fidelio behaved as if nothing unusual was about to take place, though Billy wore a continual frown and seemed very distracted.

When Charlie finally lay down in bed he felt

as though a coiled spring, deep inside him, might suddenly unravel. How could he possibly lie still until two o'clock? He wanted to begin Asa's rescue right now, before he lost his nerve.

Sometime between eleven o'clock and midnight, Charlie fell asleep, exhausted by his own imagination. He had been picturing so many different versions of Asa's rescue, his mind had finally demanded a rest.

Charlie woke up to find someone gently shaking his arm.

"Charlie. It's two o'clock," whispered Fidelio.

Charlie sat up, rubbing his eyes. "I didn't even hear my watch."

"I thought you might not. Charlie, Dagbert's not in his bed. I don't know when he left the room."

Charlie rolled out of bed. "Can't worry about that now," he whispered. "I'd better wake Billy." He pulled on his blue cape while he found his shoes with his feet.

A gentle tap on the head brought Billy scrambling out from under the covers. "What?" he said.

"Shhh!" Charlie put a hand over Billy's mouth.

"No! No!" came Billy's muffled voice. "Please, no."

"Shhh! Billy, it's only me, Charlie. It's time to go."

"Where?"

"Shhh! To rescue Asa."

"I don't want to go," said Billy, pushing Charlie's hand away.

On the other side of the dormitory, someone stirred and moaned in their sleep. Waiting to make sure that no one had woken up, Charlie whispered, "Please, Billy. I need you."

There was a long silence, and then Billy reached for his glasses. Swinging his feet to the floor, he struggled into his cape and shoes. Charlie grabbed his arm and wordlessly they crossed the dormitory.

"Good luck!" Fidelio's whisper was so soft, Charlie never heard him.

Out in the dimly lit hallway, Charlie could see Billy's huge, terrified eyes, and he felt guilty. "I'm sorry, Billy. Please don't be scared. I wouldn't ask you to do this, but you're the only person who can talk to Asa."

"Not Asa, the Wilderness Wolf," said Billy. "And I'm only scared of not being able to do the right thing."

"You will do the right thing. Come on." Charlie began to creep briskly down the hall.

The only sounds in the vast, sleeping building were the soft patterings of their feet on the oak floorboards. The great, silent emptiness made Charlie feel as though he and Billy were the only beings alive. And yet he knew that, somewhere in the darkness, Dagbert Endless and Manfred Bloor were awake, and waiting.

But no one appeared as they hurried out of the dorm, no one followed them down the narrow hall to the theater, and no one barred their way onto the stage. The dark in the theater was so absolute, Charlie had to pull out his flashlight.

"Where do we go now?" Billy whispered.

Charlie shone his flashlight across the back of the stage until he saw the trapdoor. "There!" he said.

"It'll be very dark," Billy said nervously.

"Very," Charlie agreed. "But this flashlight is pretty good." He beamed it along the hem of the velvet curtains, half expecting to see Manfred hiding in one of the deep folds. But no one was there. He tiptoed over to the trapdoor and, looking furtively over his shoulder, lifted the door by its iron ring.

"It wasn't locked," Billy observed.

"Never is," said Charlie.

"But it could be," said Billy. "There's a padlock on that ring beside the opening. Someone could shut the door and lock us in."

Charlie glanced at the rusty-looking padlock. "It's old, Billy. No one's used it for years. There probably isn't even a key to fit it. And look, it's closed. No one could open that. Come on."

Lowering the trapdoor onto the floor, Charlie began to descend the wooden steps. Billy gave the padlock an anxious glance. "Do I shut the trapdoor after me?"

"You'd better," called Charlie. He reached the foot of the steps and switched on the light.

Billy climbed in and pulled the trapdoor over his head. "I've never been in here," he said when he was standing in the room full of cupboards and trunks.

"It's the costume department." A thought came to Charlie. "We'd better find some clothes for Asa, for when he's a boy again."

"IF he's ever a boy again," muttered Billy.

Charlie opened the first trunk. He took out a thick tweed coat and put it on beneath his cape. Billy found a blue beret in one of the cupboards and a pair of green corduroys in another trunk. He pulled the beret over his head, and tied the trousers around his neck. Charlie pounced on some thick-soled brown boots that he liked the look of, wondering if he could do a swap with Asa later on. He tied the laces together and hung them around his neck.

"Should we turn the light off?" asked Billy, as Charlie headed for the dark recess behind a row of pillars.

Charlie hesitated. "No. We'll have to come back this way, when we've gotten Asa to the riverbank."

"IF we find Asa," Billy said quietly.

Once he was behind the pillars, Charlie trained his flashlight on the dark, mildewy wall. At the very end, a low, arched entrance was revealed. At that moment, Charlie would have given almost anything to have turned back. But he knew he couldn't. "Come on," he said, and was very relieved to hear Billy's footsteps padding behind him.

Slipping cautiously through the arch, they found themselves in a narrow tunnel. The low ceiling, walls, and floor were built entirely of dark redbrick, broken in places and glistening with slime. After a few meters the tunnel dipped sharply, so sharply that the boys began to slip on the damp bricks.

"Help!" wailed Billy.

Charlie lost his balance and, as he slid to the ground, he clutched wildly at the wall. The flashlight flew out of his grasp. He could hear it rolling along the ground and then it stopped. Seconds later there was a distant, dull thud.

"Sounds like it fell into a pit," said Billy in a shaky voice.

"It could have been us," muttered Charlie. "My flashlight is done for, that's for sure."

And yet they weren't plunged into utter darkness;

a soft, silvery glow pervaded the tunnel, and above Charlie's head, a small light hovered.

"Claerwen!" Charlie gazed up at the white moth. "Clear light. I hoped she would come."

"Charlie, can we go back?" begged Billy. "I don't want to fall into that pit."

"There may be steps." On hands and knees, Charlie cautiously made his way forward. When he reached the edge of the pit, he could see that an iron ladder had been fastened to the wall. Even in Claerwen's pure light he could barely make out where the ladder ended.

Billy crawled up to Charlie and peered down. "It's an abyss!" he cried. "We'll never reach the bottom. Maybe it goes to the center of the earth?"

"Of course it doesn't." Charlie tried to sound calm, but he couldn't keep a slight tremor out of his voice.

And then they heard it: a distant animal moan. It was so infinitely sad, Charlie found himself swinging his feet onto the ladder without a second thought.

THE RED KNIGHT

If the moth hadn't been with them, Charlie had no doubt that he and Billy would have fallen to their deaths. The rungs in the ladder were worn and rusty; several were missing altogether. Without a light to guide them they would surely have slipped, and it was a long, long, long way down.

But at last they stood on firm ground again. At the bottom of the pit the walls were lined with huge rocks and boulders, and there, huddled in the shadows, was a scrawny, gray creature.

"Asa?" said Charlie softly.

The beast turned its head. Its yellow eyes flashed fearfully in the unfamiliar light, and it gave a low, rumbling growl.

"What's he saying, Billy?" asked Charlie.

Billy clutched his forehead. "I don't know."

"You must know."

"I don't. I kept telling you. I can't understand their language anymore."

Realization dawned at last. Charlie had refused to take Billy seriously, because he dared not let himself believe that Billy had lost his endowment. "Does that mean you can't talk to him either?" he asked desperately.

"Don't think so," said Billy, keeping his eyes on the gray creature.

There was a sudden roar, and with bared teeth, the beast lunged at them.

"Asa!" cried Charlie. "Don't you know me?"

There came a low, grumbling growl. Charlie and Billy backed against the wall.

"Try, Billy, try." Charlie closed his eyes in panic.

Billy's response was to fling the beret into the middle of the floor. The creature snarled and sprang closer. Billy threw the trousers after the beret. The beast sniffed them, raised its head, and howled.

"I think that means he doesn't like them," said Billy.

"Beggars can't be choosers," muttered Charlie. "If

he doesn't like these boots I'll eat my hood." Anxious not to anger the creature, he threw the boots lightly to one side.

The beast trotted over to them. As it pawed the shiny boots, Charlie could see how emaciated it was. Every rib showed beneath its sparse gray coat. There hardly seemed an ounce of flesh on its whole body.

"Poor thing," said Charlie softly.

"I've remembered the sound for boots," said Billy in an excited whisper. He gave a light little grunt.

The beast looked up. It gave a short bark.

"Good," said Billy. "He said 'good.'"

"Can you remember any more sounds?" asked Charlie.

"Like what?"

"Well, can you tell him we've come to rescue him, and that he must put the clothes on quickly, before we look for the tunnel to the river?"

"Charlie, he can't put them on, he's a wolf," said Billy. "How can a wolf put boots on?"

Charlie felt very stupid. "He can't," he said glumly. "He needs more light to change into a boy."

Billy gasped. "I forgot. I keep forgetting things, but look!" Billy put his hand in his pajamas pocket and brought out a candle. It immediately burst into flame. "My guardian's magic candle," Billy said happily. "I always keep it with me."

"Of course!" Charlie grinned with relief. "I forgot about it, too. I think it'll do the trick, Billy. Hold it higher."

With light from both the candle and the moth, the pit became almost as bright as day. The moth had been sitting at the top of the tallest boulder, but now she began to fly closer to the beast. She fluttered between its ears and it snapped at her as a thin veil of sparks lit its shaggy head. She perched briefly on its back, sending a bright glow down its spine. The beast whirled around, growling and grumbling. Undeterred, the little moth swooped over the thin tail, and then, unbelievably, she spun around the beast's legs until each one was a gleaming rod of light. The beast lifted its feet with a bewildered expression, but the growling had died to a thin whine.

"He's changing," Billy whispered. "Look!"

And, indeed, the beast was changing. A thin line of red hair had appeared between its shabby ears. The long wolflike features were receding; a pale forehead could be seen; sallow, human cheeks formed around a thin mouth; and bony shoulders appeared through the sparse gray hair. With a sudden cry that could have been a howl of protest or of joy, the beast turned its back and hunched itself on the earth.

It was several seconds before Charlie realized he was staring at the thin back of a real boy. He walked toward it and, pulling the tweed coat from under his cape, gently covered the boy.

A sob echoed around the pit. Charlie sank to his knees beside Asa and said, "It's OK, Asa. We've come to help you."

Billy brought the green trousers and the boots closer. The moth had retreated to her high boulder again. She seemed to be waiting. Slowly, Asa got to his feet. With his back toward them, he pulled on the green trousers and the boots. When he had shrugged himself into the coat, he turned to face Charlie and Billy with a wan smile.

"Asa! You're you again," said Charlie.

"Yes," Asa croaked. He coughed. "Sorry. Throat's dry. Haven't spoken to anyone for weeks."

"We're going to get you out of here, but we've got to hurry. There's a tunnel that leads to the riverbank. Someone's waiting to rescue you. Your mom will be there." Charlie was speaking so fast that Asa began to look confused.

Charlie slowed down. "My guess is that the tunnel begins behind one of those boulders."

"My mom's OK, then?" Asa murmured.

"Yes." Charlie hesitated and said awkwardly, "I'm sorry about your dad."

Asa's face began to crumple and Billy said quickly, "I bet it's behind that tall boulder, the one your moth's sitting on, Charlie. I bet the tunnel begins there."

"Let's have a look." Charlie went over to the boulder and tried to shift it. "It'll take all three of us to move this," he said. "Come on, you two."

Billy blew out his candle and put it back in his pocket.

After several minutes of heaving and pushing, puffing and panting, they managed to move the boulder a few inches away from the wall. Billy was right. There was indeed a hidden entrance. With renewed strength the three boys pushed the heavy boulder another few inches. Now there was just enough space for them to squeeze into the entrance of the tunnel.

They moved in silence. Billy first, then Asa. Charlie walked behind Asa, just in case he began to lose his shape again. But the white moth fluttered close to the beast boy, making sure there was enough light for him to keep his human form.

The tunnel was, if anything, more dank and smelly than the first one. It was certainly colder. Charlie and Billy pulled up their hoods, and Asa, somewhat reluctantly, put on the beret. Charlie first noticed the water when Asa's feet began to splash, sending cold sprays at Charlie's legs.

"Do you think the river might be coming into the tunnel?" Billy asked nervously.

"It can't be," answered Charlie. "The path is a long way above the river and besides, we're walking upward, not down."

"What if the river floods?" Billy persisted.

"It hasn't been raining," said Charlie. Even as he spoke he was remembering the high river that had nearly swept them off the bridge. "Dagbert," he murmured.

A few minutes later, the water was knee-deep. "Let's go back," cried Billy.

Charlie looked back. Behind him a muddy tide was filling the tunnel. "We can't," he said. "It's even deeper behind us. Go faster, Billy."

Billy started to walk faster, but soon the water was above his knees. The current was so strong he could hardly move against it. "We're going to drown," he moaned.

Asa slumped against the wall. "It's me," he muttered. "Manfred will never let me go, he'd rather see me dead."

"It's Dagbert Endless," Charlie said bitterly. "We mustn't let him beat us. We've got to keep moving." He walked past Asa and grabbed Billy's hand. "We'll help one another. Come on, Asa. Take Billy's other hand."

They began to move again, slowly and painfully, while the white moth hovered above them, the sparkle of her lively spirit encouraging them onward. But even she couldn't stop the water rising, and it wasn't long before the swirling torrent was gurgling around their waists. Charlie had no idea how close they were to the riverbank. Perhaps the path was already underwater and as soon as they emerged, they would be swept into a flood.

When the water reached their shoulders, Charlie began to give up hope.

Far above the tunnel, Tancred Torsson was making his way across the grounds of Bloor's Academy. He was sensitive to water in all its many forms. He was aware of the tides, knew when rain was on its way, could even tell when water might pour from a heavy cloud. Tancred knew that, deep beneath him, water was filling an ancient tunnel. He could hear it rushing beneath his feet, and he knew that Charlie was in trouble. Tancred even knew the source of that drowning water. At the edge of the woods that bordered the Red Castle, phosphorescent colors lit the treetops. As Tancred drew closer, he could see Dagbert Endless leaning against a tree. His head was raised, his eyes were closed, and he was smiling.

Tancred strode up to the boy. "Stop that," he demanded.

Dagbert opened his eyes. "Oh, it's you."

"I can hear water," said Tancred. "It's drowning them. Give it up."

"Why should I?" Dagbert sneered. "I'm having the time of my life."

"Not anymore." Tancred swung his cape in a wide green arc.

"What are you doing?" asked Dagbert suspiciously.

A blast of icy air sent him spinning away from the tree. "Stop it!" he yelled as a great gust of wind swept him off his feet. A stream of golden creatures began to pour from his pocket as he turned upside down, pawing and kicking the air.

Strolling forward, Tancred caught the tiny creatures in his hands.

"No!" screamed Dagbert.

Tancred stood back and let the boy crash to the earth. Dagbert lay still for a moment and then he began to shake. His face took on a sickly green glow, his hands shone, and a luminous glint stole through his clothes. The shaking became uncontrollable.

"G . . . g . . . give . . . m . . . m . . . me . . . the . . . s . . . sea-gold . . . cr . . . creatures," stammered Dagbert.

"These?" Tancred ran them through his fingers from hand to hand. "I don't think so."

"F . . . fiend!" screamed Dagbert.

"Stop the water!"

"N . . . n . . . no!"

Tancred raised his clenched fist, and Dagbert was sent flying through the woods. Sharp twigs tore his clothes and scratched his face, thorns caught in his hair, and naked branches pulled off his shoes. When he fell to the earth a second time, his trembling had become so intense he bounced up and down on the ground. "G . . . g . . . give me . . ." he gasped.

Tancred walked up to the glowing boy. "I'll give you nothing until you stop the water."

There was a long silence and then, with a gurgling sigh, Dagbert closed his eyes and dug his hands into the earth.

Tancred began to feel a change in the ground beneath his feet. He watched Dagbert and waited. Still trembling, Dagbert dug his fingers deeper and deeper into the earth. At last, with a shaking voice, he uttered the word, "D . . . done!"

"Hmmm. I won't thank you." Tancred sauntered away.

"P . . . please," moaned Dagbert.

"Your sea-gold creatures? Come and get them." Tancred scattered the tiny fish and the golden crabs in the long grass that bordered the woods. But he put the sea urchin in his pocket. "For future encounters," he said to himself. Keeping in deep shadow, he made his way back to the school. He had noticed a light at the very top of the building and didn't want to take any chances.

Old Ezekiel had seen the spectacle from his high attic window. He had no idea that Dagbert was not alone in the woods, and was most impressed by the glowing colors streaming from the trees.

"Our very own aurora borealis." He chuckled. "Well done, Dagbert Endless."

In the tunnel deep beneath the woods, Charlie felt the current begin to ebb.

"It's going down," breathed Asa.

Soon they could see their muddy legs again. Minutes later, they were walking on damp bricks. The flood had become a tiny trickle.

"How did that happen?" said Billy.

"I think Tancred had something to do with it." Charlie grinned up at the mossy roof.

They were now walking up a steep incline. Far ahead, Charlie could see the moon, and although they fell several times on the slippery bricks, the sight of the moon gave them fresh hope. Ignoring their wet clothes and aching limbs, they crawled upward until, one by one, they tumbled out into the small grove of trees beside the path. A strong breeze had blown every cloud from the sky, and everything was bathed in brilliant moonlight.

"We're here!" cried Charlie, rolling down the bank.

The others followed. Asa was even giggling. He looked a very odd sight with his red hair straggling from under the beret, and his long coat covered in mud.

They were now, all three, shivering from wet and cold, but Charlie wanted to make sure that Asa reached Bartholomew's van. They ran along the path until the bridge came into view, and there, just visible above the stone wall, was a white van.

"Asa" — Charlie pointed at the bridge — "see that white van? Your mom's there, waiting for you."

As he spoke they felt a tremor in the earth. A distant pounding reached their ears; as it grew louder a white horse leaped down the bank beside the bridge. On its back rode a knight in a silver helmet and a velvet cloak that looked gray in the moonlight, yet Charlie knew it must be scarlet. They caught the flash of steel as the knight brought out his sword and came charging toward them.

In that moment, Charlie could only think that he'd been right all along. The Red Knight was no friend. He'd been given an invincible sword that he'd always intended to use against them.

They turned to run but there was nowhere to go. For on their other side, a huge horse came thundering at them. The ground shuddered as its great hooves pounded the path. Stiff gray feathers stood up from its head, and the knight on its back wielded a long pale lance.

"They look like stone!" Billy whimpered.

"They are stone!" cried Charlie.

Caught between the Red Knight and the gray stone Knight, the river seemed the only place to go. Charlie stood, shivering on the moonlit path, unable to move, while Billy and Asa fell to their knees, clutching Charlie's cape and yelling something incomprehensible. And then, when both horses were almost upon them, the Red Knight shouted, "DOWN!"

Charlie fell to the ground as horse and rider sailed above him. A rush of air from the billowing cloak warmed his bones and stopped the shivering.

The stone knight's lance was pointed straight at the Red Knight's chest, but at the last moment, the white horse swerved and, faster than lightning, the Red Knight brought down his sword. A bright flash shivered along the lance. The stone horse turned awkwardly on the path. The lance was pulled away and then came sweeping at the Red Knight's back.

Charlie heard a thud as the lance hit its mark. But the Red Knight didn't topple from his horse. The lance rebounded from his red cloak, the white horse pranced sideways, and the Red Knight smote the lance with his bright sword, again and again and again.

There was a mighty crack and the lance broke in two, one end thudding onto the path. The stone knight brought his mount crashing into the side of the white horse; a cry of pain filled the air as she backed away, but, as she moved, the blade of the Red Knight's sword fell on the stone knight's helmet. His head split but still he moved, wildly swinging his blunted lance. The sword flashed again, slicing the stone knight in half, cracking his arms and slashing the remains of the lance. The stone pieces dropped to the earth; the stone horse staggered and then rolled into the river.

The three boys got to their feet a little shakily, though their clothes were dry again and they couldn't feel the cold. They gazed at the Red Knight and his horse, standing so still in the moonlight. If it hadn't been for the steam coming from the white horse, they could have been taken for statues.

"I can make it on my own, now." Asa had an odd little smile on his face. "You'd better get back to school."

"Are you sure?" asked Charlie.

"Quite sure," said Asa, as the white horse came toward them.

The boys stood aside to let horse and rider pass. Charlie heard the creak of leather, the rustle of chain mail, and the heavy breathing of the horse. The Red Knight sat erect, his sheathed sword hanging from his belt, and the red cloak lying soft against his back. He paused for a moment and looked down at them. The visor hid his face, and only the glint of his eyes could be seen.

When the horse moved on, Asa walked beside it. Charlie and Billy watched the lanky figure in its long coat and Charlie murmured, "He'll be safe now."

"Probably the safest person in the world," added Billy.

As they climbed back up the bank, they failed to see a small boy and a tall woman standing in the trees.

The journey back to school was easier and faster now that the tunnel was empty of water.

"It's always quicker when you know what to expect," said Charlie, as he hauled himself up the iron ladder and out of the dreadful pit. But they weren't expecting to see what they did when they finally emerged into the room below the theater.

Charlie hadn't seen Manfred anywhere near the stage, simply because Manfred had been hiding behind the first row of seats in the auditorium. He heard the trapdoor being lowered and waited, smiling to himself, as he imagined Charlie and Billy making their way down to the pit where he'd been keeping the beast-boy. He particularly enjoyed the pictures he'd conjured up for himself, when he thought of Dagbert's drowning water pouring into the tunnel.

"Asa will drown," Manfred said to himself, "and I'll lose my useful beast, but it can't be helped. And with Billy out of the way, who cares if Lyell Bone finds Maybelle Raven's will? As for Charlie Bone, the sooner he's out of the way, the better."

But Charlie had a way of escaping trouble, and Manfred wanted to make sure that, this time, he wouldn't survive. Leaving his hiding place, he climbed onto the stage. In his pocket he had an old key that fitted the padlock on the trapdoor. He was about to fit the key into the padlock, when curiosity got the better of him.

Manfred lifted the trapdoor and descended into the costume department. It appeared to be deserted. Swinging the key and whistling to himself, Manfred popped his head around one of the pillars and squinted into the darkness. Nothing. And then, in the distance, he heard Billy's frantic wail as he slipped in the tunnel.

Manfred smiled with satisfaction. He turned back and, to his utter astonishment, came face to face with Lysander Sage.

"What are you doing here?" stormed Manfred.

"Give me the key," Lysander demanded.

"I'll give you nothing," scoffed Manfred. "Get out of here before I call Weedon."

"I'm pretty sure that Weedon is driving around the city counting white vans and wondering which one he should watch. Now give me that key."

"Come and get it!"

"OK." Raising his arms, Lysander spun around the room, threading his way between leather trunks and wicker baskets. The walls resounded with mysterious chanting, and while Manfred slowly backed toward the steps, drumbeats began to accompany Lysander's voice. Pale shades began to fill the black spaces between the pillars; slowly each ghostly shape took the form of a tall dark man. Their brown arms were encircled with gold, their bodies draped in white robes, and each man carried a tall spear.

"Illusions," muttered Manfred.

"You know they are not," said Lysander. "They are my ancestors and as tangible as any being in this city."

One of these warriors moved behind Manfred, barring his way to the steps.

"Give me the key." Lysander held out his hand.

Manfred dumbly shook his head. Clutching the key, he moved away from the steps and down the aisle between cupboards and trunks.

"Then take the consequences." Lysander uttered a long singing sound and the dark warriors moved forward. As they closed in on Manfred he gave a strangled cry. Throwing the key at Lysander, he lifted the lid of one of the baskets and leaped inside, pulling the lid over his head.

Lysander bounded over to the basket and fastened the buckle. Then, picking up the key, he sat on the basket and waited.

Surprised by the bright light filtering toward them, Charlie and Billy hesitated before they walked through the pillars. And then they saw Lysander, surrounded by his tall spirit ancestors.

"What . . . ?" uttered Charlie.

"Shhh!" Lysander pointed at the basket beneath him. Unfastening the buckle, he stood up and led the others up the steps.

Before closing the trapdoor, he called softly to

his spirit ancestors and then his face broke into a wide grin.

"What's going on?" asked Charlie.

"Manfred was going to trap you," said Lysander. "But I trapped him instead. My ancestors will keep him prisoner until dawn."

Billy stared anxiously at Lysander's calm face. "But he's going to be furious. He'll . . . He'll . . ."

"He'll do nothing," Lysander told him. "Do you think he'd want anyone to know that he hid in a basket and failed to stop you from getting back? Believe me, he's too proud for that. Now, tell me, were you successful?"

"Very successful," said Charlie.

As they tiptoed back to their dormitories, Billy whispered sleepily, "We saw the Red Knight, Lysander, and a white horse. And I think the horse was the queen that Ezekiel accidently brought to life."

"Then, perhaps, the Red Knight is the king," said Lysander.

"Has to be," said Charlie.

On the other side of the city, Mr. Brown, driving back from a very important assignment, counted no less than seventeen battered white vans parked in various places around the city. He wrote down each location in his notebook. "Something's going on," he said to himself. "Unless . . . of course. Illusions." He tore the page out of his notebook.

By then, the only white van that he had failed to see was already speeding away from the city.

CHARLIE GETS A POSTCARD

On Tuesday morning, there was a very curious mood in Bloor's Academy. Even the children who had not been involved in Asa's escape were aware of a change in the atmosphere.

Dagbert Endless lay in bed, his face covered in scratches. Occasionally, he moaned about the wind. He kept his clenched fist close to his cheek and wouldn't show anyone what he held, although sometimes between his fingers the glint of gold could be seen.

"Leave him be," said the matron. "He's the sort of boy who has nightmares."

So Dagbert was allowed to stay in bed, an unheard of thing for a boy at Bloor's Academy.

In his room in the west wing, Manfred Bloor was also in bed. He lay with his face to the wall, mumbling about ghostly warriors.

Old Ezekiel wheeled himself to Manfred's door

and knocked. There was no answer. Finding the door locked, Ezekiel rattled the handle. "Were you successful?" he called. "Mission accomplished? Asa gone? Charlie Bone finished and little Billy abolished?"

"Go away," snarled Manfred.

"Failed then." His great-grandfather sighed and he gloomily wheeled himself away.

Scrambled eggs were being served in the blue cafeteria. Charlie could never remember having had such a treat for a school breakfast. He stood at the end of the line, trying to keep his eyes open and yawning loudly.

Cook gave Charlie an extra-large portion when he finally reached the counter. "I rushed out and bought the eggs myself," she said. "Why shouldn't you children have a decent breakfast for a change?"

"Cook, you don't look worried anymore," Charlie observed.

"I know I'm not alone." She gave him a mysterious smile and then pulled something out of her apron pocket. "I bumped into your grandma Maisie this morning. What a bit of luck! She wondered how she was going to get this to you." Cook reached over the counter and handed Charlie a postcard.

There was an exotic-looking stamp on the back and his father's handwriting. A few words about the journey and the weather and then, "One day we'll take you with us, Charlie, and you'll see these magnificent creatures for yourself."

On the other side of the card, the huge tail of a humpback whale filled the sky above a vast glittering sea.

JENNY NIMMO

I was born in Windsor, Berkshire, England, and educated at boarding schools in Kent and Surrey from the age of six until I was sixteen, when I ran away from school to become a drama student/assistant stage manager with Theater South East. I graduated and acted in repertory theater in various towns and cities.

I left Britain to teach English to three Italian boys in Amalfi, Italy. On my return, I joined the BBC, first as a picture researcher, then assistant floor manager, studio manager (news), and finally director/adaptor with *Jackanory* (a BBC storytelling program for children). I left the BBC to marry Welsh artist David Wynn-Millward and went to live in Wales in my husband's family home. We live in a very old converted water mill, and the river is constantly threatening to break in, which it has done several times in the past, most dramatically on my youngest child's first birthday. During the summer, we run a residential school of art, and I have to move my office, put down tools (typewriter and pencils), and don an apron and cook! We have three grown-up children, Myfanwy, Ianto, and Gwenhwyfar.